Handsome wrestler Terry 'Kid Bacchus' Ryan is popular with the fans in the ring and with the men in the bedroom. But faced with dwindling audiences and fierce competition in Britain, Terry gambles on a tour of Europe with 'uncle' Doug, three wrestling buddies, and an unexpected sponsor, the masked wrestler Johnny Deuce.

Abroad, Terry and his team score on the mats and between the sheets, catching the eye of influential wrestler/promoter Yves Montaigne, who is eager to make Terry a star and lover.

But even as success beckons, Terry is drawn into a world of dark and dangerous sexual fantasies, and to save himself and his wrestling family, Terry must find out who his real enemies are. Are they linked to the death of his father years ago? What part did Doug play in that? And above all, who really is the man behind the Johnny Deuce mask?

Published by
NineStar Press
PO Box 91792
Albuquerque, New Mexico, 87199
www.ninestarpress.com

Warning: This book contains sexually explicit content which is only suitable for mature readers.

Print ISBN # 978-1-911153-88-7
Original Cover Art by Aria Tan
Print Cover by Natasha Snow
Edited by Elizabeth Coldwell

WRESTLING FOR

TOP

The Complete Collection

Jack Stevens

Dedication

For Cymrofight

The world's best wrestler!

PART ONE

Chapter One

He'd put up a good fight, but now...he was fucked.

Hopelessly pinned by the heavier man's weight, he tried to buck and bridge, to shift his captor, but his struggles were useless, for show only. His slim, muscular body had finally been overpowered by the near-naked, hairy thug on top of him. Exhausted and outmanoeuvred he could only lie there, grit his teeth and prepare for the inevitable.

"You ready for this?" The man on top looked down, grinning ferociously. His knees dug painfully into his captive's biceps, his hairy thighs framing the young, flushed face as he sat triumphantly on his bare, heaving chest. Slowly he drew one hand down his face to wipe the sweat from his eyes, let the hand continue down, over the sopping, dark, matted hair of his chest, sending a sudden shower of stinging sweat straight into the eyes of the lad pinned under him with a contemptuous flick of his wrist.

The boy shook his head and blinked furiously to clear his sight. Grunting loudly, he made one last attempt to be free, thrusting his hips up in a powerful, bridging motion. He was young, strong and agile, but it was hopeless. Laughing cruelly, the man on top rode the boy, let him arch his lean body up as far as he could before raising himself that little bit further with a push of his thighs and then dropping his full weight back down on him, breaking his bridge and crushing all hope of escape. Defiance blazing in his blue eyes, the winded, beaten boy glared up at the man on top of him. "Fuck you." The words were clearly mouthed but totally silent, one last secret message between them.

The older man laughed out loud. "Suck my dick," he whispered, before leaning down and forward, smothering the handsome, clean-cut features of the face beneath him with his soaked package.

"One-ah! Two-ah! Three-ah!"

Around the wrestling ring, the audience erupted into a ragged chorus of boos and catcalls as the referee sprang up from his crouched

1

position right next to the two grapplers, and signalled his decision to the ringside MC. The bell rang, the last wrestling match of the evening came to its end, and its outcome wasn't what anyone had expected. Splendid in bow tie and dinner jacket, whose repairs and missing buttons only showed if you looked really closely, the MC rose from his seat at the ring's apron and clambered in under the ropes to announce the decision.

"You getting off my face anytime soon?" The pinned youngster, back to canvas, was attempting a hissed stage whisper but his words were muffled by the Lycra-clad crotch still shoved in his face.

"Just giving the punters what they want."

"Just getting what *you* want!"

The winning wrestler gave a soft chuckle and sat back up, his arse plumped down hard on the younger man's chest. In full villain mode he raised his arms and struck a victory pose, calculated to enflame the audience, who had of course favoured the younger, blue-eyed, blond-haired 'face'. In traditional 'heel' black trunks and boots, the hair on his chest and belly plastered to his skin after the exertions of the previous six rounds, the winner slowly twisted and turned, arms flexed, so that everyone on every side of the ring got an eyeful of his sneer and show of arrogance. With a leer at an elderly lady in the front row, he kissed first one rounded biceps then the other.

"God, you're such a ham!" hissed the voice from beneath him. As he continued to play to the crowd, the man on top shifted forward, as if by accident, so that he was practically sitting on the vanquished boy's face, his arse grinding down on the smooth features beneath him in front of forty or more shouting, screaming fans, all of them blissfully unaware of just how much both guys in the ring were getting off on it.

"Ladies and gentlemen." The MC had taken his place at the centre of the ring. He paused, as if waiting for a much larger, much louder crowd to quieten. He pulled uncertainly at his garish bow tie. "In the third minute of the sixth round, after a terrific struggle, the one fall required goes to..."

The winning wrestler finally rose to his feet and strolled over to the MC, arms stretched out as if basking in the hate from the ringsiders. "What's up?" he whispered out of the corner of his mouth. "Forgot my name?"

The MC hastily covered his mic. "You were supposed to lose!" he hissed back while keeping a fixed smile for the benefit of the audience.

"So what you gonna do?"

The MC uncovered his mic. "The winning fall goes to... 'Nasty' Nick Norris."

The cries of derision rose and peaked as Nasty Nick took his victory walk round the ring, pausing at strategic points where the punters were most vehement, swapping a few crude insults with familiar faces. He despised the crowd. The crowd hated him. And they all loved it.

"And your appreciation, ladies and gentlemen, please," the MC continued, "for a valiant opponent...and unexpected loser... The teen sensation, Chris 'Kid' Bacchus!"

The Kid had also by this point risen to his feet and with one hand pressed to the small of his back, just above the line of his tight yellow trunks, as if massaging some dire injury, he let the MC raise his other arm and accepted with sportsmanlike grace the crowd's applause.

"You should've killed him, Chris!" shrieked the old woman from the front row. It wasn't clear whether her excitement was due to anger at Nick's ill-deserved victory or to being so close to a good-looking young man with the musculature of a gymnast, body glowing from his grappling, skin gleaming with sweat, wearing only the briefest, tightest trunks. The Kid nodded with exaggerated ruefulness and waved at her, wincing to drive home the point about his 'injury', before smiling with brave resignation to show what a good loser he was. The old woman sank back into her seat and fanned herself with the evening's programme.

The MC turned once more to Nick, hand held out, and Nick, finally back on script, laughed nastily in the required fashion, spurned the gesture, and slid out under the bottom rope of the ring to make his way back to the dressing rooms. "Once again please," the MC declared, "a hand for your winner, Nick Norris. And one for the loser, Kid Bacchus."

The boos and cheers dutifully came on cue then died quickly away. The bout was done, the evening's card finished, and already people were heading for the exits.

A few, mainly youngsters, hung about in The Kid's corner, waiting for him to leave the ring, hoping maybe to witness his trademark exit: a victory somersault from the top rope. The Kid glanced at the referee who was gathering the wrestlers' towels and water bottles from their corners. The man in the black and white striped shirt gave a small shake of his shaven head and he understood. Much as he'd like to have obliged the fans, a triumphant vault from the ring was hardly in keeping with the way this night's bout had ended. So instead, he waited for the referee to sit on the middle rope, pushing it down at the same time as he pushed the top rope up, so Kid Bacchus could carefully leave the ring between them the way an exhausted and probably injured teen sensation should.

"Bad luck, Chris!" a tall, thin lad in a faded, frayed POWer Promotions T-shirt said. "The bastard cheated. He was heavier than you."

"Thanks, Dunc." The Kid nodded to this familiar and most die-hard POWer fan, as if agreeing with the strange illogic.

He went to move on but from somewhere behind Dunc came the sound of handclapping, a slow and ironic echo of the previous applause. He peered into the gloom of the hall, lit only by the few lights that were still on over the ring. "Yeah, Kid," a man's voice drawled in mockery of the lad who had just spoken, "you should have won. I mean, you really should have won. That was tonight's script, wasn't it?" Dunc scuttled away as if unwilling to hear such heresy, leaving the young wrestler to face a still-seated middle-aged man wearing, in contrast to absolutely everyone else there that night, a suit and overcoat. The man stopped clapping and lounged back in his seat, an expression somewhere between amusement and boredom on his face. Beside him another figure stood, and although his features were practically invisible in the dim light and shadows of the hall, something about his stance struck The Kid as peculiarly protective of the seated man. *Bodyguard?* The idea was ridiculous, but who knew? The sarcastic speaker had certainly made enough enemies in the business.

"Up yours, Mansfield," The Kid muttered and turned away, making his way up the aisle between the seats to the exit doors.

The man laughed. "Later."

Instinctively, The Kid left the hall through the door that Nasty Nick had not used. Punters liked to think of wrestlers kept apart before and after matches, coached by separate trainers, nurturing long-standing differences and dislikes in, of course, separate changing rooms. In reality, both doors led to the same cramped room, and when The Kid entered it, his bitter enemy of only a few minutes ago was there waiting for him. To his surprise, though, Nasty Nick wasn't alone. "Thought you'd have gone ages ago."

Barry 'Baz' Collins, 'The Midlands Marvel', had been on the bill first that night, and had warmed up the crowd nicely by letting himself be worked over by Sam 'The Mad Man' Cooper. A baby-faced twenty-year-old, Sam had suffered beautifully at the hands of The Mad Man, who also happened to be his uncle. Given that his bout had been over for a good hour, and that he was supposed to be getting a lift to and from the hall with Sam, The Kid hadn't expected to see Baz still in the changing rooms. But there he was, bouncing to his feet with typical Baz enthusiasm, an equally typical broad smile on his face. "Thought I'd hang on in case, y'know, you needed anything."

The Kid looked down at Nasty Nick who was still sitting on the rickety changing room bench, leaning back against the wall, muscular legs spread wide.

"Or we could go for a drink or a burger or something," Baz went on hopefully. "Fish 'n' chips?"

The Kid glanced again at Nick whose hands were now stroking, apparently absent-mindedly, the hairy thigh muscles that had trapped his opponent's lithe body in several breath-stealing body-scissors back in the ring. "I've got...one or two things to sort out here," he said. "I'll catch you tomorrow in The Shed."

Baz hesitated for just a second, as if considering yet one more option, then nodded, his smile resolutely undimmed. "Right. Great. See you there, then." He paused in case either of the other two men wanted to add anything. When they didn't, he gave them both cheery nods and quickly quit the changing rooms.

Kid Bacchus and Nasty Nick Norris regarded each other.

"You were supposed to lose tonight," The Kid said easily.

Nick grinned still more and went to speak, but the door that had just closed behind Baz banged open again and the evening's referee entered, changed now from his traditional black and white gear into a plain black T-shirt with matching black scowl. He was already chewing on a thick cigar in flagrant disregard for any and all health and safety regulations. "You were supposed to lose," he said.

Nick shrugged. "So everyone tells me. Don't lose your hair, Doug."

It was a very old joke, but they all still used it because it always got the same automatic reaction. Sure enough, unconsciously Doug ran his head over his shaven head. "So why didn't you?"

Nick shrugged again and bent down to begin to unlace one of his long leather wrestling boots.

"Mae's furious," Doug said.

"She'll get over it."

Doug shoved a hand in his pockets, pulled out a thin wad of notes and peeled off three, holding them out for Nick. "She might. You might not." He turned to The Kid. "See you later—" his eyes flicked to the man undressing on the bench "—when you've...finished up here."

The Kid was starting on his own boots. He waved. "Later." He looked up, struck by the echo of what he had just said. "Oh, wait. D'you see Mansfield was in tonight?"

Doug nodded shortly. "Saw him. Should have had Baz throw Sam out of the ring at him. Would've taken the shine off his suit. 'Spect he'll collar me again on the way out."

"Careful. He's got someone with him. Might be hired muscle. Two on one, you wouldn't stand a chance."

Doug's disgusted expression made it clear just what he thought of The Kid's mock warning. The door closed behind his disdainful snort.

With a sigh, 'Nasty' Nick Norris, real name Phil Morris, pulled off the one boot now completely unlaced, rolled down the black sock and tossed it to one side to join the boot, then set to work on the other, his stage grin gone, replaced by a more thoughtful expression.

Chris 'Kid' Bacchus, real name Terry Ryan, looked across the small room at him. He loved the old school, plain leather boots the other man wore, soft from years of honourable service. The smell of leather, mingled with sweat and muscle rub. He'd known it since he was a real kid. It never failed to stir something deep inside him. And something deep inside his trunks, too. "So why didn't you lose?" he asked, though more than half his attention was on the second boot sliding down over his erstwhile opponent's calf, then the long black sock being pulled down, balled up and tossed to one side.

6

Phil gave a small smile, maybe at the question, maybe at the awareness of where his young companion's attention really was. "You pissed off you lost?"

Terry laughed. "Course not. It was a good wrestle. I made you look good. You made me look fantastic. The punters got their rocks off. 'S what it's all about, innit? Just means they'll be that much keener to see the rematch. Real grudge vibe going on, yeah?" He smiled openly. "And I'll definitely win the next one." Phil snorted derisively, but in his eyes Terry thought he saw something more guarded. "Believe it!" Terry insisted. "Mae's not going to let you have two in a row. As it is you'll be lucky if she doesn't put you up against Sam for your next two bouts." Terry wrinkled his nose. "And you know what it's like when Sam gets hot and sweaty under the lights."

"Not something I have to worry about any more," Phil said.

"What d'you mean?"

Phil leaned back against the wall which was still damp from the steam of the showers used by the wrestlers who had fought and left earlier. "I quit. That was my last fight. I'm giving up wrestling."

Terry laughed uncertainly, stopping when he saw the other man was serious. "You can't. I mean... Well, you can't. I mean, I know you're old..."

"Only by comparison with the 'teen sensation'," Phil said without bitterness. "And how many more years are you planning to stay nineteen, by the way?"

"Hey, with this face I could carry that into my thirties at least."

Phil snorted again and gestured at his own face. "Yeah, well, with this mug the punters thought I was in my thirties when I *was* nineteen. God knows how old they think I am now."

"Hey, c'mon. I was only joking." And Terry had been. Taunts of old age were common pro wrestling currency, even if, in reality, there were only a couple of years between the guys involved. It was as much a part of the game as the holds and counter-holds. In reality, despite the MC's colourful description, Terry was actually coming up to his twenty-second birthday. Phil had been wrestling, under a variety of ring names, for all of those twenty-two years and a few more besides. But there were plenty who were a lot older than Phil still in the game and, as far as Terry was concerned, there weren't many who looked as hot as beefy Phil did right there and then. No, Phil had never been a baby-face, but his craggy, strong features had been perfect for a heel. Now, naked apart from his coal black trunks, he looked back at Terry with those dark eyes of his, with that flinty cold expression that drove the crowds wild, and Terry felt his stomach lurch and his blood begin to pound at the thought of what that man could do to him right then, right there. And how much he wanted him to.

"I don't know," Phil said softly, his hand once again stroking his thigh, moving more noticeably to the curved line of his crotch. "I'm sorry, Tel, but maybe it's had its day. Wrestling. Our kind of wrestling, anyway."

Terry shook his head firmly, tearing his eyes away from the furry muscle of Phil's legs, trying not to think of how he'd like to stroke that coarse hair, too, run his hands up the swell of the thighs, shove his face into the older man's lap and push his tongue along that line where trunks met skin... He dragged his thoughts back to what Phil was saying. "No way!"

Phil laughed shortly, ruefully. He stood up. For a second there was an almost wistful look on his face as he regarded the lad in front of him, then he grinned, and it was all gone. Then the grin, too, vanished, and all that was left was that sneer. *That challenge*. Terry felt his cock swell, stiffen and push out eagerly at the tight Lycra of his trunks. *Seconds away?*

Without taking his eyes from Terry's, Phil hooked his fingers into the waistband of his own trunks and eased them down, over his hips, his thighs until the still damp material fell around his ankles. He kicked the trunks to one side and stood there, hands on his hips. Challenging. Like most wrestlers on the pro circuit he was wearing a second pair underneath: smaller, pale grey speedos rather than the fuller pro-style trunks. Much more sheer. Two pairs of trunks blurred the outline of what a man kept in them, an important aid to modesty and public decency when the contents were as sizable as the meat Phil packed. Sweat darkened the soaked fabric. And clearly visible was the darker, much wetter patch, right at the top of the long, thick ridge that ran all the way up the front of the tight speedos.

"God, I love wrestling you, Tel." Phil stepped in closer to the boy. "Did I ever tell you that? Did you know?"

"Yeah." It was the only word Terry could manage to get out, his brain filled to the exclusion of almost everything else with the sight and smell of the near-naked, burly man in front of him. Breathless, he stayed seated as Phil walked up to him. He went to stand but Phil slapped one broad hand on his shoulder and pressed him back down. Phil stepped in, pushing his pre-come soaked package into the boy's face, forcing his head back onto the cold tiled wall behind him. Slowly, he ground his hips into Terry's face, rubbing the hardened bulge over and over Terry's nose and mouth, moaning softly. Eagerly, Terry reached up and round to clap both his hands on the older man's arse cheeks and pull Phil's Lycra-covered cock and balls even harder onto his face. Phil gave a guttural laugh. "Fuck, yeah!" At his own crotch, Terry's cock was aching fiercely now, hard as a rock and thrusting out strong against both the pairs of trunks he wore.

Phil leaned down slightly so that now his belly was up against Terry's mouth, and greedily the lad drew his tongue along the hairy gut. When he began to mine the man's navel with his tongue, Phil cried out sharply and pulled away.

"Oh, man!" he gasped. "That feels..." Abandoning attempts to put feelings into words, Phil bodily yanked Terry to his feet, pulled his face hard into his own with both hands and kissed him passionately, tongue thrusting deep into his mouth. When he stepped back both men were breathing as heavily as if they had just wrestled another round. "Get those fucking trunks off." Only too willingly, Terry tore off first his trademark yellow trunks, then the white speedos underneath, having to stretch them out from his body far enough to get the tight material over the jutting hosepipe of cock they were restraining.

Naked except for his wrestling boots and socks, Chris 'Kid' Bacchus stood in front of 'Nasty' Nick Norris in a face-off their recently departed audience could only have dreamed of. The Kid's eager young dick was a ramrod up against his belly, hard against the lower ridges of his washboard abs. Phil stepped in close again, circling the boy's trim waist in his hairy arms, grinding his own still-covered cock against the boy's already dripping, exposed boner. Terry gritted his teeth at the rasping of the material across his exposed and sensitised cockhead, but Phil ignored any protest that might or might not have represented, pressing his mouth to Terry's again and shoving his tongue in even deeper than before. He tasted of cigarettes and mint chewing gum. Both men felt the warm slipperiness of Terry's pre-come spurt up their bellies.

Terry pulled back from the kiss, moving his mouth to Phil's bullish neck, licking, hungrily nuzzling, moving down, dragging his tongue over Phil's chest, across to the nipples where he sucked hungrily at the flesh and dark, damp hair round the hardening, puckered nubs.

Phil cried out inarticulately, and without warning wound his fingers tight in Terry's tousled blond hair, pulling the boy's head back. "Oh, man! You know what I wanted to do to you out there?" Holding the twisted hair in one hand, looking down into his face so he could watch his reactions, Phil rubbed his other hand back and forth over Terry's smooth, cut pecs, the callouses on his palms catching Terry's tender nips, making him wince and grit his teeth again. In turn, he took each roused bud between his fingers and twisted it, harder and harder. Terry gasped, grimaced... but didn't say *stop*. Phil grinned, leaned into his face and whispered hoarsely, his words breathy and hot in Terry's face. "I wanted to rip those trunks off your sweet arse, slam you face first into a corner post and ram my cock right up your tight hole. I wanted to fuck you hard, right then, right there, under the ring lights, the big, hairy bad guy fucking the cute, young blue-eye, with everyone watching, everyone yelling and booing. And everyone lovin' it."

"Fuck!" Terry felt his ball sac tighten in near climax. "Bastard!"

"It's only what they wanted to do to you, most of 'em. They like seeing cute young guys like you being mauled by bears like me." He pulled hard on Terry's now-reddened nipples. "Submit?" He yanked again.

"Shit. No way!"

Without warning Phil broke off and pushed himself back and away from Terry. He stood in front of the lad, panting as if at the end of a round, his eyes tight closed. "Fuck, I'm close," he muttered. "I'm very, very close." The glossy purple head of Phil's cock was mushrooming over the waist band of his grey speedos, liberally oozing pre-come. Slowly, Terry reached out, hooked his fingers into the waistband of the speedos, and pulled outward, fractions of an inch at a time, then downward. Phil swallowed. "Careful. Careful," he whispered shakily.

Terry sank to his knees as he eased the skimpy trunks down over Phil's thighs. Fully revealed, Phil's cock was a thing of beauty and brutality, a veined club. And Terry wanted every inch of it. Pushing his floppy hair back out of his eyes, he leaned in, lips parting.

"No!" Phil practically jumped back. "I'm...too close. Give me...give me a second."

Wordlessly Terry complied, leaning back, literally salivating, waiting. When at last he felt safe enough to move, Phil stepped away, walking awkwardly across the small floor space of the changing room to his kit bag. Returning, he stopped in front of Terry. Holding out his hands, he let the lad see the foil packet and tube he'd pulled out. Terry grinned. "Oh, yeah!"

Without hesitation, Terry stood, turned round, bent over slightly and leaned into the wall. The heat of his body made the cool lube on Phil's fingers seem icy. Phil pressed into Terry's arse crack, gently at first, then with more insistence, and Terry forced himself to relax and allow the blunt fingers to enter him. As Phil generously applied the slippery gel to his hot, aching hole, Terry's cock jumped eagerly and hardened even more, to a degree that was almost painful. When Phil unexpectedly kissed him on the neck with surprising gentleness, even as he lubed his arse, Terry's fuck muscles spasmed dangerously and his sphincter clamped down hard on Phil's reaming fingers. Both men froze, waited, waited, until with a nod Terry signalled he was in control again, and Phil very slowly withdrew his fingers.

Terry watched over his shoulder with barely controlled impatience as Phil tore open the wrapping of the condom, took the rubber to the crown of his cock, then smoothed it down with practised ease, sheathing the veined and iron-hard length. Protected and proud, Phil stepped in one last time to the younger man, and shoved him forward. Terry cried out at the contact of cold changing room tiles on the bare skin of his chest. Then he cried out a second time at the twin sensations of Phil kissing him on his shoulder while simultaneously sliding his thick erection deep up his arse with one unstoppable, unforgiving thrust of his hips. "Shit, Phil! Can't you just... Wait! I can't... Ah! Ah, fuck!"

One long drawn out, inarticulate grunt, and Phil was in the boy up to his balls. *How the fuck could I have imagined I wanted this?* Terry bit down on the inside of his cheeks and struggled to take it. *How could I have thought I could take this monster up my arse? Phil's donkey dick hurts. It bloody, fucking hurts!*

Then the older man withdrew and thrust, withdrew and thrust, his merciless, thick dick smacking hard each time into Terry's hot, throbbing sweet spot, triggering waves of near unbearable pleasure that surged throughout his entire body, washing the pain right away, and the young wrestler remembered with absolute crystal clarity why he'd go through that initial pain any day of the week, again and again, for the rest of his life. Nothing, literally nothing compared to this and, in an ecstasy of fierce joy, Terry utterly abandoned himself to the rough rhythm of Phil's jackhammer fucking. With a sound somewhere between a cry and a groan, a submission and a demand for more, Terry closed his eyes, threw his arms up over his head as he leaned into the wall, and thrust his arse out back as far and hard as he could into the man spearing it with his pitiless dick. "Fuck me, Phil! Aw jeez, fuck me hard! Yeah. Do it!"

In his ear, Phil's breathing was ragged. For a moment he paused, deep in the boy, his bull's balls slap tight against Terry's toned arse cheeks, as he whispered something Terry couldn't make out. Then he pulled back and thrust again, pulled back and thrust, back and thrust, faster and faster, harder and harder, the mutual cries and moans of the two men mingling and filling the changing rooms.

Terry knew the second Phil climaxed, felt the whole of his body stiffen against his back even as a strangled cry of release tore itself out of the older wrestler like a cry of pain. Hands balled into fists, Terry squeezed on the cock up him as hard as his arse muscles could, triggering the ripping surge of his own orgasm. The come from his unsheathed cock shot high up the white porcelain tiles he was pressed against, splashing in thick gouts before running back down the wall in sluggish rivulets. "Oh, man!" he gasped. "Oh, man!"

For long, delicious minutes they stood there as if caught in time, as physically close as it was possible for two men to be, the rasping hairs of Phil's chest, belly and thighs pressed inseparably against the unblemished smoothness of Terry's back, arse and legs. Then carefully, slowly, nuzzling Terry's neck, kissing his shoulder blades, Phil withdrew and stepped back. Terry winced, remaining for a moment face to the wall, the tiles warm now from his body heat, coming down, readjusting to the absence of the massive man in his body. Dimly he heard Phil dispose of the condom then pad barefoot back to him. He turned round. Phil smiled back at him, almost comically sheepish now the moment had, so to speak, come and gone. "I..." Phil stopped. "I'm..."

"That was brilliant, man!"

Phil laughed. "Yeah. Yeah, it was."

Terry reached out. After just a fraction of a hesitation, Phil stepped into his arms, wrapped his own around Terry's body, and for another long moment the two men kissed again.

"Still thinking of giving it up?" Terry said when they finally separated.

"Yes," said Phil, and he walked away back to his kitbag to find his towel and shower bag. "Sorry," he added as he passed Terry, still standing by the wall, on his way into the showers.

When both men had showered and dressed, Phil slung his kit bag across his shoulders. He stood by the door, as if uncertain of quite what to say. "I'm sorry," he repeated, finally.

"You're sorry?" Terry said incredulously. "I'm not."

"No, I don't mean... that. I mean..." Phil came to a halt, unable to find the words. "Just...just take care of yourself, you hear?" Terry looked at him quizzically, not troubling to hide his amusement at his mate's tongue-tiedness, which in turn made Phil, clearly unused to communication that actually involved words, even more inarticulate. The older man sighed heavily and made one last effort to say what he wanted to. "Look, it's a hard world out there, and you're still...a kid."

"*The* Kid," Terry corrected him.

"The *cocky* Kid," Phil pressed on, "who thinks he's going to walk out of every ring without a broken bone and away from every problem with no comebacks. Everything seems easy now, Tel, but this is a tough business, really tough. It's a tough world. There are things..." He broke off again.

"What?"

Phil shook his head and sighed as if still unable to find the words. "Doug knows. And your dad knew."

Terry sobered, momentarily, at the mention of his father. He'd forgotten that Phil was old enough to have known his father, even to have wrestled with and against him on the circuits. He suddenly felt uncomfortable. "Doug?" he said. "Doug's just a miserable old git."

"Just you listen to him, Tel," Phil said earnestly. "He's only looking out for you. You think you don't need anyone to do that for you, but you do, and you're lucky to have him. The world's changing. It *has* changed. Just...don't let it change you." Phil stopped, both he and Terry embarrassed by such unusual eloquence. "Stay safe, mate." He resettled his kit bag on his shoulder and opened the changing room door. "I'll see you around."

"In the audience?"

Phil gave a small laugh. "Maybe."

"Won't be the same."

Phil shook his head. "No, it won't, will it?"

"I'll try and fix it so I get myself thrown out of the ring and land in your lap."

Phil guffawed. "I'll leave my flies open. No point in wasting any time while you're down there, eh?"

Terry shoved his towel into his bag. "If you hang on a minute, I've just got to pass the keys on to Old Ted then I can give you a lift to wherever you're going."

Phil waved a hand. "Nah. 'S all right. Got the wife waiting in the car. She'll already be getting her hair off over being kept waiting. Take care, Tel. Bye!" And with one last wave he was gone.

Terry stood in the centre of the empty changing room and looked around. "Yeah," he said to himself softly. "See you around, *Nick*."

Chapter Two

Another place.

Another ring.

Another fight altogether.

The boy in trunks is called Mario: slim, a Latin lad, skin the colour of milky coffee that beautifully sets off the dark green of the speedos and boots he is wearing. Just the one pair of trunks. The lines of his sweet cock and balls are as clear as the lines of his cut abs and pecs. This audience likes to see cock. They've paid to see it. And more.

His opponent is older, late twenties, lean, sporting black boots and skin-tight black leggings, so tight they could have been sprayed on. They make his pale skin look even paler. Round his narrow waist, a white sash. It is spotted with blood. The blood is Mario's.

The audience is small, but not in the way Kid Bacchus's last audience had been. This audience is *select*. It's entirely male and every man of them has handed over a lot of money to watch this fight. They want more for their money than just wrestling. The pale man in black is not going to disappoint them. He never does.

For over forty minutes he has toyed with the younger lad, has made him grunt, made him groan, stretched and twisted and clawed his young body for the sadistic gratification of his audience. There has been no play-acting. No give and take. This has been real. The blood has been real. Now, the time has come to end it. The only way fights like this can end. The men around the ring know it. Their silence is intense, unnerving. Mario is down on the canvas, backed up against one of the corner posts. Slowly, the man in black advances on him. Mario, dazed with pain and exhaustion, holds up a hand, half surrender, half pleading. The man in black ignores it.

"No! No more! Please!"

The man in black smiles. He reaches down, digs his fingers deep into the hollows of the lad's armpits, pushes his thumbs pitilessly into his pec muscles and pulls him back up to his feet. Mario tries desperately to pull the hands away from his tormented muscles but the claw hold, so often faked in the pro ring, is very real here and completely implacable. The man digging into Mario's screaming flash with his pitiless fingers leans in to whisper in the boy's ear. "You know what they want. Time to give it to them."

He releases the hold, one hand shooting down and between Mario's legs, and with a dip then sudden thrust up, hoists Mario bodily off the mat, his booted feet flying upward, high above his head. He is held for a moment for all to see his plight, then slammed down ruthlessly, back first to the canvas. The boy gasps, arches, rolls back and forth, clasping the small of his back. This ring isn't sprung like the one Kid Bacchus had wrestled in, like normal wrestling rings are sprung. Its surface is hard and unforgiving. Its canvas is stained with marks darker and older than the ones on the pale man's sash. Mario's agonised writhing is no play-acting, and that is the way this audience likes it. As one, they lean in to inspect more closely the suffering boy, the spectacle of his beautiful face grimacing in pain, mouth open, eyes screwed shut, his tight stomach muscles pumping in and out as he gasps for breath.

The man in black crouches at Mario's side, pulls the lad into him then over his raised knee, bending his supple body in the cruel bow of a torturing backbreaker, punishing still further that battered spine. "I submit! I submit!" Mario screams.

His tormentor smiles, teeth like a wolf's. "So what?" He continues to rock the boy over his knee, one hand pressing down on his face, the other on his thigh, the bone of his knee an excruciating fulcrum, wringing out the cries for mercy that the crowd love. Their eyes stay glued to the suffering in the ring being served up for their pleasure, their breathing almost as laboured as the boy's.

When at last he releases his victim, he rolls Mario contemptuously off his knee to fall face down on the hard canvas, where he lies, moaning faintly. It is a release. It is not a mercy. It is the beginning of the inevitable end for all matches in this ring.

Reaching down one last time, the man grasps the waistband of

Mario's tight green trunks and yanks at them harshly. The boy tries to protest but he is a beaten thing. His sweat-sodden speedos are wrenched from his body and held aloft by his tormentor who displays them like a trophy to the crowd that cheers and stomps the floor. With a barked laugh he throws them out into the watching men who scrabble to catch them, the winner waving them in triumph before plunging his face into them to breathe deeply the scent of the vanquished youth's sweat and musk.

The victorious wrestler stands over the boy. He gazes down at the defenceless bare buttocks, at the pale moons of the arse cheeks, so much lighter in tone than the rest of his skin. Round the waist and just visible around the crack between the cheeks is the still paler skin left untanned by the thong the boy last wore on the beach.

The victor kneels between the boy's legs, brutally shoving them apart still further. The prone boy moans but doesn't dare provoke his opponent by resisting or protesting. The kneeling man takes his time, enjoying the sight, allowing the audience to do the same, as he unties and unwinds the sash from around his waist. Slowly he rolls the ends of the sash around first one fist then the other, pulling it taut with a sudden snap, then without warning he drops on the boy's back, leans forward, loops the sash around Mario's throat and pulls back. From somewhere in the audience there is a harshly whispered, "Yes!"

Desperately, Mario claws at the makeshift garotte and grunts in pain at the renewed torque on his back. The man riding him laughs, leans back still further, pulls the cloth still tighter. "Submit, boy?" he asks mockingly. The inarticulate choking in reply makes him laugh more, and pull harder.

In the audience, one of the watching men suddenly cries out as he comes helplessly in his trousers.

Mario's clawing becomes more frantic, his face darker. Then the clawing begins to slacken, the bulging eyes begin to close. One hand drops from the sash, shakily tries to rise again to pull at the cloth, then drops again. The cheering and exhortations for more from the surrounding men gradually dies away... then stops. There is a silence. An expectant silence.

The man on top unwinds the sash and tosses it to one side. He stands over his opponent, one booted foot planted on either side of his body. Mario's eyes flutter open. With a ragged sound he drags in a lungful of air, then another. He coughs, feebly massages his throat.

Slowly, the standing man pulls down his midnight black leggings, over his thighs, over his calves, down and over his boots, kicking them into a pile to one side so that now he, too, stands naked except for his gleaming black wrestling boots. Released at last for all the assembled men to see, his erection is curved, long, hard.

This time he uses the boy's hair, dragging him to the ropes. There is not even a pretence of resistance from the boy. He has no more resistance to give. The man pulls him up and pushes him back into the roughness of the three ropes that mark the boundaries of their small arena, pressing his arms down hard over the top one. With an effort that makes clear the ring's tension, the pale man pulls up on the middle rope until it, too, is over the boy's arms, then lets go. It snaps down, and Mario cries out as his arms are pinned with crushing pressure between the two lengths of thick, twisted hemp. Arms spread wide, he is pinioned helplessly, the ropes biting fiercely into his biceps.

Around the ring there is a shuffling rumbling as men rush to their vantage point of choice for the climax to the evening's entertainment: some wanting the sight of the naked boy's suffering from behind, some wanting to savour the sight of his body and face from the front.

The man in black boots takes his time, letting the men settle again, letting them enjoy the display he has prepared for them. As he waits, he slowly strokes his cock, now gleaming with pre-come under the hot ring lights. He steps through the ropes, out onto the ring's narrow apron, then advances slowly on the trapped boy from behind. Reaching out, he tenderly strokes Mario's beautiful pale arse cheeks that clench reflexively. With one hand he guides his cock to the tight crack between the curved cheeks. He moves it up and down the length of the crack, the hot pre-come oozing from its head tracing a line that gleams wetly. He reaches round the boy's throat, pulling his head back and around with unrelenting pressure so that he can look into Mario's eyes. He smiles. "Please," Mario whispers. The man kisses him. He feels the tightly clenched buttocks against his slick cockhead relax, just fractionally.

With a savage thrust of his hips, the man drives his scimitar-like cock up and in. Mario howls, and all around them there is an answering sound, almost as feral, from the assembled men, as each one vicariously shares the pleasure of shafting the beaten, beautiful boy. The only silent man in the hall now is the one viciously fucking Mario. His eyes glitter as he shafts the tight arse, no lube, no time for accommodation. No pity. He bares his teeth and throws his head back as he reams the twisting, struggling boy over and over. Mario writhes but his arms are held inescapably outstretched by the ring ropes.

Just for a moment, the pale man stops. Sweat makes the length of his lean body gleam like the polished marble of a Greek sculpture. With the boy still speared on his dick, he leans in to Mario's ear and licks it, drawing his tongue around the whorls of the outer ear before nipping the lobe with his sharp teeth. He whispers. "You like this, don't you, Mario? You like being helpless. Beaten. Fucked till you can't stand by the better man."

Hanging in the ropes, Mario swallows, head down. When he finally speaks, his voice is so low, only the man deep in him can hear his words. "Yes," he gasps.

His opponent nods, laughs once, then thrusts himself hard into the boy again. "You knew what you were letting yourself in for, Mario. You'd have done this to me. If you could have. Wouldn't you?" He thrusts again, forcing the boy to cry out before he can answer. Then he leans in to whisper one last time. "But you couldn't. You never had a chance. And now... it's over." He thrusts again. And again. And again.

Chapter Three

"He was supposed to lose," Mae Ryan muttered.

"He knew, Gran."

"He didn't lose."

"I know, Gran."

"So why didn't he lose?"

Terry shrugged his shoulders. "I...don't know, Gran. It was kind of complicated."

Mae scowled into her knitting, a complicated creation in green and pink. As ever, Terry had no idea what it was going to be. There was even a chance he still wouldn't know when it was finished. With Mae it was the process not the result that mattered. "Last time he works for us," she said, needles clacking unforgivingly. Not two feet from her, two young men in Lycra shorts writhed on the ground, grinding their bodies into each other. Mae knitted on, unperturbed.

"You always say that," Doug growled softly. His tone changed abruptly as he turned to address the wrestlers grappling in the ring in front of them. "Make it look like he's hurting you!" he bellowed.

"He *is* hurting me," one of the young men protested.

"Then make it *look* like he is. Sell it!"

Terry sighed. Ordinarily he loved their training/recruiting sessions in their makeshift gym-cum-ring, lovingly built up from nothing over several years, fondly referred to as The Shed, literally at the bottom of their garden, and unofficially the nerve centre of POWer Promotions. But today, his heart wasn't in it. As he, Doug and Mae, the heart, soul and brains of POWer, sat by the cobbled-together ring, each apparently caught up in his or her own gloomy thoughts, Vic and Rick, two wannabe teenage applicants to the shrinking POWer roster wrestled their hearts out in front of them, eager to show off their moves.

They were cute, Terry grudgingly admitted to himself, each in his own way, and probably boyfriends. Vic had a pert arse which his skimpy shorts did little to conceal, and his opponent was taking every opportunity to slap it with some very satisfying cracks of flesh on flesh. Rick, meanwhile, had a huge and almost obscenely noticeable bulge at his crotch. With shorts as suggestive as his partner's, it was a wonder they couldn't all tell his religion let alone his dimensions.

Yesterday, Terry would have said that the highly stimulating seeing-to he'd had from Phil would have kept him satisfied for days. Today, though, he found himself wanting more, as if the previous day's post-fight fuck had stirred up rather than cooled down his libido. Or was it, he wondered, that he just needed comfort or some sort of reassurance after Phil's odd farewell? Not wanting to recall what had seemed like a vaguely framed warning, Terry chose to focus instead on wondering just how tight Vic's arse might be, and just how large Rick's bulge could become, with the proper encouragement. *Yeah*, he mused. Vic just had to be a bottom. You could see it in his eyes that he'd just love to be wrestled to the ground by a stronger opponent, pinned, those tight Lycra shorts peeled from his body, then fucked hard till he came. But what about Rick? Would he want to watch, making mock protests until Terry was finished with Vic, before challenging Terry only to be pinned and fucked in turn? Or would he want to shove that cock of his up Terry's arse while Terry was shafting his boyfriend? Terry smiled dreamily. *A twink sandwich.* Although, technically not, if the twinks were playing the bread. So what then? A beef sandwich? Nah, he was too lean to be beef. Then maybe...

"Ah. No. You're breaking. My back."

Vic's completely unconvincing cries of pain broke Terry's dreams and brought him back to a less exciting reality. He would have loved to try and teach Vic and Rick how to moan and groan with a hell of a lot more conviction than they were demonstrating at the moment. But that would have been sex. When it came to wrestling he had to admit, after nearly twenty minutes of watching the boys fluff moves, repeat routines and spectacularly fail to 'sell', there was nothing he could do to make either of them worth watching in a pro ring. A sideways glance at Doug and the latter's sour expression made it obvious he thought the same thing. "Why don't they just save it for their own bedroom," Doug muttered, "instead of making us watch?"

"So this is where you go to scrape the barrel, is it, guys?"

Jolted from his melancholy musings, Terry turned round sharply to the sound of the mocking voice. Two men were standing in the gym doorway. Mansfield. And the other had to be his silent companion from the night before.

Mansfield strolled easily into the cramped space of The Shed like he owned it, looking around with evident amusement and even more obvious contempt. The man with him, wearing the same large, shapeless overcoat as the previous night, held back in the doorway, only entering when the older man frowned and beckoned him in impatiently, and even then only taking the smallest possible number of steps required. He was wearing some kind of cloth cap that just didn't go with his coat, and which Terry assumed was a trendy fashion statement. Whatever it was, it made him as anonymous as he had been last night and that, Terry considered, was probably the real point of it. He mentally dismissed the man and turned his attention back to the speaker. "Mansfield," he said sourly.

"Mr Mansfield," said Mae primly.

Doug growled. It wasn't clear how he had addressed the new arrival.

"What can we do for you, Mr Mansfield?" Terry's gran asked with a deceptive sweetness.

"I was very curious, Mrs Ryan," Mansfield said, "about this..." He waved his hand around to take in their surroundings. Terry bristled. The Shed and its ring had been a Ryan family labour of love, and for Terry himself a place of refuge and not inconsiderable pleasure of many different kinds. The man in the expensive suit and the barely restrained sneer made him suddenly aware of how very small, how very... *homemade* it was. Unconsciously, his hands balled into twin fists. He made them uncurl by sheer strength of will.

"I've heard so much about it," Mansfield was continuing, "from some of the men who are now working for us. Oh, and that reminds me." He gestured to his silent companion who hurriedly reached into one of his pockets, drew something out and handed it to him. Mansfield passed it on to Mae who inspected it, sniffed then passed it on to Doug. Doug barely glanced at it before flicking it to Terry. It was a small business card in garish red and yellow with a website, e mail address and telephone number, dwarfed by the letters *CMP*, with underneath the explanation: *Critical MASS Promotions.*

"MASS?"

"A pun, young Terence," Mansfield said, with that provoking smile again. "Mansfield and Sons." He gestured to the man at his side. So, a son. Not a bodyguard. Terry looked at him again to reappraise him, but the man was looking down as if deliberately avoiding his eyes and the fringe of his cap completely obscured his face. *Fair enough. If Mansfield was my dad I'd be ashamed to look anyone in the eye, too.*

"So what does the second S stand for?" Mae wondered out loud.

"I can guess," said Doug, with a snort that for him was the equivalent of an uproarious laugh.

"Now, now, Douglas. Let's not be bitter. Let's not start things on the wrong foot."

"Start things?"

Mansfield clasped his hands behind his back as if preparing to address a congregation. In the crude ring behind them, Vic and Rick had stopped their grappling, finally aware that something else was going on, and were listening, still tied up in each other's arms and legs, a panting and mildly sweaty human knot. "As you know," Mansfield began, "for some time now I have been making overtures of...friendship to you and your small...company." Terry, Doug and Mae snorted as one. "I believed that together we could have flourished rather than spending our energies in competing against each other in a cruel world. And I do mean *world.* You may be happy pootling round this tiny island of ours, Terence, but I'm already putting feelers out in Europe. And after Europe..."

"With the crap you put out as wrestling?" Terry interjected. "Give me a break. You couldn't..."

Mansfield raised one hand, and Mae raised one eyebrow. It was the latter that made Terry rein in his temper and listen.

"Now, however," Mansfield went on, "things have changed. *My* company has grown, prospered, reached what you might call—" he coughed lightly at his own small joke "—a critical mass, ready to explode outwards. Hence our new *nom de guerre*." His tone and facial expression changed, both becoming harder. "And I find I am in more of a position to *take* what I want, when I want it."

"You aren't taking us anywhere, Mansfield."

"Perhaps. But then neither is anyone else."

Terry and Doug exchanged puzzled glances. Only Mae looked as if she finally understood where this was going, and she was nodding sadly to herself.

"Although I haven't been able to make friends with you, I have been able to make many other new friends in the business: wrestlers, promoters...venue managers."

Terry bit his lip as light at last began to dawn.

"That's the problem with our little branch of show business, isn't it?" Mansfield oozed. "We're so dependent on the goodwill of others, specifically those good people up and down the country who hire us their halls and sports centres and fields and ballrooms or whatever for us to put on our little shows. Why, without them we just couldn't survive at all. Could we?" The last two words were delivered at last with an unmasked venom. He paused.

"So you're saying...?"

"I'm saying that POWer Promotions was a good operation...in its time. It had a good run. But times change. And people have to move on."

In his head, Terry heard a faint echo of Phil's parting words. Was this what he had meant? "Bullshit!"

"Terry!" Mae snapped.

"Sorry, Gran."

Mansfield smirked laconically.

"There'll always be a place for good, honest British pro wrestling."

Mansfield laughed. "Honest?"

"You know what I mean," Terry said hotly. "Guys who actually wrestle, not stand and shout scripts at each other. Bouts between wrestlers who know more than just one move each." Mansfield cocked a glance at Rick and Vic, still locked in each other's limbs. Rick waved back happily at him.

"Wrestlers like you, you mean?"

"Yes. Like me. And...and..." Terry's eye also fell on Rick and Vic. Vic waved at him. "And others," he concluded.

Mansfield tutted. "Terence, you are so young. So naive." He sighed theatrically, "But, if you really believe that, join me."

"I..." Terry stopped, for the first time lost for words. "*What?*"

"Work for me." Mansfield gestured again to the man at his side. "And my sons." He took a step towards Terry, implicitly cutting Mae and Doug out of their exchange. "Look, son. Your kind of operation is dead. Your audiences are drying up. People want showbiz razzmatazz these days. They want what they see on the telly. It's all about the storylines now, not the moves. I've put on shows where the wrestlers haven't even laid a finger on each other and the audience has still gone wild for it. The way you're going... Well, pretty soon, let's say you might find it hard to get yourself booked into any kind of venue at all. But if you join me I can use you. Trust me. I'll look after you. Even give you the kind of bouts you like. Some of the time."

"And in return?"

"In return?" Mansfield gave a short, barked laugh. "Why I pay you, Terence, of course. More than you're paying yourself at the moment, I'll wager."

Terry genuinely struggled to work out just what game this man was playing. "You could pay anyone. There are loads of guys out there as good as me. Maybe even better," he added grudgingly. "So why say you want me?"

Mansfield wagged a finger at him, and Terry dearly wanted to snap it off. "Don't put yourself down, Terence. You're...good."

"Yeah. I am, aren't I?"

"And you've got a name," spat Doug.

Mansfield glared at Doug and snorted. "The family name? Do you really think there are still enough fans out there who remember The Bacchus Brothers, or who even care that one of them was our Terence's father? Please. Let us be realistic."

Doug shrugged his thickset shoulders. "You tell me. You're the one trying to buy it."

Mansfield narrowed his eyes as he regarded the compact, powerfully built, former Bacchus Brother. "I am here," he said, with unpleasant softness, "to deal with the organ grinder, not the monkey."

From the mats, there was the sound of a smothered snort. It might have been Vic laughing at the monkey idea. It was more probably Rick reacting to the word 'organ'. Mansfield turned so that his back was to Doug and he was facing Terry. "What do you say, Terence?"

Terry's small gym, usually home to the grunts and groans of physical exertions of all kinds, was suddenly still. He knew all eyes were on him, waiting for his decision. He didn't keep them waiting long.

"I say..." he began slowly.

"Terry," said Mae in a warning tone.

Terry took a deep breath. "No," he concluded.

Mansfield blinked as if unable to reconcile the word with its delivery. "No?"

"No."

On one side of him, Mae was chewing her lip thoughtfully. On the other Doug just nodded once and that was that.

Mansfield took a few more seconds as he struggled to take in what was obviously an unexpected and unbelievable answer. When it came, his response lacked any of the gravitas or even the originality he'd obviously been struggling for. "You'll be sorry!" he snapped, and he turned on his heel and stalked from the small shack.

Surprisingly, Mansfield Junior hesitated.

"Get out," Doug rumbled.

Even more surprisingly, given the sheer level of threat Doug had managed to load into just two words, the man still hesitated, until a curt, "Martin!" from his father made him turn and leave The Shed, too.

"Er, do you think...?"

Terry looked round. Vic and Rick had hastily untangled themselves, thrown on T-shirts, grabbed their kitbags and were now standing looking anxiously out through the doorway after the departing Mansfields. "Do you think, maybe, they might, y'know, be...er...hiring new wrestlers, like, well, now?"

Doug fixed them with a cold, hard look. "Go and ask them," he said, very, very softly. A simple suggestion had never sounded scarier. As one, Rick and Vic bolted through the door.

Terry, Doug and Mae were left alone to contemplate the consequences of what Terry had just done and what it meant for their futures.

"Terry…" Mae began.

"I think I'd really like to be alone for a bit, Gran."

Mae looked to Doug who nodded. She patted Terry gently on one arm, the way she always had since he had been a very little boy and had needed comforting. "We'll be back in the house, then. When you need us. C'mon, Doug."

Chapter Four

Terry sank down onto the small stool by one of the ring's corner posts and considered what he had just done. It was the only thing he could have done, wasn't it? Why, then, did he feel that it might just have signalled the beginning of the end of the life he loved? In his mind he ran through the encounter with Mansfield again. The threats had been obvious. But there was something else. Something nagging away at the back of his mind. He gazed around him, taking in the ring, the weights in one corner. The mirrors. *"I've heard so much about it,"* Mansfield had said. *"From some of the men who are working for us."* Terry frowned. *"Some of the men who are working for us."*

Phil!

With a wordless yell of anger, Terry kicked out at one of two small dumbbells on the floor nearby. Was that what Phil had been trying to warn him about the previous night? That he was going to sell him out? But why not just tell him? There was no way he could have been scared of Terry. *I'm not Doug! We could have talked. We could have sorted something out, as long as it didn't involve more money. We could have...* Terry stopped as realisation kicked him in the face. *But then Phil wouldn't have got his farewell fuck, would he?* By being so two-faced, Phil had got to screw him twice. With another, louder, yell of fury, Terry lashed out at the second dumbbell.

"Sorry I'm late, I..." Baz came to a halt in The Shed's doorway. He took in the sight of Terry's face and the dumbbell skittering across the floor to crash against a wall which shook alarmingly. "Er, bad time?"

"Yeah. You could say that."

Baz continued to hang back in the doorway as if nervous about actually stepping across the threshold. "Were Laurel and Hardy really that bad?"

"Who?"

Baz tried a grin. "Vic and Rick. The try-outs."

"Ah, right. No. I mean, yes. Yes, they were bad. Shit, actually. But that's not why..." Terry trailed off. Baz was a sweet guy, a dependable wrestler and the last decent recruit POWer had made. But there was nothing he could do about the situation Terry found himself in, so what was the point in even trying to explain? "Look, mate, this is just not a good time right now, okay? Those two dickheads have gone and I'm...I'm just not up for any more training today."

Baz ducked his head a couple of times in what might have been nods. "'S okay, mate," he said. "Not sure I'm up for anything like a workout myself, not after what Uncle Sam put me through last night. I could stick around for a bit if you like." He glanced in the direction of the kicked dumbbells "Help you tidy up maybe?"

Terry gave a small laugh, but shook his head. "Cheers, but no, really. I'm just going to close up and..." He stopped, not sure what he was going to do. What was there to do? "I'm just going to close up," he concluded.

Reluctantly, but with the cheeriness that was his trademark, Baz accepted it would be best for him to go, and after getting a promise from Terry that he would call when next he was running a training session or, even better, when next he had a bout lined up, he said his goodbyes and left. Terry stood for a moment looking at the closed door, and for the first time wondered whether he would be calling Baz to book him for another fight. Whether he'd ever be booking anyone ever again.

With a heavy sigh, he turned back into his beloved gym and trudged over to collect the abused dumbbells and to restore them to their rightful place in a rack.

Behind the weights rack was one of The Shed's full-length mirrors. Looking up from replacing the weights, he found himself staring into the reflection of his own eyes. "Wanker," he said dispassionately to his own image. "Prat," he added as he thought about how easily he'd been played by Phil, how easily he was being squashed by Mansfield. *Mind you*, he couldn't help thinking as his reflection stared back, *there's no denying I'm a good-looking wanker and prat.*

He turned his head from side to side, vaguely wondering if his misfortunes could be read yet in his features. He'd been told often enough he was handsome so it would be kind of stupid to deny it. He knew he'd been lucky with the wheat gold hair and striking blue eyes, perfect for a wrestling 'face'. But the body? That was something you had to work at. That was something he felt he could take pride in.

Only too willing to think about something other than his gloomy prospects for a moment, Terry pulled his T-shirt up and over his head and let it fall to the floor. Unselfconsciously, he studied the naked torso revealed. At five ten, he was actually one of the taller wrestlers on the circuit. As a very young kid he'd wanted to be even taller but then he'd discovered how being just a couple of inches under six foot actually made any muscle he put on look even better. Slowly he turned his upper body, first right, then left, keeping his legs fixed, his hips square to the mirror, an old bodybuilders' trick designed to make the waist look even narrower. Not that he had anything to worry about on that score. Rigorous and protracted crunches, sit-ups and leg raises had given him abs like ridged steel and a waist measurement to make women and a hell of a lot of grown men sigh.

He leaned in to look even more closely at his reflection. It wasn't really vanity. Well, almost not entirely. It was coming round time for some new publicity photos for POWer's posters and website, and he wanted to make sure he hadn't picked up any bruises or rope burns from the previous evening's fight. Or from what had happened afterwards. For the moment he deliberately put to the back of his mind the thought that maybe those pictures wouldn't be needed now, and made himself focus instead on his inspection.

Nope. He slowly scanned his unblemished skin. *Nothing there.* He struck a few poses, fists clenched and on hips, again emphasising that waist, then down on one knee, one arm flexed to show off his biceps, impressively defined in one still so young, then standing again with arms out to the glass as if inviting his reflection to lock up with him. He nodded. *Looking good. Muscle mass building nicely with no loss of definition. Clean-cut pecs. Still lightweight of course, but heading into middleweight fast.* He ran one hand through his hair. No wonder the punters loved him. He gave a small frown. Would they still love him if he lost all his hair like Doug had? He dropped the frown. Course they would! With or without hair he'd still have that jawline, still be able to

31

call up that cheeky come-hither smile. Nah, no need to worry. He'd always be a looker. His eyes fell to his crotch. A pity he couldn't put his best feature on display.

Terry glanced across to The Shed's door. It was closed. He looked back to his full length reflection. Unhurriedly he dropped the soft cotton jogging trousers he was wearing. Underneath, he was going commando. *Well, it always feels so damn comfortable.* Proudly Terry took in sight of the cock he had been blessed with. Hanging free between his legs from its nest of soft gold hair, his endowment was generous indeed. Who knew how many more bums on seats POWer Promotions would get if the paying punters had a clearer idea of just what it was the exciting young wrestler in the ring had hidden in his trunks? Of course, Mae'd have a fit! He turned round fully, looking over his shoulder to get a view of his back and arse: a tasty V of muscle tapering down to two tight buttocks with not an ounce of fat in sight. He flexed his arse cheeks in turn with amused satisfaction. *Now those are what you call pert.*

He turned round again to face the mirror and his sizeable tool. He stroked its length thoughtfully. *Nude pro wrestling. That would be cool. Or hot!* There were definitely a few wrestlers on the circuit he'd like to get down and grapple with in the buff. And doing it with people watching and cheering... *Very hot.* He'd need a new ring name, though. 'Kid' just didn't prepare an audience for the adult-sized meat he was carrying. So, what could it be? Caught up in delicious dreaming, his melancholy of a moment ago temporarily and very deliberately forgotten, Terry's stroking became gradually heavier, faster. *The Python? The Firehose? The Yardarm?*

His mood, and his member, lifted. He closed his eyes and took hold of his stiffening dick with both hands. Who would he really like to get to grips with, bollock naked in front of a crowd? Paul Prince, that stocky, hairy-arsed Yorkshireman he'd wrestled last month? Straight, so they said, but he'd seemed mighty keen to make as much body contact as possible with Terry, keeping on the holds for much longer than had seemed necessary. Maybe he'd been enjoying the sensation of a lithe lad twisting and squirming against his body at least as much as Terry had enjoyed doing the twisting and squirming.

Or what about veteran Johnny Angel, with that hot retro anchor tat on his left delt? Johnny had been in the business for years, and could tie opponents twice his size in knots, but was enough of a pro to realise a good bout had to have some give and take in it. And besides, he knew just how damn sexy he looked when he played the jobber, caught in some villain's 'inescapable' submission hold and moaning like a man taking cock. In at least two of the bouts they'd had, Terry had had to release him from holds he was working on him because the sight and sound of Johnny selling his 'suffering' was just too much of a prick-tease and had brought Terry close to coming in his trunks.

Wanking full on and with vigour now, Terry let his mind run through a gallery of horny wrestlers, some he'd actually fought, some he hadn't but wanted to, and pictured each of them naked and up for it. Steve Stone. A bull of a man, grizzled and standing at nearly six feet six. Five stone heavier than Terry, so they'd never wrestled each other, but they'd tagged once. Terry had played the much lighter, younger jobber and Steve had been the experienced 'older brother' figure, his old school leotard straining over slabs of chest muscle and a well-rounded gut. He'd spent most of their match pantomiming anguish from his corner outside the ring while Terry was twisted, stretched, clawed, posted and thoroughly 'squashed' by two skinhead heels until he was finally able to make the tag and save the day. Terry had fond memories of Steve playing the devoted partner, clapping him affectionately on the back, on the shoulder, on the arse, the hand always lingering longer than it really needed to, the victory hug at the end that bit tighter, and damper, than it should have been. Terry had had high hopes of a little *après*-match fun with Steve, until he'd seen the even bigger guy waiting backstage for him after the bout with their two dogs and the ride back home. But if they could ever meet again. Alone. Naked...

Terry's dick was throbbing expectantly in his hand now. *Shit!* Never mind Paul, Johnny and Steve. If only he could have a wrestler, *any* wrestler, in there with him right then!

"'S bigger than I thought."

Terry span round at the sound of the voice, hand jumping, first from his cock then back to it in a futile effort to hide what was by then frankly unhideable. "What?"

The figure in the doorway gestured. "This. Your gym. Bigger than I thought. When they told me in the house that it was in the shed at the bottom of the garden, I thought it'd be tiny, but this…" He strolled in, dumping the kitbag he had slung over one shoulder onto the floor. "It's cool." He stood, staring around himself, and Terry didn't know whether to feel relieved or irritated that the newcomer didn't seem at all phased, or even interested, in the massive standing member he was struggling so unsuccessfully to conceal.

"Er, right. Thanks." Terry scrambled for his discarded jogging bottoms and hurriedly pulled them on. "And just who the hell are you?"

"Mark," said the new arrival, apparently completely unbothered by Terry's abrupt tone. "Word on the grapevine was you were looking for new wrestlers."

Always. Once. When we had a business. Now… He opened his mouth, went to tell Mark that it was over, that he'd come too late. That POWer Promotions was as good as closing up for business. And then, jogging bottoms finally back in place with drawstring pulled tight, he took his first real look at the other man. And he changed his mind. "Might be," he said.

Mark was an inch or two taller than him, maybe a stone and a half heavier, mid to late twenties. Jeans and leather jacket. Buzz cut black hair. Face… Not strikingly handsome, not strikingly ugly. Quite bland, actually, apart from the sexy black stubble. But then, who cared about the face at times like this? He was a wrestler, or at least, wanted to try out as one, and a wrestler was exactly what Terry had been wishing for. Things, metaphorically and literally, were looking up again. "Brought any gear?"

Mark slipped his holdall off his shoulder. "Course," he said, unzipping the bag. "We going for it, then?"

Terry took in the tight sweep of his jeans across his arse in glorious close-up as Mark bent over his kitbag. "Yeah. I think we are."

Mark wasted no time and no further words, happily stripping down then and there, pulling on the dark purple trunks and matching ring jacket and the black boots he'd bought, rich with the smell of new leather. Terry had to rush around gathering his own kit together so as to keep up. By preference he'd have gone for his favourite tight, light blue trunks. Sheer and cut high over the thigh and low over the waist, they showed his package off to perfection and had plenty of give for a healthy hard-on. In combination with his white boots and his hot body they were a cock-raiser *par excellence.* But, rushing now, he could only find his standard black boots and a pair of red speedos. *Okay, your basics it is. That's fine. The boyz always like the red speedos!* Quickly he pulled the gear on, trying to snatch sideways glances at his new opponent as he did.

Mark had already climbed into the ring and taken his position in one corner, waiting for him before Terry had finished lacing up his second boot As quickly as he could, Terry tied off his boots, and, forsaking the ring jacket, vaulted over the top rope in best Kid Bacchus style to face his challenger. "You wrestled professionally before?"

"Nah."

"Wrestled pro-style?"

"Yeah. Some. Mostly just fooling around. You ready?" Mark unzipped his ring jacket, pulled it off and threw it carelessly over the corner post. He stepped up to the centre of the ring, swinging his arms around in vague windmilling gestures that Terry guessed were meant to pass for warm-ups.

Raw. Terry stepped forward to square off. *Keen but raw. And with definite potential.*

Mark was in good shape, gym-solid with pleasing bulges in all the right places: shoulders, arms, thighs and, Terry was really pleased to see, trunks. The light hair across his pecs was as black as on his head, and a thin line crossed his stomach from chest to waist. Terry looked on appreciatively, following the line of that hairy trail with his eyes as it made its uneven, sexy way over Mark's belly into the promising depths of his trunks. The explorer in Terry was very keen to find out just exactly what lay at the end of that trail. He had a warm feeling they were both going to enjoy this wrestle very much indeed.

Mark held out his arms, his stance technically accurate for a wrestler's lock-up, but stiff and awkward. He was scowling, like a man tackling some particularly difficult mental problem, or getting ready to tear another man's head off. *Okay, let's just relax him a bit here.* Terry reached out a hand for the traditional pre-match handshake. Mark responded with a vicious forearm smash straight into Terry's chest, and the next thing Terry knew he was flat on his back looking up at the overhead strip lights. "Whoah. Now hold on a minute there, fella." He clambered back to his feet. "Just a..." He never even saw the second smash coming. *That strip light's blinking a lot.* Once again he lay, back to the canvas, looking up. *Must be on the way out.*

A second time he clambered to his feet. "The thing is," he got as far as saying, before Mark was on him, a meaty arm wrapped round his throat, dragging him back down to the mat and squeezing hard. Terry choked, yanking uselessly at the solid biceps throttling him, and his world swam, turned yellow, and began to fall away. Frantically he slapped at Mark's thick arm, struggled to gasp out his submission. Mark squeezed even harder...

Several seconds later, Terry was looking at that strip light again. *Yup. Definitely on the way out. Right.*

More carefully this time, he climbed back to his feet, making sure his eye was on Mark and there was a safe distance between them. No more surprises. And no more Mr Fall Guy. Someone had a lesson to learn on what pro wrestling was really all about.

Mark stepped forward, the scowl replaced by the start of a grin. *Getting cocky, eh?* Terry swiftly turned side on to his man and shot out his elbow with expert aim and just the right amount of force. It rammed unerringly into Mark's belly with a pleasing smacking sound followed by the equally pleasing whoosh of air forcibly expelled from Mark's lungs. Mark doubled over, and Terry moved in close, jumped up and came down, driving his elbow down with him, this time into the back of Mark's head. Mark dropped like a sack of coal to the mat and Terry was on him. With practised ease he caught the man's arm, pulled it round, pushed it up Mark's back and wrung an instant submission from his opponent with a savage backhammer.

Terry released his hold and sprang back to his feet, wary of angry reprisals. He wasn't normally that brutal with a rookie, but the man had asked for it and had to learn. Mark rose, too, gingerly swinging and massaging the arm that'd been twisted nearly to breaking point, and Terry stepped in and swept both his legs from under him with a quick reaping motion of his own long leg, threw himself back on top of the man, wrapped his strong arms round Mark's head and twisted hard. Not subtle, not even a move good enough to be graced with a special name.

But it did the trick nicely. Mark's second submission was gratifyingly swift.

When they rose yet again to face each other, both men were breathing heavily and moving much more warily. Mark moved first, head down, lunging at Terry. Terry didn't dodge, taking the charge, letting the heavier man drive them both back into the ropes, then using the energy of the rebound to drive Mark over and onto his back once more, pulling his legs up way over his head so that his purple-clad arse was pointed helplessly towards the ceiling and he was pinned there easily. "One! Two! Three!" Terry cried out, slapping the mat at each call as the man underneath him squirmed, thrashed and swore colourfully. "Gotcha!" he proclaimed, throwing the beaten man's legs to one side. He squatted back, hands on his hips, sucking in lungsful of air and watching carefully for Mark's reactions.

Mark just lay there looking up, his belly, crossed by that teasing hairline, rising and falling as he, too, sucked in much needed air. "That," he gasped at last, "was fucking fantastic! Abso-fucking-lutely fantastic." He pulled himself up into a kneeling position and faced Terry. "You have got to show me how you do that."

Terry grinned. He'd been worried Mark might have a strop and storm out, or even try to take a swing at him. He could have handled either, but neither would have led to the conclusion to this bout he was hoping for. "Okay. But look. That might have been a good scrap..."

"Fucking brilliant."

"...but it wasn't great wrestling."

Mark frowned. "How'd you mean?"

"Look at us." Terry held out his hands to take them both in. "Knackered."

Mark sat up brightly. "I'm up for another round."

Terry drew himself up as well, not wanting to be outdone in the fitness stakes. "Well, yeah, I am, too, of course, but that's not what I mean. We've been wrestling for about what, five minutes? And already there's been three submissions, one pin and a couple of near knock-outs. That's enough for half a dozen bouts. We've got to last for half an hour at least. At this rate one of us will have killed the other within the first ten minutes."

"Bouts don't last that long on the telly," Mark said uncertainly.

Terry sighed. "They used to. And they still do, the way we do them. If all audiences wanted to see was two guys beating shit out of each other they'd be happy with boxing, or cage-fighting. Wrestling's got to give 'em something else. We give them moves, a bit of gymnastics, skills." He stopped for a moment and, for the first time, looked pointedly and unashamedly directly at Mark's body. "And something to look at." Their fierce, sudden exertions of the last few minutes had brought out the sweat from both of them. It lay on Mark's skin with an oil-like sheen, accentuating the sliding movements of the muscles under his warm skin. "If the guys who are fighting have got something worth showing."

Mark's frown cleared as suddenly as it had come. "Fair enough," he said amiably. "I can see that." He looked at Terry's body as appreciatively as Terry had just looked at his. "I like looking at guys' bodies. I like people looking at my body." His hand had fallen to his lap and was pressing none too subtly on his crotch. "You like looking at my body?"

"Yeah."

Mark nodded, as if really it was the only answer possible. "Good."

Terry nodded. "Good."

Mark ran his hand over his close-cropped hair. "So. Wanna fuck?"

"Er, yeah." Terry tried not to double take. This man's speed in all things took some getting used to. "Why not?"

Without any more preamble, Mark tugged at his purple trunks, leaning back and lifting his legs to pull the trunks up and over his boots before flinging them the way of his ring jacket. Only then did he rise to his feet to stand over the still-seated Terry. His cock was thick and very, very hard, standing to excited attention over a large, swinging ball sac in the nest of jet black hair that lay at the end of that teasing glory trail. He wrapped a fist around it and pumped it vigorously several times before stepping into Terry and swinging it heavily back and forth across the young man's face with meaty slaps like a flesh truncheon. "Suck on that, mate." He reached out with his free hand before Terry could even begin to answer, clapped it around the back of Terry's head and pulled him into his crotch, forcing his engorged cock into Terry's mouth and way down his throat. Terry struggled not to gag. Mark, completely unconscious or uncaring of his difficulties, pumped his hips powerfully into Terry's face. The one hand stayed clamped to the back of Terry's head, while the other reached up to work his own nipples which had sprung to eager hardness. He threw his head back, eyes shut tight in pleasure. "Yeah! Oh fuck yeah!"

Terry sucked manfully on the solid meat in his mouth, reaching round with both hands to grab Mark's bare buttocks to keep himself balanced, his palms sliding over the sweaty cheeks. "Yeah. Yeah!" Mark was moaning in time to his thrusts. "Suck on my big dick. Suck on it." With a face full of wiry crotch hair, Terry did as he was told. "Yeah. Oh fucking yeah!" Terry's mouth filled with the salt of Mark's liberal pre-come. Just like his wrestling: fast and to the point. No problem. Terry moaned, sucked harder, and got ready for the gusher. *No choice here between spit or swallow.*

He was caught off guard when Mark pulled out, leaving him open-mouthed as a goldfish. "It's okay..." he began.

But Mark had turned round, his fist once again at his cock, pumping hard, and he was down on his knees on the mat, leaning forward on his one free forearm, forehead down to the canvas, bare buttocks pointing up at Terry's face. He broke off from his wanking for a second to look round, reach back and slap his own glutes hard. "Up my arse, mate!" he shouted. "Fucking get your cock in me!"

Thrown off balance for just a second at the abrupt change of direction, Terry swiftly recovered and, never one to look a gift horse, or a willing arse, in the mouth, rose. He jumped out of the ring and dashed over to his kit bag and its store of lube and rubbers, tearing off his trunks as he went, almost tripping in his haste. "Right. Just...hang on. Don't...don't go anywhere." Diving back into the ring, Terry flung the tube of lube to Mark to do with as he wished, feverishly tore the condom out of its foil and rolled it the full length of his own, now blue-steel cock. Armed for the battle, he turned to face Mark's sweating butt cheeks. "My God, that is a great arse," he breathed.

"Fucking well fuck it then!" Mark cried out.

Terry dropped to his knees behind the gasping, wanking man, and positioned the tip of his sheathed cock on the arse crack, the thin line of coal black hair nestling within a stark contrast to the pale curves of the hard cheeks. He took a deep breath and slowly leaned forward and pushed. Mark's muscles relaxed and took the length of him in at one go then gripped, hard. Terry couldn't help it. He cried out.

Mark howled. "Oh yeah! Come on!" He beat the mat with one hand, then let go of his own cock with the other and, using both arms, pushed himself up and back from the canvass and harder into the cock spearing him. Terry cried out again, louder, as he lost his balance, falling backward so that he breakfalled automatically, ending up once again looking up at that damn strip light but this time with a sweating, moaning wrestler squatting on his tentpole dick. Mark drove himself down hard on its sheathed length, pushing himself up with powerful thrusts of his thighs, then sinking back down on it, driving both of them inexorably into a frenzy. "Fuck me! Come on! Fuck me!" Mark cried out and, more than willing to oblige, Terry thrust his hips up again and again to meet Mark's downward squats, forcing himself deep up into the arse slamming down onto him, goaded to still harder, fiercer, upward hip thrusts by Mark's repeated cries. Finally, the shouts became one long wordless howl, Mark's arse slammed down and clenched tight on Terry's cock and Mark's come geysered up and out, falling far from both their bodies in a warm torrent on the canvas.

"Fuck me!" Mark gasped, pushing himself up one last time and off Terry's cock.

"I think," gasped Terry, panting like a man who had run a marathon, "I just did."

"Right. Come on, mate." Mark dropped like a heavy sack to the canvas and lay there, back to the mat, careless of lying in the small lake of come he'd jettisoned from his well-stocked cobs. "Give me what you've got."

Easing off the condom and chucking it to one side, Terry eagerly straddled the prone man, gazing down at the chest, the face, as he worked his hot cock with his hand.

"You want to come, yeah?" Mark goaded.

"Oh, yeah."

"On my tits. On my face?"

"Oh, yeah."

"Well come on, then. What's stopping you?" Without warning, Mark shoved both hands under Terry's arse, pulled the lad's tight buttocks apart and slipped two fingers straight up and into his hole. Terry cried out in surprise and pain as the unlubed digits stabbed deep but true, straight into the wildly throbbing heart of his arse, triggering an uncontrollable orgasm that fountained over the man under him, gouts of come splattering down all over his face and chest. "Yeah! Give it up! All of it!" Mark grinned and ran his tongue round his lips, licking up Terry's plentiful salty jism as it rained down on him.

When at long last he came to himself again, Terry had somehow slid off Mark's body and was lying next to him on the mat, both of them staring dazedly up at the ceiling. It was Mark who finally broke the silence. "That light needs fixing," he said.

Terry got up. He came back with towels and they took turns wiping each other and the mat down. "So, did I pass the audition?" Mark asked.

Terry nodded. "Oh, yes. Oh, very much yes."

"Sound."

Mark threw the towels to one side and flopped back on the canvas. Terry lay next to him, his head on Mark's outstretched arm, his naked side against Mark's. It felt...good. "That was just exactly what I needed."

Mark looked sideways at the lad. "Needed?"

Still basking in the post-sex glow, Terry waved a hand airily. "'S nothing. Hell of a day, that's all."

"Tell me about it."

Maybe I'm getting cynical in my old age, but I'd kind of expected Mark to be a wash-and-go merchant. Having had his shag, Terry hadn't thought Mark would stick around very long. *Phil hadn't!* He was surprised. But it was a nice surprise. "Well. If you really want to know..."

He told Mark everything. About Mansfield, Critical MASS, the apparent near end of POWer Promotions, even about Phil's leaving, which he hadn't meant to but which sort of came out with all the rest. Mark listened to it all, head propped up on one arm, from Mansfield and son's first appearance back at the last public bout to their visit and threat just before Mark's arrival. When Terry had finished, Mark regarded him, none too concerned. "Is that all?"

"Er, yeah."

Mark pulled Terry's naked body in closer with the arm the lad had been lying on, and with the other hand squeezed a naked arse cheek. "Well, that's easily sorted."

Yeah. Right. But Terry lay and listened. And as he did, bit by bit, incredibly, his scepticism gave way to something like hope and then to actual belief that things really could be 'sorted'. This guy was just exactly what he and POWer Promotions needed. "That's...brilliant!" he exclaimed when Mark finished outlining his ideas.

Mark shrugged a shoulder and gave a lazy grin. "That mean I get a second fuck?"

Terry leaned in close, kissed him, and happily reached for his cock. *A friend with benefits and a business plan. Yeah. Brilliant!*

PART TWO

Chapter One

"Europe."

"Fuck off."

"Doug!" said Mae automatically.

"Sorry," said Doug, equally automatically.

"Europe," Terry said again, as if perhaps simple repetition could win the day.

"Fuck. Off."

"Doug!"

"Look, this could go on all night at this rate."

"Terry," said Mae in a placatory way, even as she glared at the unrepentant Doug. "We've talked about Europe before."

Terry held his hands out in front of himself to forestall her arguments. "I know, I know. And why? Because Europe still has promotions like ours. They still want to see the kinds of bouts we put out. Not the sort of showbiz crap Critical MASS and others like it are into."

Mae and Doug exchanged glances across the small kitchen table at which all three were seated. "And we've always come back to the fact that we just don't have the resources, the contacts to crack the market over there," she said.

"Plus, The Hardman here—" Terry cocked a thumb in Doug's direction "—has his thing about crossing the Channel."

"So what's changed?" growled Doug.

Terry took a deep breath. "I've got the contacts."

Mae looked surprised. "What kind of contacts?"

"Promoters. Venue holders. All the kinds of people we need."

"How?" said Doug.

Terry took another deep breath. "I've met someone." He looked to Mae, as much as anything to avoid the sarcastic look from Doug. "His name's Mark. You've already met him. He's the guy who came here to the house the other night and you sent him down to the ring."

"Mark...?"

"Smith. Yeah. It turns out he's just back from Europe. He's training to be some kind of entertainment entrepreneur, on some sort of scheme to find out how they do things over there, what the market is after. And he's mad about wrestling."

"Handy coincidence," Doug suggested drily.

"Not really. I mean, he wouldn't have looked me up if he hadn't been into what we're into, would he? In fact, it was being in Europe and seeing the sort of wrestling they've still got going over there that kind of relit his interest. He's been travelling around for a couple of months now, learning how things work, even getting some wrestling in, and making the contacts. He just didn't know how it was all going to come together until he came back and...bumped into me."

"Bumped?"

"Yeah."

"Handy coincide..."

"You've said that, Doug. Sometimes things work out, y'know? The world isn't always doom and gloom."

"And it isn't always fun and games, either."

"Money," said Mae with a sigh, putting down her knitting and verbally forcing herself between the men in her life. "You know it always comes down to money, Terry. And we haven't got any. Not enough to finance some grand European alliance."

"I know, Gran." Terry reached down into his kitbag. He pulled out an already dog-eared card folder, took a sheaf of papers from it and spread them out on the kitchen table. "And this is the plan we've come up with. Mark's come up with," he added with reluctant honesty, "but only after I agreed." Mae re-donned her glasses and scrutinised the columns. "A tour of Europe that puts POWer back on its feet and on the map. The whole thing is designed to be self-financing, almost from the start. More than that. We go during Britain's off season..."

"Which is just about any season these days."

"...and we can bring in more in three months than we'd make in a year here. Plus, we big up our rep, get bookings for another year at least, hook up with some of the better wrestlers they've got over there, bring 'em back here for bigger and better shows than anything Mansfield can put on, backed up by the new promoters we've linked with. We'd still be wrestling. I'd still be wrestling." He looked at Mae and Doug. "We'd still be in the business."

Mae, the woman who for over forty years had guarded POWer Promotions' finances with the tenacity of a bulldog, studied the rows of numbers. "He seems very thorough, your new friend," she said grudgingly.

"Like I said, it's what he's training to do." Terry didn't like to add that actually he, too, had been surprised when Mark had turned up the day after their wrestle with the wallet of printouts. The organised expertise they represented hadn't quite squared with Mark's blunderbuss approach to wrestling. And to sex. But then that was Mark's job, or the job he wanted to do. Some guys approached work and pleasure in very different ways, he guessed. Not everyone could mix the two as easily as he liked to.

Mae handed the all-important sheet of monetary promises to Doug, who took it reluctantly. "But these figures, the whole organisation, are based on taking at least five wrestlers on this tour."

Terry nodded. "Yeah."

"So, who you taking with you?" Doug asked bluntly.

Terry took a deep breath. "You thinking of coming out of retirement?"

"Fuck off."

"Doug!"

"Right. Then it's Baz, Eric and Jonesy. They're the only ones who can commit to that sort of time away at the moment. I know because... I checked with them."

"Already?"

"Yeah."

"And?" Doug waited. "I know your new friend Mark is the one who's good with numbers, but even you must see that's still only four wrestlers altogether, counting you as well."

"And there's that *almost* you slipped in back there, Terry," Mae added. "This scheme is self-financing, *almost from the start*. But not *actually* from the start. It'll need an initial outlay of..." She pursed her thin lips and squinted as she did the mental maths.

"I know, I know," said Terry hurriedly. "I know how much we need." He looked at Doug. "And I know we need a fifth wrestler." He took a deep breath. He'd recognised all along that this would be the tricky part. "And the solution is the same to both. Mark."

Mae frowned. "Mark's going to...lend you the money? Terry, we can't..."

"He's going to give it to us. Well, invest it, really."

Mae looked dubious. "I thought you said he was studying business. Doesn't sound like he's much of a businessman yet."

Doug was more openly sceptical. "What does he want in return?"

Terry came out with Mark's condition. "He wants to wrestle with us."

Doug looked like he'd been slammed into a corner post by a heavier heel. "Is he trained? Does he have any experience? Does he know one end of a ring from another? Can he even...?"

Terry raised his hands. "He's new, yes. He's...raw. But he's got potential. Really, he has. Like I said, he got some wrestling in while he was travelling. And...I've started training him."

"I'll just bet you have."

"And I want you to work with him, too. You taught me almost everything I know."

"I taught you *everything* you know...about wrestling. I just didn't teach you everything *I* know."

Terry grinned. "Whatever. It kills me to say it, Doug, but you are still the best trainer in the business. Bringing Mark up to speed will be no trouble at all for you. You'll see." Terry spread his hands out to both of his family. "The thing is, we need him if we're going to do this. And...and he really wants to do it. *I* really want to do it." He stopped. Instinct told him this was the sticking point, the crucial moment when he would or wouldn't win over the two people who mattered most to him in the whole world: the grandmother who'd raised him like a mother, and the uncle figure who, in fact, had been more than a father to him.

What he hadn't mentioned, of course, was the last condition Mark had stipulated before he agreed to help. That one Terry was definitely saving till Mae and Doug agreed to his plans. If they agreed. Anxiously, silently, Terry waited.

"I've wrestled abroad..." Doug began.

"I know," Terry butted in. He couldn't help himself. This was the old, old story. "You and Dad wrestled there as The Bacchus Brothers," he said in a sing-song tone suggestive of frequent repetition, "and you had a Really Bad Time." He punctuated the last phrase with air speech marks. "You've told me. Many times. Though you never go into the details." He stopped, looked Doug in the eye and waited. Doug glared back at him unwaveringly, but said nothing. Terry sighed. "So, no change there then. But Europe's a fu−" he caught Mae's warning glance "−a very big place. We don't have to go...wherever it was you went. And besides, that was a long time ago."

"Not that long."

"Things have changed. They have electricity and everything now."

"Terry," his gran said warningly.

Terry held his hands up. "Sorry, sorry. Look, all I'm saying is we need this. I need this. And whatever it was happened to you and Dad when you were there needn't happen to me. Especially−" and he took another deep breath "−if you'll come along to make sure it doesn't."

"What, like a manager?"

Terry brightened. "Yeah."

"Sounds like you're managing things pretty well yourself. You and your 'friend', Mark." Doug mimicked Terry's air punctuation.

"So, I'm taking charge a bit more. This is the family business, yeah? That's what I'm supposed to do, isn't it? I'm growing up."

"You've a way to go yet."

"Then come to look after me. Come as my roadie. Come as my nanny. Anything. Just...come."

There was an awful silence in the kitchen, and now it was Mae's turn to look back and forth between the two males at her table. Either of them would be happy to take on guys twice their size in a ring and would most likely come out the winners. But at that moment, Terry knew, Mae could happily have reached out and knocked both of their heads together, and there wouldn't have been a thing either of them could have done to stop her.

Doug took a very deep breath, let it out slowly in a long sigh and nodded with resignation. He stood up and turned to leave the table. "I'd better go and find my passport, hadn't I?" he rumbled. "Or get a new one. Last one's bound to have expired."

"It's so old you've probably got hair in the photo," Terry called out after him as he left the kitchen. The grunted response was cut off by the kitchen door closing after him, which was probably just as well for Mae's sensibilities.

Left alone in the kitchen, Mae and Terry regarded each other for a moment, then Terry punched the air. "Yes!"

Mae smiled sadly. "That's a big thing you've got him to agree to, Terry."

Terry nodded. "Yeah, yeah, I know."

Mae shook her head. "I doubt it."

Terry sobered slightly. "You know, don't you, what it is that happened to him and Dad when they were out there?"

Mae looked down at the knitting that was still in her lap. "Of course, I do," she said softly.

"You've never told me about it."

"You've never asked."

"It was always made pretty clear that I shouldn't." Terry looked at her closely. "So?"

Mae hesitated, and in a woman normally so decisive, that slight pause made Terry more uneasy than anything she had said so far. "I'm sorry, Terry," she said reluctantly. "It's not for me to tell you. It's Doug you have to ask."

Terry made an exasperated noise. "Then I'll never know. He just clams up whenever we get anywhere near the subject."

"Perhaps. But up until today he's always said he'd never leave the country again." Mae picked up her knitting. "And now you've got him going to Europe with you. Things change, Terry. People change. Doug'll tell you what happened when the time's right. For both of you."

Chapter Two

Another place.

Another room.

A man is sitting before a laptop screen. He reads the email that he has just received. He smiles. *"Merci, mon ami. Merci beaucoup."*

"It's happening?"

The question comes from behind the man, who frowns slightly. "Did I say that you could speak?"

Carefully, unhurriedly, he closes the laptop down before rising and turning to face the source of the question. The young man on the bed looks up at him nervously. He's probably not yet twenty, though his soft curly hair and smooth body make him look slightly younger. He's naked. The bed is large. Its sheets are made of silk. So are the ropes holding the youth spread-eagled on the mattress.

The man walks slowly up to the bed, and then around it. He likes to look at the lad tied like this from every angle. The young man swallows and tries not to look scared, but he is, and the man knows it. He likes that.

The man sighs and sits down on the side of the bed. He reaches out, and the lad flinches, but the man makes a soothing noise, as if to pacify a small child, and lays his hand gently on the side of the boy's face, stroking it thoughtfully. "Yes," he says in a soft voice. "It's happening." His hand moves down, stroking the boy's neck. "Do you want to know more?"

"I..." The boy stops, uncertain. The man is fond of games, but mistakes can be...costly.

The man laughs quietly. "You want to know," he says, as if explaining something to a child or a simpleton, "what I am going to do when he is here?"

The boy nods, telling the truth but not sure if he has given the right answer.

The man smiles. It's a small, cold expression. "I could tell you. Or I could show you." His hand strokes the boy's neck, moving down to the line of his collar bone, over his hairless chest to the pink tenderness of his nipple. He toys with the soft flesh, smiling slightly as it hardens at his touch. "Which would you prefer?"

"I..." The boy stops, uncertain. "I..."

The man pinches the nub of the boy's nipple, his perfectly manicured nails biting deep into the sensitive flesh. The boy gasps, twists in an effort to escape the sudden pain, but is held by his silken restraints. He clamps his teeth down together in an effort to prevent any more sound. The man doesn't like too much noise. Not at first.

The man smiles again, showing perfect white teeth, and releases the now inflamed bud of flesh. He lets his fingers trail across the boy's fine skin till they reach the other nipple. He is even crueller with this one, pinching harder and pulling at the soft flesh, twisting till tears spring to the eyes of the young man who is still struggling not to make any sound. At last the man stops, and the boy cannot help letting go the pent-up breath he has been holding in an exhalation of relief. "*Bien. Très bien.*" The man leans down and the boy's body stiffens, but when the man's lips touch first one tortured nipple then the other, it is to brush them with the lightest kisses. The boy can't stop himself. He groans. "There are lessons that must be learned. I will become...the teacher." He strokes the boy's hair. "And there is a debt to be paid. I shall collect."

The man sits back, regarding his willing captive steadily, head tilted to one side as if fascinated or maybe even surprised by the angry red welts he sees on the boy's chest. "Such a little thing," he muses. "Such a little thing." He leans down again and gently places a kiss on the left nipple, licking the pained bud lightly with the tip of his tongue.

The boy groans again deeply, eyes closed, body responding to the man's expert touch. "*Maître,*" he whispers.

The man turns to the other side of the boy's smooth chest, leans in. This time he takes the nipple not between his lips, but between his perfect white, hard teeth.

"*Maître!*"

Chapter Three

"He's late!" Doug snapped.

"I know," Terry snapped back.

"He should be here by now."

"He had business to sort out."

"*This* is his business, while he's working with us."

Terry bit back his reply. Doug was right but that didn't help.

They were exactly two days into their *POWer Takes Europe* tour, as they had provocatively entitled it, and at the first venue on their wrestling itinerary. Mark had arranged the hire of a serviceable minibus which they were going to use in conjunction with the camper van he had used for his own European tour earlier that year. The plan had been for him and Terry to cross the Channel in the van with the rest of the POWer contingent following on in the minibus. The first hitch, however, had come just as the wrestlers were loading the minibus, when Mark had phoned to say he'd been held up and that Terry would have to go ahead with the others and make the crossing without him. Terry had been narked at missing the fun time he'd been anticipating alone with Mark in his camper, but had been reassured by the prospect of the many more opportunities for similar pleasures there'd be in the weeks that lay ahead.

The crossing had been smooth and problem free. Doug had been like a smouldering volcano from the off, his bad humour growing ever worse the closer to the continent they got, but on arrival he'd proved an excellent roadie, shepherding the POWer guys through customs and out onto the road quickly and efficiently, even managing to impress his companions with his few words of workmanlike French. To Terry's relief, all the paperwork and directions Mark had supplied seemed spot on, too. They'd spent their first night at quite an attractive little *pension* about fifty miles out of Paris, and had found their first wrestling venue the next day with no trouble at all. Terry had even started to relax a little. Until now.

Mark had phoned to say he'd be with them that night at their lodgings but hadn't arrived, then the next day he'd phoned again to say he'd be with them before they arrived at the venue for that night's wrestling. But now here they were, already onto the second bout of the night's bill, Mark due to wrestle in the third, making his professional debut for POWer...and he wasn't there!

Terry and Doug sat ringside, alternately looking up at the bout in progress in front of them and over their shoulders at the hall door, increasingly desperate for signs of Mark.

Given that they were a British team wrestling French wrestlers in a French town, there'd been little doubt from the outset who the punters would be rooting for. Baz had gone on first for POWer/England. A trim, fast lightweight with a Union Jack plastered teasingly across the arse of his speedos, he'd been well matched against another skilful lightweight, and had gone down at the end of the fourth round, much to the approval of the biased audience who'd been particularly appreciative of their boy's wicked leg-spread on the cheeky Brit that had forced his crotch open so wide the inflammatory flag had been pulled way up his butt crack.

Eric was in the ring now. A cheerful, Buddha-shaped middleweight in a low-cut harlequin leotard, Eric's ring persona was the wrestling joker: happy to play the fool, swap jokes with the punters, and look like a complete fish out of water about to go down at any minute. And, of course, when his opponents took him at face value, underestimated him and lowered their guard—which they always did, even the ones who had known him for years—that was when Eric waded in and wiped the mats with them, usually to the resounding approval of the punters. It was an old wrestling truism that you had to be bloody good to pretend to be really bad, and Eric was the living proof. It never failed. Except tonight.

"I told him after the third that he had to keep it going till at least the sixth."

Terry glanced at his watch. There was barely a minute of the fifth round left, and still no sight of Mark.

54

"Eric was well pissed off," Doug continued. "Wanted out then and there."

Terry nodded glumly. He could understand why. Back home Eric was a crowd favourite. Mums and little kids in particular adored his clowning. Here, though, the crowd wasn't getting the script. As a foreigner, Eric was automatically the bad guy, and not speaking a word of anything other than English, there was no way he could win the punters over with his usual saucy quips. But worst of all, tonight he was up against Jean-Claude Gilet, a tousle-haired, fiery lad of only seventeen (or so the publicity said), born and bred in that very town, and so very much the local hero. The crowd was up for blood, and it was Eric's they wanted.

To be fair, young Jean-Claude wasn't bad, Terry had to admit, and pretty damn cute in sheer red tights and white leather boots. Terry had even managed to forget about Mark's non-appearance for a few minutes as Eric had abandoned his attempts at playing the likeable rogue and had laid a series of bear hugs on the lad, wrapping his solid arms around his much slighter opponent, and pulling him hard into his ample body, his round belly completely enveloping the other's smooth, flat stomach. Jean-Claude had sold his suffering very fetchingly, twisting and groaning in the older man's grip, punching helplessly at the relentlessly squeezing arms, making it look as if at any minute he was going to break, to beg the heavier man to stop, and submit, but never quite. Eric, a showman at heart, carried him round the ring in his crushing hold, so everyone could get a good look from every angle at the punishment he was inflicting on their boy. But Jean-Claude still had a lot to learn, and the simple fact was the much bigger, more experienced Eric could have won the bout easily a quarter of an hour previously.

The bell for the end of the round rang and Doug rose again to perform his duty as Eric's second. "Tell him he's got to make this last round go right to the end!" Terry hissed.

"He won't be pleased," Doug muttered before climbing into the ring with his bucket and bottle. Ten seconds later, the look Eric shot Terry over Doug's shoulder as Doug towelled him down made it very clear he wasn't.

The MC announced the sixth and final round in French, the bell rang and Doug ducked back under the ropes to take his seat next to Terry. "Eric says you can…" Doug began. Whatever obscene suggestion he had been about to report back was drowned out by a sudden roaring and cheering followed by a thunderclap of applause.

"Wha…?"

To give him his credit, Eric had tried. When the bell had gone he'd strolled over to the middle of the ring and held his hand out in exaggerated, mock gentlemanly fashion. Back home, that was the well-known signal for the face and heel to go through a whole pantomime as to whether the good guy should follow his natural sporting instincts to take the hand and shake but thereby put himself at risk of the bad guy punching him in his unprotected gut. Both men would appeal to the audience to agree with them. Much fervour for and against would be generated. Eventually, the good guy would give in to his nature and play the gent, reaching out for a sportsmanlike handshake to begin the final round, receiving the villain's fist in his stomach for his pains. Played well, two wrestlers could spin that one out for well over a minute. In France, though, they didn't seem to know the routine, or if they did, Jean-Claude, possibly as fed up at being waltzed around by Eric as Eric was of dancing with him, decided to ignore it. Eric reached out his hand and, quick as a fox, Jean-Claude ducked under it, rolled forward, came up behind Eric, pulled him back and pinned him for the fastest three count from the French ref that either of them had ever seen.

"You're going to have to go on," Doug shouted at Terry, as the MC was struggling to make the official decision heard over the wild cheering of the crowd, delighted at the local boy's win.

"Shit! Where's Jonesy?"

"He's not here. He'll be feeding his face at a French McDonalds if he can find one."

"Shit! Again!" Furious as he was, Terry couldn't be angry with their good-natured Welsh mid-heavyweight. Technically limited, Jonesy filled out POWer's ranks at the heavier end of the spectrum. Given his lack of enthusiasm for gym work and training generally, at just twenty Jonesy was very probably at the peak of his career, and it couldn't be too much longer before his fondness for fast food and fizzy drink caught up with him, slowing him down and filling him out. At the moment, though, his boyish good looks tended to carry the day and make up for his lack of actual wrestling skills, and he could usually be relied upon to provide a sound, 'cooling down' last bout. When he was there. But tonight, he was not.

Terry's was supposed to be the final fight on the card. The local promoter had promised him a good opponent, and their wrestling should have been the best the night had to offer, sending the audience home happy and hoarse. "All right. I'll get ready." Terry rose. "But tell Mark when he shows that I..."

"He's here."

Both men turned to see Baz, changed back into civvies, dashing down the aisle towards them. "He's here. And..." He looked uncertainly at Terry and Doug.

"And? And what?" Doug demanded suspiciously.

"And...I guess he's ready." Baz ducked into a seat and deliberately fixed his attention on the ring.

Doug turned back to Terry. "What...?" he began.

Now, Terry thought, was the time to let Doug in on that one last condition of Mark's. "I meant to tell you. Mark was very keen... Well, actually, he insisted that if he was going to help us..."

A sudden crackly recording of Verdi's *Entrance of the Gladiators* cut him short and heralded the arrival of the wrestlers everyone was waiting for. Terry and Doug watched as the French wrestler, Simone LaGuerre, made his entrance, followed, at long last, by Mark. At least, Doug assumed it was Mark. "Oh! Fuck!"

Terry laughed. "I think he looks damn hot."

LaGuerre was determinedly old school: a tall light-heavyweight in black pro trunks, suspiciously black hair, slicked back either side of an otherwise smooth pate, thick Zapata moustache and a scowl.

"*LaGuerre* means 'war'," Baz shouted over helpfully.

"You don't say," Doug answered sourly.

"*Et, d'Angleterre, un lutteur de mystère. C'est... Johnny Deuce!*"

Mark marched down the aisle, up to the ring, ducked under the top rope, swung his leg over the middle rope, and strode to the centre of the ring with a confident ease that belied the fact this was his first pro match. Bang in the middle of the roped square, he raised his hands high in approbation, and, in spite of themselves, the audience applauded. Because, as Terry had said, he did indeed look hot. He'd gone for white: white tracksuit top, trunks and boots, and on each boot and down one side of his trunks was a simple design in black: a playing card, the two of clubs.

And then there was his face. Or rather...there wasn't.

"You never said anything about a mask!" Doug protested.

"You don't like masks."

"Masks are crap."

"And that's why I didn't say anything about it."

The mask, too, was white—wrapped around the top half of Mark's head Zorro–style, leaving the bottom half of his face exposed, and tied off at the back in a rakish tail. Enough to conceal his identity but not hide his grin at all. And Mark was grinning. Broadly. He was plainly loving this. And in spite of itself, the audience seemed to be loving him.

LaGuerre's scowl deepened as he threw off his old-fashioned dressing gown and performed a few perfunctory, primitive warm-up moves on the ropes in his corner. Sunk back into his chair, Doug scowled, too. "That mask's a fucking disaster. Gives his man something to pull on."

Terry's eyes were drawn down to Mark's well-filled, salt white trunks. He knew what he'd like to be pulling on at that moment. Yes, Mark really was enjoying himself. That was plain to see.

The ref called the two men together, and Terry forced himself to watch in a more professional manner. His cock was being less disciplined but he was wearing baggy tracksuit bottoms and no one would be able to tell. If he stayed sitting. With a programme open on his lap.

Like his two compatriots who had gone before, LaGuerre had been expecting to be the crowd's favourite. Faced by this younger vision in white, he felt himself sliding against his will into the object of their dislike. As the ref rattled away in rapid French and his English opponent leaned in and nodded as if he actually understood, LaGuerre slapped his hairy pecs with both hands, signalling his eagerness to get started, much the way a gorilla signalled its eagerness to tear a puny human's head off. Pep talk over, Mark held out his hand to his opponent who unwisely ignored it, bringing on a smattering of boos. The bell rang, and the bout began.

"He's got to win," Doug said simply and without much hope. Terry knew exactly what he meant. If Mark lost, then Team POWer/England would be down three bouts. With only one bout left on the card, the overall victory of the French in their mini tournament would therefore have been decided, making the outcome of the last fight largely irrelevant. But there was also the other reason why Mark had to win. Masks were a risky gambit. They raised the mystery, but there was the unwritten rule: you lost the bout, you lost the mask. To be a man of mystery you had to be a winner. Always. Terry leaned in keenly. He quickly saw that LaGuerre was a seasoned pro and a rough-houser, easily two stones heavier than Mark. 'Johnny Deuce' had had some intensive training with Terry, and had a natural pit bull style of attack that often served him quite well. But he'd never stepped into a pro ring surrounded by an audience before in his life. Mark had been very insistent on wearing that mask. Terry wondered how he was going to take losing it so quickly.

LaGuerre came in fast and strong: forearm smashes, head butts, kicks. The crowd didn't like it but he seemed to have already abandoned any hope of winning their love. Terry grimaced. Mark was tough—he knew that from first-hand experience. He could soak up that kind of punishment, and dish it back, too. When the Frenchman realised he couldn't just power his way to victory maybe he'd resort to his technical skills. Then Mark would really be up shit creek. Except...

Terry leaned forward even more closely, blinking in surprise. Mark wasn't soaking up the punishment. He was avoiding it! LaGuerre lunged forward; Mark dodged. Mark feinted; LaGuerre kicked out...and missed. LaGuerre lunged forward again, both arms outstretched, and Mark twisted and escaped, leaving his hairier, heavier opponent floundering in the ropes and drawing on the laughs of the audience.

"I taught him that move," Terry said to Doug. He didn't add that he'd never dreamed he'd taught him so well.

"I give him to the end of the second," Doug snarled, but Terry noticed that he, too, was leaning forward, watching the wrestling closely. Terry smiled to himself and said nothing.

The end of the second round came, and, contrary to Doug's dire prediction, the bout was still wide open. There'd been hard fighting on both sides, nasty backhammers and wrenching leglocks that had made Terry wince in sympathy. But as the seconds leaped into the ring to wipe down their sweating charges with their rough towels and proffer the traditional bottles and buckets, Mark was still standing in his corner, bouncing lightly up and down on his toes, while the Frenchman sank back against his blue corner post and glared at him across the canvas.

"He thought you were easy meat," Doug said as he wiped the towel across Mark's glistening upper body.

Mark grinned. "Didn't you?"

The bell rang for the third and Mark bowled out of his corner, forcing Doug to scuttle out of his way which raised another appreciative laugh from the audience. LaGuerre took a very noticeable deep breath and lumbered back up to his feet. Slouching like a bear approaching its prey, he planted his booted feet solidly in the centre of the ring and waited, glaring at the younger man who was making a fool of him on his home turf. Menacingly he raised his hands, arms outstretched in the recognised invitation to a lock up. Mark bounded in, full of youthful confidence and was felled by a fist slammed hard into his stomach. "Referee!" Terry yelled, surging to his feet and gesticulating angrily at the ring.

Doug pulled him back to his seat. "Get a grip," he growled. "You're worse than the grannies back home."

"But that was real!" Terry hissed.

Doug nodded. The boy was right. There had been nothing fake or pulled about that punch. LaGuerre meant business. Doug leaned in closely to see how Mark was going to deal with it.

In the ring, Johnny Deuce was still doubled up on the canvas, clutching at his stomach and gasping for breath. The referee had apparently not seen his countryman's blatant foul. *He's counting him out!* On the count of nine Mark forced himself to his feet again, and Terry gave a tight smile at the small nod of approval he saw from Doug. But before either of them could comment further, LaGuerre was on their man again, clapping both hands down onto his muscular shoulders, and digging the thumbs hard into the corded delts on either side of his neck in a crippling 'nerve hold'. Mark cried out in genuine pain, his face twisting in agony as the vengeful LaGuerre sneered and bore down with all his might, forcing the Brit to his knees, until his masked face was humiliatingly on a level with LaGuerre's crotch.

"*Oui? Oui?*" LaGuerre demanded of the crowd, twisting his head to left and right to address them all as he piled the pressure onto a suffering Johnny Deuce, the trapped masked man kneeling helplessly before him, clawing hopelessly at his wrists. But if the veteran Frenchman expected the home crowd to be behind him in this cruel punishment of the upstart 'invader' he was mistaken. A chorus of boos swept round the hall at his mistreatment of the dashing *homme de mystère*. LaGuerre looked genuinely astonished, but the reversal of expectation just seemed to inflame him still more and he redoubled his efforts to wring a submission out of the Englishman by brute strength alone, bearing down on him even more brutally.

"The fucker's gonna take his head off if he keeps that up!" Terry shouted.

"He's got balls," Doug muttered.

With a bellow of frustration, LaGuerre finally conceded defeat in his efforts to wring a submission from his man this way, and released his hold. Raising one foot, he leaped high into the air and came down, slamming his one boot hard into the back of Johnny Deuce's neck. Mark toppled forward, pole-axed, onto the canvas and lay there, feebly clutching his neck, the prints of his opponent's fingers bone white on his flesh, rapidly flushing an angry red at the release of the cruel pressure. All LaGuerre had to do now was drop on top of his man and pin him for a three count. Both Terry and Doug knew Mark could have nothing left in him after an all-out attack like that, where literally no punches had been pulled. Terry was shouting a stream of outraged invective. Doug was shaking his head and already rising to do his second's duty and escort the beaten man from the ring.

Then LaGuerre made his mistake.

An ugly leer on his face, he dropped to his knees by his stricken opponent. But instead of going for the easy winning pin he went for the mask. Reaching out, he began to untie the knot at the back of the man's head. With a roar and a speed that took both Terry and Doug by surprise,

Mark exploded up from the canvas, smashing a startled LaGuerre backwards. As the Frenchman fell, Mark hooked both his legs and dived forward with them, so it was LaGuerre's shoulders that were pinned to the canvas, arse in the air, his body folded crushingly in two with Mark's weight pressing down on him. The referee's count might have been slow, LaGuerre's struggles might have been frantic, but Johnny Deuce's pin had every last scrap of desperate strength left in the wrestler's body. And in the end, that was enough.

Exhausted, Mark flung the loser's legs to one side and clambered to his feet, raising his arms in victory. And the crowd went wild. Applause and cheers rang out even louder than they had for Jean-Claude's victory in the previous bout.

Doug was actually open-mouthed. "Fucking hell!" he said, eventually.

"Doug!" said Terry, in mocking imitation of his gran's disapproval of such language. But as he added his own frenetic claps and whistles to the cacophony in the hall, he knew that Doug's swearing was the most glowing praise this unfailingly dour and taciturn man could ever have given.

"Move it!"

"What?"

"Move it!" Doug snapped again. "You're up next."

"Shit! Right!"

Chapter Four

Caught up in the moment, Terry had indeed forgotten that he was next on the bill. Leaping up from his seat, he dashed up the aisle past rows of punters still applauding Mark/Johnny and shoved his way through the hall's double doors into the corridor outside, out of sight of the audience. There, he stripped off his tracksuit bottoms, revealing his long, white leather boots and the pale blue trunks he'd chosen for his European debut. Yeah, looking good and ready for action. Eager for the fray, he bounced up and down on the spot for a minute and stretched out his muscles.

Baz re-entered the corridor. Terry grinned, eager for the fight, but the smile faltered when he saw the young man was wearing that worried expression again.

"He's not here."

Terry shook his head, momentarily confused by this apparent rerun of what had happened earlier. "You mean Mark? But he's just..."

Baz shook his head. "No. Your guy. Jacques, whatever it was. The guy you were going to wrestle. He hasn't shown up."

"Oh, great. Oh, shit!" It had all seemed to be going so well, right up to this, the night of their very first card. And now, it had all turned, as they said here, to *merde*.

Abruptly, the doors from the main hall burst open and LaGuerre stormed through, spluttering a stream of very fast, probably very obscene French, followed by an agitated second who seemed to be doing his best, and failing, to calm his man down. Five seconds later, a still grinning Johnny Deuce followed them through the door. *"Enchanté!"* he called out after LaGuerre, who snarled spectacularly and slammed the doors of the changing room behind him in the face of his second. "Lovely man," Mark said.

"That was brilliant!" Terry threw his arms round Mark who hugged him back. But when he went to kiss him Mark pulled away.

"Pas devant les enfants."

Terry blinked in surprise. "Eh?" Mark inclined his head at the people around them. Terry laughed. "It's France. Guys kiss each other all the time." And kiss was the very least of what Terry wanted to do just then. The sight of the victorious wrestler, bare skin gleaming with sweat, the smell of him, the damp warmth of his body against his was rousing very strong reactions within Terry in spite of the other guys around them. Sensing Mark's continued reluctance he let go and stepped back. *Later.* "Smooth moves in there." Mark shrugged but immediately winced. Terry stepped in close again to take a look at the welts around his neck. He whistled. "Bastard! You're gonna have some bruises there, mate."

Mark nearly shrugged again but wisely held back. "I heal quick," he said simply, then he stopped, finally taking in the expression on Baz's face. "What's up?"

Baz brought him up to speed.

Mark frowned in thought. "Okay," he said slowly. "I guess what we could do..." Whatever he had been about to suggest was cut off by the slamming open yet again of the hall doors and the rapid emergence of the MC. Spotting Terry, he immediately let loose a stream of French and rapid gesticulations. "He says what are you doing hanging around here, you're needed back in the ring now," Mark translated.

Terry's head began to spin. French wrestling seemed an incomprehensible whirlwind, and he suddenly wondered if all the tour was going to be like this. And if it was, could he cope? "Ask him what's the point when there's no one to wrestle?" He double-checked Mark. "And when did you get so good at French?"

"You knew I'd been working over here. Kind of hard not to pick up the language if you're trying to see how their businesses work, y'know. How'd you think I made all those bookings?"

"I guess..." Terry scratched his head. "I just didn't think you'd be that...fluent."

"Thanks. Okay now, you, *faites attention.*" He turned back to the agitated MC, translated Terry's words and listened to the quick-fire response. Behind the mask his eyes widened slightly, as if in surprise. "Well, that's a turn-up for the books."

"What? *What*?"

"They've got a substitute. At the last minute."

"Okay, so where is he?"

"He's..." From within the hall there came a roar that outdid anything they'd heard that night. "He's in there."

As one, the Englishmen rushed to the doors and threw them open to see who was getting such a reception. It was incredible. Every man, woman and child in the place was on his or her feet applauding.

"Who the hell is he?"

"*C'est Yves Montaigne*," said the MC, his voice swelling with what seemed to be patriotic fervour.

"It's Yves Montaigne," Mark translated, unnecessarily.

"Who?" said Baz and Terry.

"Only," Mark said, "one of France's top wrestlers. Only the headliner at all the big bouts in Paris for the past three years."

"And he's the substitute?" Terry said incredulously. "Here? No offence," he added to the MC, who smiled and nodded, clearly not having understood the insult.

"Turns out he was in the audience. Volunteered to step in when he was told they were a man down."

A red-faced Doug rushed up. "Will you get your fucking arse in here? There's a couple of hundred punters about to bust a blood vessel if we don't give 'em some fucking wrestling."

Terry threw his shoulders back and clenched his fists. "All right, then," he said. "Let's show them how it's done." He caught Mark's eye and winked. "Catch you later." He left them, pushing his way through the doors and into the riotous hall.

Nervous as hell but determined to give the crowd the best show they'd ever seen in this backwater, Terry ran down the aisle, leaped agilely up onto the ring apron and vaulted over the top rope, landing on his toes and bouncing eagerly on the sprung canvas. His first sight of Yves Montaigne was of a tight, hard arse in sheer, plain grey trunks pushed out towards him as Montaigne leaned into his corner, stretching his back and hamstrings. *Nice.* Montaigne turned round. *Very nice!*

His unexpected opponent was probably in his late twenties, maybe an inch taller than him, maybe a little lighter, but cut like a knife: pecs, abs, biceps so clearly defined it hurt. Glossy hair cut short like a skull cap. Skin smooth and gleaming the way only an expensive waxing could get it. His ring gear was simple: grey trunks, black boots, white socks just visible over the top. Terry sized his man up. Nothing showy yet somehow everything managed to say *class*. He'd heard some Frenchmen could do this effortlessly. He just hadn't expected to see it in the ring. He unzipped his ring jacket with just a touch of teasing slowness, passed it to Doug, and proceeded to limber up, giving the punters—and Montaigne—their first opportunity to get a look at *his* body, and tried hard not to feel like some English country bumpkin meeting a Parisian aristocrat.

The two men met up in the corner of the ring. Montaigne extended his hand. "Good evening," he said, in perfect, accentless English. "I am very pleased to meet you."

Terry struggled to deal with the unexpected formality and to draw on what little French he could remember from school. "Hi," was all he could come up with. Montaigne smiled, and Terry felt himself relax a little. *Hey, he's just another wrestler. Just another fantastically good-looking wrestler.* Feeling the familiar stirring in his trunks, Terry forced himself to concentrate on the bout at hand.

The referee launched into rapid and, to Terry, completely unintelligible French. "It is merely the usual formalities," Montaigne murmured, looking down at the canvas as if he was listening. "Just nod and the crowd will think you understand. They will like that."

"You want them to like me?" Terry whispered back. "You going to play the heel?"

Montaigne smiled, still looking down. "Why should things be so simple, *mon ami*? There's a bit of heel in all of us, *non*?" The referee finished. The two men shook hands and stepped back. The bell rang for round one.

Looking back, Terry would describe the next thirty minutes as the best time he had ever spent in a ring without getting his cock out. Montaigne was indeed a superb wrestler, and he knew the game wasn't just about looking good: it was about making the other guy look good, too. And if both guys were good to begin with, the results were explosive.

For six, increasingly sweaty rounds, the two men swapped holds and counter holds, muscles straining, limbs twisting, hands slapping thighs, chests, arses as they grunted and groaned, pressed and pinned, pulled and stretched each other in a variety of lingering holds. Within a minute, Terry knew he and Yves were on exactly the same wavelength: both wanted the crowd to be as turned on by their wrestling as they were themselves.

"Enjoying yourself," Doug growled sardonically, as he seconded between rounds two and three.

"Yeah," Terry panted.

"Not a question," Doug said drily.

Terry glanced down at his trunks. Two layers but they weren't hiding the growing contours of his enthusiasm. He glanced across the ring at Yves. The other wrestler tipped his water bottle in his direction in an ironic salute. The long vertical line in his own trunks made it clear he was enjoying the bout every bit as much as Terry. "The French just don't care, do they?" Terry whistled appreciatively.

Doug scowled. "No, they damn well don't."

Terry was both surprised and disappointed when the bell for the sixth rang. He'd never known a bout fly by so quickly. Only five minutes of it left. He determined to make the most of them. Feigning a standard lock up, he threw his arms round his opponent's waist and locked on a bear hug. Yves struggled in the brawnier boy's grip. His skin was hot and slick. Hidden from the audience between their straining bodies, Terry felt the undeniable pressure of the man's hard cock pulled up against his own. As he played up his struggles for the crowd, the Frenchman ground it back and forth across Terry's aching erection. Terry gasped and pulled the man in even tighter, unable to help himself.

Yves groaned and the audience roared, taking his moans of pleasure for moans of pain. He let his head fall forward onto the muscles of the lad's shoulder, as if momentarily losing consciousness, bringing his lips close to Terry's ear. "You like this? Yes?"

His body smelled of expensive cologne, the last thing Terry had ever expected to smell in a wrestling ring. Terry gave a hard jerk to his hold as if ratcheting up the pressure. There was a hot spurt of pre-come as their cocks slammed into each other, and Terry hoped the sweat pouring off both of them would disguise the quickly spreading damp patch in his trunks. "God, yes!"

Yves gave a sudden twist of his supple, sweat-slippery body and was suddenly out of the surprised Terry's grasp. A shove in the boy's chest sent him reeling backwards into the ropes, which stretched then catapulted him back and straight into the Frenchman's arms. And now it was Yves's turn to lay on the bear hug. He held Terry lower than the boy had held him, hands clasped in a wrestler's grip just above the small of Terry's back so that he could pull up slightly as well as squeeze. As a wrestling move it pressured the ribcage, making it harder to pull in a decent breath. It also brought added pressure to bear on their hard cocks, sending stabs of pleasure through Terry's groin. "How far do you think we can take this before anyone notices?" Yves breathed into Terry's ear.

"Oh, man, let's find out." And Terry in his turn twisted and 'escaped', coming up behind the Frenchman this time to lay on a full strength bear hug from the rear, flexing his biceps hard around the Frenchman's wiry body, with the thick, straight line of his cock rammed up hard against Montaigne's Lycra-covered buttocks.

"Mon dieu!"

"Yeah!" breathed Terry.

For a good two minutes, the grapplers swapped bear hugs, front and rear, the escapes getting more imaginative, more unexpected each time, the hugs apparently crueller and harder. Maybe it was the pure athleticism, or maybe the punters, too, were picking up on the raw sexual vibe, but the hall was wild, cries of encouragement making the rafters ring, first for one man, then the other. Terry'd never known anything like it. He didn't want it to end. But judging by the urgent, near uncontrollable pulsing throb at the base of his cock, it had to. *And bloody quickly, too!*

Yves gave one last jerk and squeeze, the loud cry it wrung from Terry having nothing to do with 'selling' and precious little to do with pain, either. "Time for the climax, *hien*?" he whispered. He relaxed his hug, just slightly, and Terry braced himself for some change in grip. It didn't come. For a split second Yves's guard was down and Terry's wrestling instincts kicked right in. Almost without conscious thought, he twisted out and round, brought his man down with a shove over his outstretched legs and folded him tight for a pin.

"*Un! Deux! Trois!*" The thud of the referee's hand coming down on the three count was lost in the uproar from the crowd, and for a second, Terry thought they'd gone mad with anger that some upstart Englishman had conquered their hero. But as he lay panting across Yves's prone body, he gradually became aware that they weren't protesting. They were applauding. More, they were on their feet, cheering.

Unsure of where exactly he was any more, Terry looked around until he saw Doug. To his relief Doug was already in the ring and running towards him with a towel. Under the pretext of helping his exhausted charge up, Doug shoved the towel into his hands. "You need this," he said disapprovingly. Terry nodded gratefully, and took hold of the towel, letting it fall in front of him to cover the prodigious tent in the front of his pale blue Lycra trunks. Glancing across, he noticed Montaigne's second had leaped into the ring, too, and was rushing to offer his man similar camouflage.

The MC clambered into the ring to deliver the outcome in an accent so thick Terry didn't even recognise his own ring name in the stream of French, and only knew the cheers and applause were for him when Yves sportingly stepped up and raised his arm, turning him around for all to see and cheer. When the two men embraced in a very Gallic way, the noise, incredibly, went up one more notch. "You let me win," Terry said, having to shout to make himself over the clamour even though the two were so close.

"France two, England two." Yves nodded to the wildly applauding fans. "Now they will want a rematch, *oui?*" He smiled. "So we are all winners."

☆☆☆

It took Terry ten minutes to make it from the ring back to the changing rooms through the jostling fans demanding *les autographies,* and along the way he lost sight of Yves. Doug was waiting for him. "Baz and Eric are back at the hotel," he said. "Jonesy's probably back there, too, unless there's a two for one offer on at the local burger bar. You want me to hang on, give you a lift?"

Terry looked round the changing rooms. He'd thought Yves would be there also, as was the usual practice back home, but he wasn't. He'd also hoped that Mark would be there, waiting. But he was disappointed there, too. Terry felt some of his tremendous high begin to evaporate. "I don't know," he said. "Maybe I'll..."

The door opened and Mark looked in. "Oh, hi."

Terry's spirits lifted once more. Mark had changed back into jeans and a tracksuit top, although... Terry gave a small laugh. "Still got the mask on?"

"Improvement if you ask me," Doug sniffed.

"Yeah, well. Still some punters around. Got to keep up the air of mystery, right?"

"Biggest mystery is how you got away with it in the ring tonight."

"What do you mean?"

"He should have killed you."

"Well, thanks to Terry's training he didn't, did he? Terence has worked miracles with me. In the ring."

Doug sniffed so hard it was a wonder his face didn't implode, but he said no more. Mark had earned the right to be a bit cocky. For this night, anyway. He looked from one young man to the other. "Fine," he snapped finally. "I'll go then, shall I? Wouldn't want to get in the way of any more 'training'. I'll see you...when I see you."

"Yeah," said Terry happily, eager for Doug to leave the two of them alone.

"I did good tonight, yeah?" Mark said as Doug passed him in the doorway.

"You won," said Doug without looking at him. "Don't push it." And he was gone.

"Praise indeed," said Mark drily.

"Actually, it was." Terry waited. With Doug out of the picture and the pair of them flooded with testosterone, adrenaline and fuck knew what other chemicals after their exertions in the ring, he'd fully expected Mark to be all over him, tearing his trunks off and screwing him then and there on the floor. But Mark was still standing close to the door, and Terry couldn't even get him to meet his eyes. *Okay, maybe it's my turn to take the lead.* He dropped the towel he was holding, pulled down his own trunks and stepped out of them to stand less than two feet from Mark, hands on hips, naked apart from boots and socks, his cock a stout, hard rod pointing unmistakably in the other guy's direction. "Want to scrub my back in the shower?"

"Oh, yeah! I mean...shit! I mean..." Mark took a step forward like a man pulled against his will on an invisible string towards the young, very willing wrestler in front of him. But then, abruptly, he stopped, as if through a sheer effort of will. "The thing is," he said slowly. "I've met someone."

"Met someone?"

"Yeah. One of the punters. You know. I'm—er... I'm on a promise."

"Right." Terry gritted his teeth. "Haven't heard it called that for a long time."

Mark gave a small, almost nervous smile, a mile away from his usual broad grin. "Yeah, well, I don't know what the French for that is."

"And you so fluent."

"Yeah. Right. Anyway. He's waiting. So, er, I'm taking him back with me."

"To the hotel?"

"*Pension*," Mark automatically corrected, "but no, not there. I'll be spending the night in my camper van."

"Ah. Right. Handy. For that kind of thing."

"Yes. Yes, it is."

"Good thing you brought it, then."

"Yes. Yes it is."

"Okay."

"Okay."

"Goodnight, then."

Mark hesitated, as if there was something more he wanted to say but didn't know how. "*Au revoir*," he said, then turned and was gone.

Terry stared bitterly at the closed door, before throwing himself onto a bench and tugging at the long rows of laces in his boots. Wrestling boots looked unbelievably hot on but were a bugger to get off. Finally unlaced, he pulled them off and flung them angrily to one side, followed shortly afterwards by his socks till he sat alone and pointlessly naked in the changing rooms. By this time his full erection had passed but his cock was still thick and heavy, hanging dispiritedly against his thigh. Terry stroked it briefly, vaguely considering a wank, but Mark's brush-off had soured his mood and dampened his ardour. Grabbing a towel, he headed gloomily for the shower.

The forceful stream of hot water against his body went some way to making him feel better, and as he soaped himself all over, hands running the length of his smooth, muscular frame, the idea of a good hard hand-shandy began to seem appealing again. He took his cock in one hand, cradling his hanging ball sac in the other. He thought of Mark in his tight white trunks and boots. *And where the hell did he get that Johnny Deuce business from? I'll have to ask.* He thought of that chest. That arse. That smile. Terry shook his head. Thinking of Mark smiling then going out to fuck another guy wasn't doing his hard-on any favours. Then, seemingly from nowhere, he caught the smell of Yves's cologne again and three things happened almost at once: his mind spilled over with intensely erotic memories of Yves's body in his arms; his cock sprang instantly and urgently to full attention; and the shower curtains whisked back, leaving him open for all to see. Or at least for the one man who was standing there to see.

"Outstanding," said Yves, looking with undisguised appreciation at the meat in Terry's hand. "That is the word, *non?*"

Yves had obviously already showered elsewhere, and was dressed in jeans and white shirt of such simple style they had to be expensive. He held up a large cotton towel and opened it out. Terry turned the shower off and stepped forward into its folds, and into Yves's arms. Yves closed the towel around him. "I will be your second, yes?" he murmured, and for a few moments he just held him there, enfolded in the thick material, before beginning, carefully and thoroughly, to dry the boy off, smoothing the towel over his firm pecs and ridged abs, across his broad shoulders, down the tapering sides of his body, over his ribs that rose and fell as Terry's breathing became faster, shorter. Terry closed his eyes and allowed the Frenchman to do what he wanted, go where he liked. Yves moved round him, smoothing the towel down the length of Terry's arms, his back, and then slowly over the curves of his buttocks. Terry shivered, and let his head fall forward slightly. Yves's breath on the nape of his neck made the hairs there stand on end.

Yves knelt to gently rub dry the back of Terry's legs, and when that was done moved so now he was kneeling in front of the young man. Terry opened his eyes to look down and met the steady, dark gaze of the Frenchman looking unwaveringly back up at him. Yves began to towel off the front of Terry's legs, all the while keeping his eyes fixed on Terry's, working up the calves, the thighs, until all that was left untouched was the matted damp patch of golden fur round his balls and groin from which Terry's cock was thrusting tall and proud.

Yves cupped Terry's balls in the heavy cotton and gently, carefully squeezed. Terry's breath caught in his throat. Yves reached in deeper, slowly drawing the towel across the pulsing soft spot behind Terry's balls, and Terry gasped softly. At length, Yves stopped, and Terry stood, waiting, eyes still closed, heart pounding so much in his chest he thought it must have been visible. He heard the soft thump of the towel falling to the floor. When the kiss came, it sent a shockwave through his body that tied his stomach in knots, and set his arse ring and nipples afire. Yves had leaned in and very gently kissed the tip of his wet, purple cockhead. Terry swallowed. He'd never been brought so quickly, so desperately to the edge of coming before. If Yves took his cock in his mouth now he knew he wouldn't be able to control himself—he'd shoot long and hard down the Frenchman's throat. He had to stop, pull back, say something. But he simply couldn't.

"You are staying at *La Fourgere?*"

Terry blinked, forced himself to focus. Yves had stopped, was leaning back on his haunches speaking to him. *Thank God! Damn it!* "Yes." The word came out a croak. He cleared his throat and spoke again more clearly. "Yes."

Yves gave a small laugh. "Very economical and very...adequate. I am staying at *La Gallette."* He stood up. "Would you like to spend the night with me?"

If Terry didn't turn up at their hotel later he just knew that Doug would have the mother of all fits. The evil-tempered, pit bull bastard of a man would bust a gut worrying about what was happening to him and would give him absolute hell the minute he saw him again. Terry didn't hesitate for a minute. "Yes," he said again.

Chapter Five

Outside the hall, only a hundred metres away, round a darkened street corner, Doug contemplated the ruined front tyres of the aging minibus the POWer group was using and swore. Someone had been very creative with something very sharp. Cursing volubly, Doug opened the back door and rummaged around for the tyre jack and spares. He'd known letting Terry put up the jaunty POWer logo on the van's window had been a mistake. Red rag to a bull, or at least to those of the French punters who had thought two victories for the English that night had been two too many.

Doug whirled at a sudden sound behind him, the jack in his hand raised defensively. The streets were empty, silent now, or was that...? He stepped forward. He'd thought he'd seen something, a shadow move across the street. But now it was gone.

Behind him, someone stepped forward, stood a moment just watching him, then slowly moved nearer, arm outstretched, six feet away, three feet away, one foot...

Doug whirled round, tyre jack raised high. "Any closer and you'll be eating this, pal!"

The figure stopped dead in his tracks and raised his hands. "Whoa there, short, bald and dangerous." He took one step to the left so that the pale illumination of a street light fell fully on his face. "You don't want to brain your team's star player right at the start of the tour, do you?"

Doug lowered the jack, though only grudgingly. "Mark! I thought you were with Terry."

"Yeah? Well... Something came up."

Doug snorted. "Right. So where is he now?"

Mark shrugged. "Dunno. Maybe something came up for him, too."

Doug swore but turned back to the minibus, kneeling to begin to loosen the nuts on the first wheel.

"He's a bit old to need a nanny, Doug." Doug worked on in silence. "Or do you see yourself as more of a bodyguard?" Mark stepped closer, leaned over the squatting man. "You'd make a good bodyguard, man. All that muscle. All that attitude."

Abruptly Doug stood and spun round so that the two men were face to face, only inches between them. Doug's face was like thunder but, after the briefest hesitation, Mark merely grinned back. For a second or two neither of them moved, then very slowly and very carefully Mark reached out and rested a hand on Doug's upper shoulder. When Doug continued to stare at him without moving or saying anything, Mark gave the arm a small squeeze and moved it slowly up to the shoulder. "Yeah," he said, "you've still got the muscles all right, haven't you? Why don't you wrestle any more, mate? You could still pull the punters. If you get my drift."

"You'd like that, would you?" Doug said, with unusual softness, making no protest as Mark's hand moved up over his shoulder to his neck, his thumb stroking the side of Doug's face, rasping against the stubble.

"Yeah."

"Like to see me in trunks and boots?"

Mark moved in even closer, eyes fixed on Doug's mouth. "Fuck, yeah."

"Me and you in a ring together, muscle against muscle, man on man?"

"Yeah!"

"Me, too."

"Yeah?"

"Yeah. You know why?"

Mark's eyes were on Doug's mouth, his head angled now, moving in closer, closer. "Why?" he breathed softly.

With impressive accuracy and no warning, Doug's hand shot forward and into Mark's crotch, grabbing a generous handful of solid cock and balls and squeezing, hard. "'Cause then I'd fucking cripple you!"

Mark's eyes and mouth opened wide, but he said nothing, made no sound, and held his ground. "Straight to the point, eh, Dougie boy? I like that." Rather than pull away, Mark pushed his hips forward, further into Doug's steely grip. "Like the feel of that?"

"Do you?" Doug gave a sharp twist to his hold.

Mark's lascivious grin wavered but it held. "Kind of. Though you could maybe, y'know, up the love."

Doug laughed, without the slightest touch of humour. "You're a big man." His attention to Mark's pride and joy was driving it to a hard-on that neither of them could deny.

Mark laughed, too, but the sound now had an uncertain edge. "It's all because of you, Dougie boy. And all for you, too, if you want it."

Doug's expression was unreadable. He held the stiffening meat another few seconds then let go, as if dropping something extremely unpleasant. "Fuck off," he said calmly. "And if you hurt Terry..."

Mark raised one hand, while his other gently massaged his mauled jewels. "Hey, hey! I'm not about to hurt Terry, okay? That's not what I'm about."

Doug regarded him coldly. "I don't know what you're about. "But I'm watching you."

"I'm just a guy out for a good time, Doug."

"Yeah. Right." Doug slowly, deliberately turned his back on Mark and knelt down again to his work on the wheels of the minibus.

For a moment Mark stood watching him, but when it became clear the man had nothing more to say to him, he shrugged his shoulders, turned and walked off.

When Mark's footsteps had faded away completely, Doug laid down his tools and leaned back on his haunches. For a while he just sat there, staring into space, completely oblivious of his surroundings. At last he spoke, just one word, softly at first then louder, again and again, and as he said it, he punched at the hard rubber of the tyre in front of him, over and over, until his voice broke and his knuckles bled. "Geoff!"

☆☆☆

Two streets away, Mark turned a corner to find his camper parked under a streetlight, and another man leaning against it. "That went well," said the man.

"You were watching?"

"Of course." He gestured to Mark's crotch. "Need something on that?"

Mark laughed out loud, sauntered over to the other man and kissed him. With their arms around each other, they climbed into the camper.

PART THREE

Chapter One

La Gallette turned out to be over three kilometres out of the town. Yves drove them there in a very fast, very expensive car. *How much do wrestlers make over here?* Terry had thought when he saw the car. *Must be a fucking mint!* he decided when he saw the hotel Yves was staying in. He couldn't help whistling out loud, immediately feeling like a prick for being such a rube. But Yves seemed to take it in good part and shrugged modestly.

"*Le Catch*, wrestling, pays a little better here than at home, I think. There are so many more...opportunities in Europe. I am surprised it has taken you so long to come over to find out for yourself."

"Yeah, well, my family's kind of always been against travelling, y'know."

"Your family?"

"Yeah. Well, Doug mainly. He's the, y'know—" Terry waved his hand over his head in a polishing gesture "—bald guy."

Yves laughed. "*Ah oui. Le chauve.* He is your father?"

Terry shook his head. "God, no! Sort of an uncle. My dad's best friend. They wrestled together as brothers years ago, but they weren't really."

"And your father is...?"

"He's dead."

"*Ah, c'est triste,*" Yves said, and nodded sympathetically. Terry felt a bit embarrassed. He hadn't been looking for sympathy. He'd been a very small child when Geoff Ryan had died.

"And your mother?"

Terry usually lied whenever this question came up. He'd say she was dead, too, and change the topic quickly, and people were always more than happy to let him do that as no one liked talking about dead mothers. The truth was Sally Ryan had left the family not long after he'd been born. He knew that wasn't his fault. Mae had always made that perfectly clear. But he still lied about it. Until now. Not asking himself why, and not having the time to consider it anyway, Terry told Yves the truth. "I never knew her. She left," he said simply.

Yves gave a small expression of sadness but also shrugged, as if it was just one of those things that sophisticated people dealt with all the time. "Families," he said. "They are complicated."

Terry looked at him, and realised that he wanted really, really badly to kiss this man.

Together they walked into the plush reception, and as Yves signed in and picked up the key, Terry saw the concierge looking at him, taking in his T-shirt, jeans and trainers, and their complete absence of designer labels. Terry knew he was in a class establishment when the emaciated old guy didn't let his disapproval show by so much as the raising of an eyebrow—and yet he somehow he still managed to make it felt. It didn't bother Terry one jot. In front of him, he had a close-up view of Yves's tight arse in his most-definitely-designer-label jeans as he leaned over the front desk, and suddenly all he could think about was that in just under ten minutes he'd have an even closer view of those tight buttocks without any obstructing denim. He hoped the rooms had thick walls. He had a feeling things were going to get noisy.

☆☆☆

They had their arms wrapped round each other and their tongues deep in each other's mouths the instant their room's door had closed behind them. *Now this is real French kissing!* They tottered round the room until they collapsed on the king-sized bed, Terry on top of Yves. In a flash, the Frenchman had his legs round Terry's waist. For a second he lay there, smiling, then with a sudden constriction of his thighs, he squeezed viciously. "I didn't get the chance to use the bodyscissors on you in the ring." He laughed. "You like?"

Terry gasped, from surprise and from having most of the air squashed out of his body. "Fuck, you're strong!"

Yves laughed, and squeezed again, harder.

"Okay. Okay." Terry laughed, as much as he could while breathless. "I submit. I give!"

Immediately the Frenchman relaxed the pressure. Without releasing the hold he leaned up and caressed Terry's face, kissing him on the cheeks and chin. "I am sorry. I didn't mean to hurt you." He smiled. "But I have my honour to regain, yes? You gained the victory in the ring. I must—what do you say?—regain face." He kissed Terry on the mouth, tenderly and deeply, and Terry would have let him crush the life out of him with those powerful legs there and then just so long as he carried on kissing him like that.

Finally breaking away, Yves leaned back slightly, took hold of the bottom of Terry's shirt and drew it up over his head, kissing the lad's flat stomach, rounded chest muscles and nipples as each was revealed. Terry unbuttoned Yves's shirt, the Frenchman shrugging it off as soon as it was completely undone. The two men were eager to feel the warm press of naked skin on skin. Even through the denim of two pairs of jeans, Terry could feel the urgent solidity of Yves's cock. He scrabbled for the belt. "Take it off," Yves whispered.

"Oh, I'm going to."

"*Non.* I mean, take it off. All the way. The belt."

With a puzzled smile Terry complied, unclasping the stylised silver buckle of the belt and pulling the length of soft leather out from round the waist of Yves's trousers. He went to drop the belt at the bedside with the rest of their discarded clothes.

"*Non.* Use it."

Terry hesitated, feeling slightly stupid, wondering if he was missing something in translation. Yves lay back on the bed and stretched out, reaching behind him for the slats of the bedhead. "Tie me," he said.

"Oh. Ah. Right." Terry looked down at the man under him. His arms thrown back like that, Yves's lean musculature was even more striking. His mouth was slightly open, his breath short and fast in anticipation. His eyes fixed on Terry's, defiant and supplicating at the same time. "Oh, man." Terry thought he was going to come then and there. "Look, I'm not sure if I... I mean, I've never...oh shit!" Yves had leaned up and run his tongue over his taut belly, and Terry's whole body had thrilled as if plugged into the mains. Swiftly, he looped the belt around his willing captive's wrists, lashing him to the bed slats, then sat back to survey his work. Yves lay there, staring up at him, helpless, and silently daring him.

Terry tore at the flies of Yves's trousers, pulling the denim down and away. Yves's briefs were plain white cotton, the glistening crown of his cock already thrusting clear over the waistband. Terry eased them down over the pulsing, jumping length, down his sinewy legs to be thrown somewhere off the end of the bed. Yves lay naked now, his erection like a veined bolt up his belly. He said nothing as he continued to gaze up at Terry, twisting his hands as if pretending to escape his bondage, arching, pushing up his groin, thrusting his splendid cock into the empty air.

Terry leaped off the bed to pull down his own jeans and boxers. Naked and steel-hard, he stood looking down at the bound Frenchman. Heart pounding in his chest, he climbed back onto the bed, his knees either side of Yves's thighs. Very slowly, taking his weight on his forearms, he lowered his body onto Yves's, inch by inch, until the length of his cock lay along the length of Yves's and the Frenchman gasped. Terry pressed down, lightly at first, then with more and more pressure until Yves cried out and yanked sharply at the restraints over his head. Terry clamped his mouth down on Yves's mouth, stifling his cries with his thrusting tongue, grinding his cock harder and harder into the Frenchman's.

Yves bucked up hard, but Terry bore down, driving the lithe wrestler back into the mattress, even as his tongue drove deeper into his mouth. Hot pre-come spurted from both cocks, lubricating so the frottage was quick and easy, and before too long Terry knew he was on the very edge of one fucking enormous orgasm. Looking down at the gasping man underneath him, he guessed Yves was very nearly there, too.

Yves looked back up at him. "Sit up," he said.

Not quite knowing what Yves had in mind, and fighting every instinct to grab the man's ankles, shove them up and over his head and ram his meat hard into the puckered little arsehole laid bare, Terry did as he was asked.

Yves shifted, arched more strongly than he had yet, and this time it was Terry who cried out helplessly as the length of French cock under him slid the length of his arse crack, pushing aside the firm cheeks, teasing his own tight little hole. The ring muscles there twitched and ached with familiar pleasure and need. "Take it!" Yves gasped.

Terry's head was spinning. One second the top, the next the bottom, even though he wasn't the one tied up. All he had to do was sit back, relax those toned glutes of his just a little and Yves would be in him faster than that French ref could count to three. And Terry wanted it. He wanted very badly indeed that thick meat spearing into him, piercing the ache, making it hurt, then making it sweet. And he realised that Yves wasn't giving a damn about condoms.

With an enormous effort of will, Terry dragged himself off Yves's body and the bed. "Hang on," he gasped. "Just...just don't go anywhere!" Frantically, he searched for his discarded jeans and the lube and condoms he'd squirrelled away in the pockets. Returning to the bed, he once again straddled Yves, holding up the foil squares and tube.

Yves groaned again, more loudly as the boy slowly eased the rubber down the length of his hot, visibly throbbing cock, the necessary care at this vital moment a literal though unintended cocktease. "*Vite!*"

"Yeah!" Terry gasped, not having a clue what *vite* meant. The condom tightly fitted, Terry lubed himself liberally, without taking his eyes off the sheathed ramrod he was about to take up his arse. *Man, that thing is like the branch of a tree!* Way out of proportion to the comparatively small frame of the French wrestler. He put the tube to one side, looked again at the monster he was about to sit on, and reached again for the tube and another generous slathering of gel. Every little helped.

Fully lubed and aching so hard it hurt, Terry squatted over Yves's crotch. Reaching behind himself, without taking his eyes off Yves's face, Terry took hold of the sheathed cock, guided its head to his greased arse crack, then oh so slowly let himself fall back onto its unyielding length. He let its thick girth stretch his ring muscles and penetrate deep, forcing himself to ignore the sharp pain until, finally, his cheeks were pressing down on the Frenchman's balls and he was well and truly skewered by French cock.

For a moment both men held the position, Terry, eyes closed, swallowing as he worked to accommodate the size of this man in him, Yves, eyes wide open, clearly revelling in the sight of the young man riding him, eyes blazing with dark passion. Then, with no warning, just a savage buck of his hips, Yves drove himself hard and deep into Terry's body and held himself there, making the boy cry out in mingled surprise, pain and pleasure. Terry cried out again as Yves repeated the motion, harder and harder still. His strength was incredible. Terry should have been the guy in control but it was bound Yves underneath him who was dominating the fucking. Opening his eyes, Terry saw the look of almost feral pleasure on the Frenchman's face as he pounded with powerful thrusts of his hip muscles again and again up into his arse, smacking again and again into the fiercely aching sweet spot deep within.

With a helpless yell, Terry came, trails of thick come geysering out over the length of the Frenchman's twisting, bucking body, his fierce orgasm followed only seconds later by the cries of release from Yves himself, and a stream of French Terry had no hope of understanding but which he really hoped was absolutely and utterly filthy.

It took a long time for Yves's cock to lose sufficient rigidity for Terry to comfortably ease himself off the man. He tiptoed away from the bed to dispose of the condom, aware even as he did of the stupidity of trying to be quiet now after all of the noise the two of them had just been making. Returning to the bed, he looked down at Yves. The Frenchman was lying back, arms still above his head as if deliciously stretching, his lips curved in a small smile. Terry leaned over and kissed his chest. He reached for the loops of belt around Yves's wrists. Yves opened his eyes and smiled again. "Not yet," he whispered, and he raised his head to kiss Terry on the lips.

Incredibly, wonderfully, underneath him he felt the undeniable hardening of Yves's cock again, already. "Shit!" he breathed. He grinned. "I mean *merde!*"

Yves laughed softly. "You are learning," he whispered.

The breath caught in Terry's throat as he felt his own cock begin to swell and rise once more. "*Oui!*" he gasped.

Chapter Two

It was going much better than even he had ever expected it would. And Terry was truly pissed off.

Two weeks in, and POWer had travelled over two hundred miles in its journey southeast through France, wrestling almost every night in a succession of towns and villages against a variety of independent promotions in a mix of styles from singles through tag matches, battle royals and cage matches. Some of the crowds had been so small as to hardly be deserving of the name, but some had been quite decent, one or two actually quite large, with two of the bills shown on local television channels. The responses had been good, the money was coming in and POWer Promotions was getting its name known.

And as they travelled and wrestled, the British boys learned. They found out how to tailor their routines and ring personalities to their new European opponents and audiences. As a result, and to their surprise, their reputation spread, preceding them to the halls they visited so they'd even hear calls of "*Vivez les Anglais!*" on arriving in a new venue. Eric in particular was pleased. Gloomy at first that 'the foreigners' just didn't get his clown act, to his bemusement he found himself becoming the centre of a cult, with small groups of devoted followers, almost equally divided between the under tens and mumsy women wearing T-shirts bearing the same gaudy check pattern as his trade ring jacket and leotards, and cheering his buffoonish ring antics. "Maybe I should take star billing a bit more often!" he'd suggested half-jokingly to Terry. Terry had laughed. Doug had snarled.

Jonesy had been pleased to discover that the French did indeed have McDonalds and that you could order the food you wanted just by pointing at pictures of it, while Baz had surprised everyone by quickly learning enough of the language to charm the punters who were drawn to his boyish good looks. He'd tried to teach Terry some but Terry had said no given that he could get what he wanted without speaking, to which Doug had said, "Fucking *vrai!*" which had made Baz snort with laughter though he wouldn't explain why.

So why, Terry asked himself, sitting in the minibus by Doug as they drove to the next venue, was he so pissed off? The answer, he knew, was simple and the reason it had taken him so long to accept it was that it was also such a bloody annoying cliché.

Men.

More specifically, two men.

Most specifically, Mark and Yves.

And maybe Doug, too.

There could be no complaint about the work Mark had done for them. True to his word he had mapped out their itinerary, booked matches, venues and lodgings well in advance and done all of the necessary paperwork so that when the boys arrived at *pension,* hotel or bed and breakfast, town hall, village hall, sports centre or, on one occasion, abandoned monastery, they really had very little to do other than get into or out of their gear, wrestle, eat or sleep. Which was just as well as otherwise, keeping track of Mark was proving to be a bloody nightmare. "I thought *you* were a tom cat," Doug had grumbled, as Mark had cried off going back to their lodgings with them yet again after a fixture.

"Given half a chance," Terry had snapped. It was looking pretty clear that Mark was deliberately giving him the cold shoulder. Terry had been looking forward very much to repeats and reworkings of that energetic and highly enjoyable sex they'd had back in The Shed. What he'd got was less than a handshake in the ring. Even when it came to tag matches, Mark had seemed quick to make sure he was partnered with one of the others rather than with him.

It just didn't seem to make any sense. Mark had come on to him in the first place. And he was bloody good looking, right? So maybe, Terry was forced to consider, Mark was one of those bastards who had a guy once then had to move on to the next and the next, like some sodding horny bumble bee flitting from flower to flower. *Maybe I've been lucky. Up until now the only guy I've known like that is me.*

Or maybe the reason was altogether more obvious and familiar.

On a few occasions Terry had watched Mark and Baz talking and laughing. "He's helping me with the language," Baz had said, but Terry didn't remember French lessons being that funny at school. What surprised Terry was how jealous that thought had made him feel, and in turn, how lousy, and largely because of that he'd forced himself to ignore the idea. That, and the fact Baz was just too hail-fellow-well-met, too ready to smile and joke with everyone for Terry to believe the worst of him. *Besides, he's not as good looking as me, either. And definitely not as good a wrestler. First or last bout material, probably for as long as he stays wrestling. And just an all-round good, decent guy.* No, Terry decided, Baz definitely wasn't the reason Mark wasn't shagging Terry.

But then there was the situation between Mark and Doug. That was really getting on his tits.

As the tour progressed, Mark built on his initial success and his popularity in the ring. He continued to win and so held on to his anonymity, and as his reputation as '*un homme mysterieux*' spread, it became more and more necessary that he did win. But he was still a raw talent, still working out his own real ring style which, as a result, varied wildly from show to show and was heavily dependent on the calibre of the guys he was up against. If they let him, he could show flashes of real technical skill that were surprising in someone so relatively inexperienced, but too often he would fall back into the bull in a china shop ways he'd shown Terry when first they had wrestled. And although the punters seemed to like him and his air of mystery, Doug continued to hate the Johnny Deuce mask gimmick with a passion. "It's corny. It's crap. It goes," he said.

"It's sexy. It's mine. It stays," Mark had replied cheerily. So it had. More than that, Mark had taken to wearing the mask quite a lot more than Terry thought was strictly necessary, always immediately to and from venues, sometimes even when they were having breakfast or supper together. "It's method," Mark had said. "Living the role," he'd explained when Terry hadn't understood. It was bizarre but it was funny how quickly they all, apart from Doug, got used to it. And in any case, Terry was pretty sure he knew the real reason for it. Mark just wanted to piss Doug off. He certainly seemed to put more effort into it than he did into being with Terry.

Now, when they had crossed the border into Germany today and Mark should have been there with them, he had again failed to show. As ever, the paperwork he had prepared for them had been spot on, and Doug had once again surprised all by having enough rudimentary German to get them over the border with no problems. But, Terry thought bitterly, that wasn't the point. Mark had, of course, copped off the previous night, though he had assured them he would be with them the next morning before they left France. But he hadn't shown, only linking up with them several hours after their crossing on the *autobahn* leading to their first German fixture.

Then, there was Yves.

Terry found it hard to get the Frenchman out of his mind: his slim muscularity, the smell of his cologne, his smile. His cock. Oh, man, that cock splitting his arse, over and over. He wanted that again, and next time he wanted to drive his cock deep into Yves too, wanted to see how a sophisticated continental reacted to a scally Brit lad ploughing his furrow.

When they'd parted early the morning after their first meeting, Terry had felt curiously shy and uncertain—*gauche*, except he didn't know that word. There was something so different about Yves from any other wrestler Terry had ever known. Make that, different from any other *man*. Yves made his living wearing Lycra and fighting in a ring, and yet he still had a certain something about him that Terry could only describe as 'classy'. To his surprise, Terry found he liked that. Of course, the downside was that next to Yves, he felt rough as a badger's arse, and definitely not in the same league. He'd been reluctant to ask if they would meet again in case Yves had laughed at him. Besides, it seemed highly unlikely they would. Their first meeting had been the result only of the purest coincidence. Terry had thought it might just have been possible that Yves had looked reluctant, wistful, maybe even sad at their parting, but part they had and that, as Baz had tried to teach him, had almost certainly been *le fin de l'affaire*.

But even if they were to meet again, Terry doubted Doug would allow anything to happen.

Terry had hoped that after the success of their first show, Doug would chill a little. The reality was he seemed to get even more bloody-minded and cussed. And it wasn't all down to Mark's constant wind-ups. He'd been an absolute bastard to Terry the day after the night he'd spent with Yves. Terry knew his 'uncle' had been worried about his unexplained absence, and had even experienced a brief moment of guilt about it, but that had died in the face of Doug's unremitting bad humour. He took to sticking so close to the boy all the time it was the most Terry could do to get a dump on his own. And as for copping off... It was just as well his one night with Yves had been so good, otherwise he'd be bursting from frustrated sexual tension. When Terry had been fifteen, Doug had taken him to one side and given him a toe-curlingly graphic talk about the birds and the bees, with emphasis on the males of both, what they wanted, what they did to get it, and what you had to do to make sure you didn't come down with any nasty bird-bee related illnesses. After that, he had never, ever commented on anything Terry had said or done in his sex life, and he didn't now. But he made it abundantly clear that if anything else was going to happen while they were in Europe, he was going to be part of it. And not in any way that was at all interesting or appealing.

Which brought them to today and Felsburg, their first stop on the German leg of their 'Grand Tour'.

The POWer crew arrived in their two vehicles a couple of hours before the evening's programme was due to kick off, and pulled up outside a small café to discuss the prospective bouts. "So, how am I going to be wowing them tonight?" Eric asked as he happily tore chunks out of a croissant and dunked it into the large cup of milky coffee. Having dunked biscuits, cake and sandwiches into tea and coffee all his life, and having been slagged off for it by friends and family who thought it was a slobby habit, he'd been delighted to find this was a perfectly acceptable custom on the continent, and now used it as evidence of his increasing sophistication and the fact that travel did indeed broaden the mind.

Doug consulted the papers that Mark had given him earlier and the details of their boys' opponents that evening. "Pieter Mielke?" he said uncertainly. He squinted at the handwriting. "Is that Mielke or Vielke?"

Mark shrugged his shoulders. "Can't remember," he said without looking.

Doug gritted his teeth but read on. "It's a catch match. He's a lot lighter than you." He paused and looked pointedly at the croissant. Eric munched on regardless. "But he's tipped for big things. It would be...diplomatic if he won."

"We'll see," said Eric, and he got up in search of another croissant.

"Jonesy, you're up against Franz Werner. Same stats. You're on after Eric so see how that one goes and play it accordingly. Top of the bill is to be a tag match. They're putting up a father and son team. Bernard and Stefan Schoenfeld." Doug stopped, put the paper down a moment and looked up, eyes narrowed in thought.

"What's up?" asked Terry. "You know them?"

"I thought..." Doug shook his head and picked up the paper again. "I thought I remembered the name."

"What? You mean someone from when you and Dad were over here?"

"Fuck!" Mark laughed. "Is anyone still alive from those days?"

"Yeah, me!" growled Doug. "So he could be." He shook his head again. "But I doubt it. The man I'm thinking of...wouldn't have a son."

Mark shot a glance at Terry and raised an eyebrow, but Terry refused to rise. "So who's going up against them?" He already knew who it wouldn't be. "Mark and Baz or me and Baz?"

"You and me," said Mark quickly.

Now it was Terry's turn to look surprised. "You and me? You want to tag with me?"

"'Course. We haven't yet, have we? High time, don't you think?"

"Well, yeah. It's just, I thought..."

"What?"

How to say what he thought without sounding lame? "Nothing." He looked across at Doug. "Is that right?"

Doug blinked as if Terry's question was dragging him back from thoughts elsewhere. He looked down at the papers. "Yeah," he said simply.

"Great," said Mark, and in his face Terry at last saw that look again he'd first seen in The Shed. "It's been too long since we had any action together."

"And what about me?" asked Baz.

Doug consulted the papers. "First bout. You're up against someone called *Das Ungeheuer.*"

"Okay," said Baz.

"It means 'monster'."

"Fucking great," Baz sighed.

Chapter Three

In fact, *Das Ungeheuer* turned out to be a perfectly pleasant twenty-something, his lurid ring name based on some joke or reference that the Brits never got to the bottom of. He and Baz opened the bill with six rounds of good, clean, scientific grappling that ended in an unusual draw and appreciative applause from the audience. After they'd showered, the two young men headed off for a friendly *bier. Knowing Baz, that's all they'll share.* Somehow Terry found it hard to imagine Baz actually having sex with anyone. He was just too…nice. He sighed, taking in the sight of the German lad's pert arse and shy smile. Seemed a waste. Still, there was no need for him to feel downhearted. His own prospects for the night had unexpectedly turned out to be good. All he and Mark had to do was be brilliant in the ring, then extra-specially brilliant dodging Doug's eagle-eyed and heavy-handed surveillance afterwards.

Eric's bout was less successful than Baz's. The serious-minded punters didn't warm to his shenanigans the way the French finally had, and the kid he'd been anticipating having to let win turned out to be so good it was as much as Eric could do to stay in the bout, let alone think of winning it. In the end, he lasted five rounds before falling to his opponent's relentless energy and varied attacks, losing to a skilfully executed pinfall. While the athletic young German in tight gold trunks and matching boots pranced and bounced about the ring in victory, Eric left the hall totally knackered and in a foul mood.

Which brought the bill to the main bout: Mark and Terry versus father and son Bernard and Stefan Schoenfeld.

"Father and son," Mark scoffed, as he and Terry stood in their corner watching the Germans enter the ring and take up their position in their corner. "Yeah. Right!"

Terry regarded their two opponents carefully, searching for signs of family resemblance. Apart from their ring gear, there was little similarity. Bernard was definitely a wrestling veteran: the hair on his chest grizzled, the hair on his head thick but iron grey, his face well-lined, and the single tattoo on his forearm a patch of lines and colours blurred by time. That didn't mean, though, that Terry was as ready to scornfully dismiss him as Mark was. With his more experienced eye he sized up the older man, taking in the wiry physique and the assurance in his moves as he ducked under the ropes, entered the ring and began limbering up. There was still a real fluidity to his movements, and he met the eyes of the young Brits across the canvas with calm confidence. The punters, who presumably knew him, were buzzing happily, clearly expecting a good fight, not some squash job of a grappling has-been at the hands of upstart foreigners.

Terry turned his attention to Stefan Schoenfeld. Late teens, possibly very early twenties, his hairless chest and pale blond curls made it hard to judge his age. A good two or three stones heavier than his 'father', stocky, but in a puppy fat kind of way. He moved around the ring with an adolescent gawkiness that contrasted with his partner, his warm ups confined to grabbing the top rope and leaning back to stretch out arms and back muscles. There was strength there, Terry didn't doubt, but he already had the feeling that the real threat from this team was going to come from its senior member.

All four wrestlers stripped to their wrestling gear, the Brits and Stefan taking off their ring jackets, Bernard taking off the old school dressing gown he had worn to the ring. In turn, they were given the once over by the referee who ran his hands over their upper bodies and checked the soles of their wrestling boots, a procedure that was more ritual than practical. Mark, of course, was in his Johnny Deuce kit, and Terry had gone along with a pair of white speedos and boots with a single black stripe down the side of each to complement him. The Germans were in matching purple—Bernard in tights, the boy in a leotard cut low over his stomach—their boots polished black leather with purple stripes down the side. Terry let his eyes linger appreciatively on the young lad's leotard. Cut very low over the stomach, he noted approvingly, and high at the sides over the thighs, showing just a hint of butt cheek round the back and tight enough to make the arse crack very visible, very tempting.

Terry found himself wondering if he was to hoist the boy up in a suplex or piledriver, pulling at that leotard as he would perfectly legitimately have to, would the sheer Lycra be pulled deep into the lad's tight crack in a classic wedgie, giving the ringsiders an eyeful of more of their local lad's beefy arse cheeks than they'd ever have dared to hope for. Completing their ring gear, each of the Germans had a single word embroidered in Gothic script at his hip. Bernard's was '*Vater*', Stefan's '*Sohn*'. Maybe, maybe not, Terry decided, but still, for some reason, it really worked for him. Chalk and cheese individually, the Schoenfelds together, were an unexpectedly sexy tag team combination.

Terry and Mark stood ring centre in front of their opponents, all four with head down, frowning as if concentrating on the instructions and warnings the referee was barking at them and nodding as if to show acceptance. By now, Terry at least was well used to pantomiming agreement to a stream of foreign words, none of which he understood. The four men shook hands and Terry couldn't help noticing how much firmer the older man's handshake was than that of his 'son'. The bell rang. Terry slapped Mark on the back as his partner left the ring to take his position on the apron outside the ropes, then crouched and prepared himself to lock up with whichever of the Schoenfelds was staying in the ring to wrestle him first. It was Bernard.

They circled, Terry grinning as per usual, the German poker-faced. They closed in and locked up, each throwing his arms around the shoulders of the other and leaning in, in an initial test of strength.

Their first session against each other lasted well over five minutes, longer than most rounds in a singles match and rare for a tag, and Terry loved every minute. Bernard was a wrestling genius. Not a movement was wasted, not a fraction of effort misplaced. He flowed from hold to escape to counter hold, over and over. He was what wrestlers called 'light', selling his holds as if he was pouring all of his weight and strength into all of them, but actually bringing little real pressure to bear on his opponent. Terry, after allowing himself to be displayed in the holds, was able to 'escape' then respond in kind, showing his own repertoire of moves and routines which Bernard also generously sold.

Terry knew, though, that this concession to showmanship might last for the first half of the bout, maybe slightly more, but he couldn't rely on Bernard's giving and taking for the whole of the match. Sooner or later, the veteran would really go for a fall or submission. Indeed, Terry quickly found that if he didn't stay on top of his game, Bernard would have him immediately. When Terry made a misstep, Bernard had reacted with lightning speed and had swept his opponent's feet out from under him and jumped on top of him in an early pinfall attempt that Terry had only just managed to twist out of. When he jumped back to his feet, Terry was mentally kicking himself for his carelessness but outwardly grinning more broadly than ever. This was his idea of great pro wrestling. Bernard remained as apparently solemn as ever though perhaps there was just a slight upturn of the lip in what might have passed in Germany for a smile.

The older wrestler definitely knew how to handle a boy's body in the ring, and Terry couldn't help mentally translating that into thoughts of what Bernard might do with a boy's body in a bed. He certainly wouldn't have objected to having that wiry grey chest and belly hair rubbed in his face. He'd bet the German had a thickly hairy ball sac, too. He could picture Bernard's balls rasping over his face, his lips, imagine taking them into his mouth, teasing them with his tongue...

It was a loss of focus, just for a second, and the next thing Terry knew he was caught up in a tight headscissors that had come like lightning out of nowhere. Belly down to canvas, Terry's head was trapped between the German's thighs, his face pressed tight into that crotch and his brains being squeezed out of his ears by the German's ruthless constriction of his quads around his skull. His daydream of nuzzling between Bernard's legs had come true, but too soon and not at all in the way he'd been fantasising. The older man slapped at his own thighs and pushed his hips upward, the textbook way of increasing the pressure and selling the hold. The movement also happened to press Terry's face still harder into his crotch. Terry in turn slapped at his tormentor's arse, selling the pain, but also let his hands linger on the silky curves of the sheer Lycra before slapping them again. With no trunks line, it almost felt like Bernard was naked.

Bernard responded by increasing the pressure, pushing his hips up still higher so that Terry's handsome face was buried even deeper in his crotch, only the thinnest layer of purple Lycra between his Teutonic tackle and Terry's nose and mouth. Bernard wasn't holding back now and Terry was really hurting, but right at that moment, he didn't care. From his suddenly acquired intimate vantage point Terry now knew for certain that Bernard was wearing nothing under his tights. He groaned deeply and the audience around them cheered, taking the muffled sound as a sign of the young foreigner's suffering in their man's hold. On the apron, to the confusion of the audience who heard it, Mark guffawed, and on the front row of seats, Doug tutted and raised his eyes. Both knew Terry better. He was enjoying himself.

For a good thirty seconds Terry 'struggled' with his head between Bernard's legs, reading the German's package with his face the way a blind man read a braille book with his fingers. Bernard wasn't hard, not yet, but he was heading that way, and he was big. Terry could definitely make out the contours of something very thick and long grinding into his face as Bernard worked his scissors hold. With his face completely obscured and hidden from the audience, Terry opened his mouth wide and let the Lycra-covered balls press in past his lips and onto his tongue. He sucked once and heard Bernard hiss hard, even above the roar of the crowd, felt the sudden reflexive tightening of the quad muscles enveloping his head before the more slow, forced relaxation. The German could have released then and there if he hadn't liked what the horny Brit had just done to his bollocks. But he didn't. Unseen still, Terry smiled in the privacy of the older man's crotch.

Ten seconds later, Terry gave the obligatory twist and hand stand and 'escaped' his opponent's hold. As both men leaped to their feet and circled each other again, the crowd applauded Terry's skill and Bernard's near 'victory'. On the German's face was an expression of regret, obviously at having lost a possible winning move. Or more probably, Terry thought, because he was no longer having his ball sac tongued by a good-looking young stud in trunks.

Though he was literally and metaphorically having a ball, by this point Terry knew it was time to give his partner his share of the limelight. Besides, much more of that kind of action and his enthusiasm would be far too visible for all to see. Accordingly, if reluctantly, Terry spun away from his opponent, stepped up to the ropes and reached out to let Johnny Deuce slap his hand and take his place in the ring.

Bernard, too, tagged out. As he ducked under the ropes, Terry tried to catch the veteran's eye, but Bernard's attention was wholly fixed on Stefan as he took the place of his 'father' and squared up to Johnny. Really selling the concerned father act, Terry thought, as he took in Bernard's convincingly anxious expression. Okay, he was beginning to see where the 'plot' of this bout was heading. It was a standard. As it turned out, Terry was even more right than he had expected.

Chapter Four

As Terry had suspected, Stefan had little of his father's skill, which was perhaps not so surprising in one so young. Stefan charged into Mark like a young bull, actually driving the masked man back into the ropes, so forcing a break. The two quickly went on to exchange a series of forearm smashes to each other's chests that had zero finesse but had the crowd quickly whipped up and shouting. A mistimed smash on Stefan's part saw Mark clamping his powerful arms around the boy's head and neck and dragging him down to the canvas to lay the hold on hard. Stefan thrashed and pounded the mat, Mark grunted and leaned back, upping the pressure of his headlock mercilessly, and Bernard leaned as far across the ring as he could in an obviously vain attempt to reach his son's flailing hand to save him by tagging him out.

Terry grimaced. He could see already how it was going to go between the two men on the canvas. Both inexperienced and both too headstrong to allow the other to look good, their wrestling would descend quickly into undisciplined brawling, far-removed from the skilled technical wrestling he and Bernard had given the crowd.

The classic pattern to a bout like this would be for Mark to rough Stefan up some more before tagging Terry back in. Terry would then work the boy over in more imaginative ways, letting him get close to reaching his despairing father's hand again and again but always pulling him back at the last minute. This would allow Bernard plenty of opportunity to act the concerned/outraged parent and should drive the crowd into a frothing frenzy of righteous indignation at the treatment of the local and youngest man in the ring. Mark would then step back in to score the first fall over Stefan, who would be forced by the rules to begin the second session in spite of his 'weakened' state. He would, however, finally make the tag with his father who would be able to leap in and avenge his son's punishment and humiliation, taking an equalising fall over Mark.

After that, the possibilities were more varied. Ideally, there should be at least one moment when all four men were in the ring at once, laying into each other. The poetic justice the crowd would love would be if Bernard used his skill to gain a second and winning fall over Mark, but Terry doubted very much that Mark would allow it. Terry's mind wandered again. Images of Bernard caught up in Mark's brawny arms being slowly squeezed in a bear hug, his slim, hairy body crushed against Mark's; experienced maturity helpless and suffering in the grip of brash youth, that heavy purple package squeezed tight up against the heavy tool in Mark's white trunks. Terry blinked, shook his head and forced himself to concentrate on the real ring action playing out in front of him. He found it was going nothing like he had expected.

Mark had run a chain of postings on the youngster, repeatedly whipping him across the ring and slamming him back first into three of the ring's four corner posts in turn so that the lad fell to the canvas, clutching his back as he arched in pain while Bernard made great show of his unhappiness and desperation to help his boy. Stefan reached up pleadingly towards Bernard, calling out, "*Vati*," but Mark stepped in and grabbed the outstretched hand, pulled him up by it, spun him round and sent him crashing yet again into a turnbuckle. Terry winced. The corner posts were, of course, padded and the impact rarely as bad as the wrestlers made them seem. But even so, he could tell that Mark was putting all of his strength into hurling the burly boy into them, the whole ring actually shaking from the impact of Stefan's body against the pads. That agonised look on his face was probably not all acting. Neither was all of the anger on Bernard's face. As Mark's brutal treatment of his opponent continued, Bernard's expressions and gestures of dismay and anger became less exaggerated, more genuine.

Then Mark made his rookie mistake. Stefan was down yet again. Clapping both hands around his head and ignoring the ref's pleas to wait until his man got up from the canvas under his own steam, Mark hauled the lad back up to his feet and sent him cannonballing into a corner post, but this time careening towards his home corner. The boy smashed front first into the turnbuckle and fell like a sack of potatoes but at the feet of his 'father', who only had to lean down to swipe his hand to be allowed to replace him in the ring. Pausing just to lift Stefan to his feet and guide him to a position of safety outside the ropes, Bernard turned to face his son's tormentor. From across the ring Terry could see the murderous look in Bernard's eye. If he'd been facing that, he'd have been very wary indeed and braced for the fight of his life. Looking to Mark, his heart sank as he could see quite clearly from his tag partner's stance and expression that he was completely unaware of just what he was now facing.

Expecting an even easier time of it against the lighter wrestler, Mark was completely unprepared for the speed at which the veteran launched himself towards him. Even Terry barely had time to blink as Bernard threw himself in a forward roll that carried him the length of the ring, bringing him up right behind Mark. Slamming his sinewy forearm into the Englishman's broad back, Bernard knocked him to the mat, flipped him over and damn nearly had him in a pinfall before the bigger, stronger man just managed to power his way out and back to his feet again. Bernard twisted, tripped him, turned and nearly pinned him again. Again and again, the more skilled man took his significantly bigger opponent to the mat and almost held him there for the three count, brute strength alone enabling Mark to force his way out each time. Terry could only watch open-mouthed. The speed, skill and stamina of the older man were incredible, and he was giving them all a masterclass in attack wrestling. There was nothing feigned about this, and no give and take for show. Bernard was furious at what his young tag partner had been subjected to and was going for the first fall in revenge. In addition, and more to the point, he was making Mark look a complete fool.

The crowd roared its approval, and Terry leaned as far over the ropes as he legally could, arm outstretched. His desperation to tag was also quite real this time. He had a bad feeling that what had started out as a good pro bout was now spiralling rapidly out of control.

Stunned and disorientated by the German's attacks, Mark staggered from one narrow escape to the next, only his greater size and strength saving him each time. But Bernard's blitzkrieg was wearing him down, and Terry thought it was mere seconds now before the vengeful father would have the pin he was looking for.

Then, with a roar of fury and frustration, Mark struck. On his knees with Bernard standing, leaning over him, eager to take hold just as soon as his man got to his feet again, Mark punched up, straight and hard between his attacker's thighs, driving his fist hard into the veteran's Lycra-clad balls. Bernard collapsed in agony. There was stunned silence across the hall. Even Terry could hardly believe what his partner had done. It wasn't the illegality, for all that he and Mark were supposed to be good guys. It was the totally unfeigned reality of the move. There was no doubt in anyone's mind that the anguish on the face of the man rolling around on the canvas clutching his crotch was completely and utterly real. The hall erupted into outraged thunderous condemnation.

"Johnny! Johnny!" Terry shouted as loud as he could, in a vain attempt to be heard over the punters' noise, bouncing up and down on the bottom rope, arm outstretched in an attempted tag. But Johnny couldn't hear him, or wouldn't listen. Enflamed by being made to look so foolish by the older man, Mark was deaf to everything: his partner's pleas, the vocal disapproval of the crowd, the referee's admonitions. All he wanted was Bernard Schoenfeld and payback time. Reaching down, he pulled the older wrestler up to his feet by his grey hair, wrapping his powerful arms round the German's trim waist and hoisting him bodily off the canvas. For a second, Terry thought his earlier wish had come true and Mark was going to lay on a bear hug. Instead, carrying the still stunned German, he turned to face a post and walked, gathering speed until he was running full pelt into the corner. At the last minute he let go of the wrestler, slamming him back first into the corner post, his own weight following on immediately in an impact that drove every last scrap of air out of the veteran's lungs. Terry felt the crash reverberate throughout the ring.

Bernard would have fallen to the mat but Mark roughly shoved his hands under the German's armpits, hoisted him to his feet again and took hold of the top ropes on either side of his opponent's body. He took a step back while still holding on, then charged into him, driving his shoulders into the man's exposed and helpless gut. He stepped back and did it again. Then again. The crowd were on their feet protesting this maltreatment of their favourite, and the referee was trying frantically to stop the brutal punishment without actually getting pulped between the two wrestlers' bodies himself. Only after he had delivered six shoulder charges into Bernard's stomach did Mark leave off, standing back to raise his arms and affect surprise at the anger of referee and crowd alike, while Bernard slid slowly down the turnbuckle padding to the mat, wheezing and clutching his gut and ribs.

The referee spoke quickly and harshly to Mark, jabbing his fingers at his sweating chest then signalling furiously to the ringside MC who announced something Terry had no way of understanding. He assumed it was some kind of public warning, the first step to disqualification in pro wrestling and an unthinkable thing for a team of 'blue eyes' who were always supposed to follow the rules. He tried to catch Mark's eye, but Mark was already crouched and regarding the gasping form of his opponent in the corner, impatiently waiting for him to get up again so that he could resume his ruthless assault. The referee had no choice but to begin a count. "*Ein, zwei, drei...*" Terry thought it was all over. The crowd was shrieking at Bernard to get up. Stefan was shouting at the top of his lungs, urging his father to rise. On the seven count, the older man finally stirred. On the eight, he began to struggle to his feet. He just made it by the nine.

Mark immediately pushed the referee to one side. He stepped in, scooped the groggy German up bodily in a crotch hold, paraded him helplessly to the centre of the ring and then slammed him down harshly, back first to the mat. Bernard had time to arch only once in agony before Mark dropped on him, elbow first into his tenderised gut, then lay across the top half of his body, chest to chest, holding one of Bernard's arms with his hands while trapping the other with his boots, keeping him easily pinned to the mat for the full three count of the first fall.

The English were in the lead.

As Stefan leaped over the ropes to dash to help his partner up, Mark swaggered over to his corner of the ring. For the punters, Terry clapped him on the back as if proud of his achievement, nodding and smiling like a loon, but as he leaned into him he hissed into Mark's ear, "What the fuck are you doing?"

"Winning the match. What does it look like?"

"You don't have to kill a man to do that!"

Mark shrugged. "Shouldn't step in a ring if he can't take the lumps, should he?" And his tone changed, became harder. "And he shouldn't have made me look such a prat."

"That's not hard, sometimes," Doug spat as he stepped up to do his second's work. He should have towelled Mark down, wiping off the sweat his exertions had worked up before offering him a drink from the water bottle he had in his bucket. Instead, he threw the towel at Mark so he could do his own rubdown, and dumped the bucket with a clang at his booted feet, letting him fish out the water bottle for himself. Mark just laughed.

"It's a show, Mark," Terry reminded him. "We're putting on a show."

"I thought you were the one who didn't like the fake stories."

"It's..." Terry struggled to put pro wrestling's elusive balance between sport and entertainment into words. It was hardly the right time and place for that particular discussion. "That," he said, indicating the visibly shaken Bernard who had finally been helped up to his feet and back to his corner by his boy, "is not good."

Mark shrugged again. "Sometimes, Terry, I don't think you know what you do want."

Terry stepped back and looked at the figure in white mask and trunks, the very image of a pro wrestler. "Maybe I don't." Mark leaned forward as if he hadn't caught what Terry had said, but before Terry could repeat it he saw the MC leaning for the ringside bell with his small hammer. "Let me take over," he said quickly.

Mark shook his head, and gave his mask a small readjustment. "Got to play by the rules, Terence. Same guys start who finished the previous round."

"Then tag me quickly."

"You're the boss." Mark shrugged again and stepped out eagerly to the centre of the ring. "For the moment."

The bell went and Bernard was still propped up against his corner post being fussed over anxiously by his second and son. For a moment, Terry wondered whether the other team was going to literally throw in the towel and forfeit the match. It occurred to him there was a very real possibility that the ferocity of Mark's attack might have cracked if not actually broken one of Bernard's ribs. It would have been a victory for the Brits, but a poor way to end a bout. And if word spread on the circuit that the POWer wrestlers were actually injuring the guys they were up against, pretty quickly the invitations to venues and events would dry up and their so far successful European tour would go down the pan.

With an obvious effort of will, however, Bernard rallied, waved aside Stefan and the second, and walked slowly, haltingly into the centre of the ring. He raised and stretched out his arms for a classic wrestler's lock up, visibly wincing as the movement pained his punished chest and belly. With complete disregard for the invitation to a clean resumption of their grappling, Mark stepped in close. He brushed the German's arms apart with two outward pushes of his own, before swinging his right arm back in and up in a ferocious, unrestrained forearm smash that caught the other wrestler under the chin and literally lifted his booted feet off the mat, sending him sprawling once again back to canvas. Mark nodded as if at a job well done, then turned and sauntered back to his corner accompanied by a chorus of catcalls and boos. "You wanted it quick," he said cheerily, reaching out his hand to tag Terry. "Done. You're in."

Terry ducked under the ropes and stepped into the ring, unsettled as much by the unaccustomed boos he was now getting on his partner's behalf as by what Mark had just done. It was up to him to pull this match back from the nasty brawl it had become. But how? Some kind of balance had to be restored, but to let Bernard gain the upper hand again now when he was so obviously still reeling from his beating would have stretched the credulity of even a pro wrestling audience. He had no choice but to move in, lock on an arm bar and take his man down to the canvas as if he were continuing Johnny Deuce's 'good work', and going all out for a two-nil victory over the Germans. But even as he grunted and twisted his face in supposed sadistic effort, Terry brought very little pressure to bear on the joint, and he maintained the hold for as long as he could to give Bernard time to at least begin to recover himself. When he heard a whispered, "Danke," he knew that Bernard understood what had been done for him. He relaxed and let the German skilfully twist and throw him, so that he was on top and Terry was now having his muscular arm worked over. He stamped his booted foot on the canvas as if enraged at his own carelessness, and the crowd cheered and hooted its approval both of a return to skilled wrestling and of their local man's being on top again.

Terry and Bernard grappled for another minute, Bernard's movements undoubtedly slower than before but improving as the seconds passed, and still exceptional if given a chance to shine. Terry could sense that the time was now right for father to tag son, and for he and Stefan finally to get to grips. Feigning a misstep, he let Bernard escape a leg-lock to a scattering of applause from the audience, but instead of the older man reaching out and bringing his son in as he'd expected, Bernard sprang forward and took him down in a side headlock. Surprised at what was generally a move used at the start of a match rather than at this stage, Terry sold the hold, even as he wondered what Bernard's gambit was. As he struggled, Bernard leaned over him so that their faces were practically touching, each hiding the other's from the audience, and whispered to him rapidly in German. The tone was urgent, the words staccato and quick, but Terry couldn't understand one of them. "*Ich...*" Terry began falteringly, not having a clue even how to say he didn't understand, but before he could get any further than that, Bernard hauled his head up then slammed it down to the mat, and Terry was obliged to act pained and stunned, even though the German had skilfully pulled him back a fraction of an inch before his skull actually made contact with the canvas. While Terry earned his Oscar, Bernard stood, walked over to Stefan and tagged his son into the ring.

Within less than a minute, Terry knew there was little he could do with Stefan. The lad had strength and weight and dogged enthusiasm, but none of Bernard's skills. Terry could easily have put him in hold after hold as the boy knew few avoidance tactics and almost no counters, but his inability to sell the 'suffering' inflicted by a Boston crab or a camel clutch would have quickly left the audience bored. From a personal point of view, Terry had enjoyed trapping the boy in a scissors hold, squeezing his beefy body slowly between his thighs, but Stefan's stoic struggles and apparent determination not to show any pain, even when Terry really put some force into his squeeze, robbed the move of much of its pleasure. In an attempt to make the fight look like more of a contest, Terry allowed himself to be put into a backhammer, but almost immediately had to twist and somersault out as the inept boy had nearly dislocated his shoulder by shoving his arm way too high up his back.

The only thing he could do, Terry realised with a sigh, was to take complete control of him and waltz him around the ring for a minute or two until he could get him close to '*Vater*', who could tag him. Then he and Bernard could put on some real wrestling for the punters again. But then the young idiot gave him a clumsy but powerful shove that sent him stumbling back into the arms of his tag partner. Terry had no choice but to tag Mark in. "Try not to kill him," he hissed as he reluctantly took up his tag rope outside the ring and grimly waited to see just what Mark would do this time. He didn't have to wait long.

There was an undoubted excited tension in the air as the two wrestlers squared off, which Terry had to agree was good for the match as a whole. The crowd was eager to see how 'their' youngster would try to avenge his father's brutal treatment at Johnny Deuce's hands earlier. Terry could see that the lad did indeed step up his game, attacking more aggressively against his new opponent, but still, the outcome was never really in doubt. Terry might have been able to string out Stefan's inadequacies as a wrestler to create at least a competent match, but Mark simply wasn't good enough even for that. And the anger he had felt at his treatment at the father's hands seemed still to be burning strong. Within two minutes, the fight had degenerated again into an exchange of forearm smashes and postings, with Stefan on the receiving end of almost all of them. The stocky boy was quickly reeling from Mark's unrelenting assault. The crowd was on their feet now, urging their boy on, even though they could tell it was hopeless. It was only a matter of time. Terry looked across at Bernard and was struck by the look of bleak inevitability on his face. He wasn't even trying to reach out to tag his son. For a second their eyes met, and again he could tell that the older man was trying to communicate something to him.

There was a crash from the centre of the ring, a mingled cry of excitement and disappointment from the crowd, and both men's attention was pulled back to the action on the mat.

Mark had Stefan trapped in the start of a classic Boston crab submission move. The boy was belly down to the mat, Mark standing astride him, back to his head. He had reached down and pulled up

Stefan's booted feet, tucking them securely under his armpits. All he had to do now was sit down on Stefan's back, pulling on his legs, and the torque on the lad's spine and thighs would do the rest. A young, bullish wrestler like Stefan could sometimes power his way out of this hold by forcing his legs out straight and unseating his tormentor, but generally only with the co-operation of the guy laying on the crab, which Mark certainly wasn't going to give, and definitely not after the sort of battering Stefan's back had taken. Terry readied himself for Stefan's submission and his team's 'victory', nervously wondering just what the crowd's reaction would be. To Terry's annoyance and unease, however, Mark was taking his time. He remained standing with his opponent trapped underneath him, playing with the boy and the crowd, actively stoking their fury. "Yeah? Yeah?" he taunted as he made as if to sink into the hold again and again only to hold back. He turned as he teased, so that he could face the punters on each side of the ring in turn, dragging his victim around with him as he did so. Only when he had addressed all four sides of the hall did he begin to lower himself slowly into the Boston. "Get it over with," Terry muttered through clenched teeth. It was obvious to everyone that Mark had won. There was no way the boy was going to get out, even he must have seen that, and no way he could take the pressure a muscular man like Mark could bring to bear on his back. Mark had brought the crowd to the peak of its excitement; now he should finish it.

But he didn't. Slowly he sank down, only to rise again a little then sink some more, repeating the move over and over, drawing out the torture, but also giving the lad chance to accommodate to each slight increase of pressure before upping it still more. And Stefan was taking it. *"Nein! Nein!"* he gasped, beating the mat with his fists, his head thrashing from side to side, the sweat-soaked hair lashing backwards and forwards across his face and eyes. Gradually the shrieking in the hall died down, the spectacle in the ring the object of a horrified fascination. Just how much punishment could the young lad take? "Submit! Submit!" Terry was hissing, and not because he wanted Mark to win, but because he wanted Stefan's suffering to stop. His hands balled into fists, and still the crab went on. There! Mark's arse had come down so that it was resting on the boy's head, Stefan's body now literally bent in two with the masked man riding him pulling back fiercely on his legs and exerting horrendous pressure on his spine. Then Mark pulled back even further, lifting Stefan's lower body off the mat, the Boston manoeuvre taken to its limits and beyond. The referee was on his knees, face pressed close to the boy, screaming at him in German to submit.

And from his position just feet away from the grapplers on the mat, Terry could see two things most of the punters couldn't. Firstly, the position of Mark's hands, clawing deep into the flesh of Stefan's thighs. Secondly, the thick, hard lump at the bent boy's crotch with just the hint of a dripping cockhead thrusting over the line of that oh-so-low leotard. Incredibly, but undeniably, Stefan was being turned on by the pain and public humiliation of Mark's submission hold.

Fascinated by the sight, Terry actually jumped when a sudden roar exploded around the hall. The referee was pushing at Mark, trying to dislodge him from the young German's back. The MC was ringing the bell furiously. The match was over. Mark had won. *Stefan must have submitted!*

Terry looked at the beaten boy, lying face down on the canvas now that Mark had been pried from him by the referee. No doubt he would find it difficult to stand for a while, not least because his back had been bent further against nature and for longer than Terry had ever seen, but also because if he did then everyone would see the massive boner he had stretching his leotard. The boy's head twisted and Terry found him looking up from the canvas directly at him. He didn't look defeated. He looked...disappointed. He had the glazed expression of a teenager interrupted mid-wank by his parents. Terry glanced at the referee. He'd never seen a ref look so relieved that a bout was over. He wondered whether the lad had actually submitted at all, or whether the ref had just claimed he had to put an end to it. From across the ring, Bernard ran to help his son up. Terry noted with wry amusement how quickly the older man wrapped a towel around Stefan's waist. An odd gesture, unless you knew just what it was he was trying to conceal from surrounding eyes.

"So when did you become a heel?" Doug snapped as Mark and Terry made their way back to the dressing room, down an aisle lined with jeering, booing punters. Terry had never been so pleased to leave a ring, and had never been so uncertain he'd be able to make it to the dressing rooms in one piece.

Mark was grinning proudly. "It's all about putting on a show, old man."

"Terry put on the show. You put on a beating. You made us look like amateurs."

"Amateurs? We won!"

"People don't come to see us win, you muppet! They come to see us wrestle. What you were doing wasn't wrestling."

"Welcome to the twenty-first century, Doug. This is how we do it now. Right, Terry?"

Unwilling or unable to answer the question, Terry ripped off his ring gear as quickly as he could, grabbed a towel and headed for the shower, leaving the two men to argue. When he emerged, Doug had gone. Mark was also stripped of his gear and looked as chirpy and upbeat as before, apparently completely unfazed by Doug's stinging criticism. A large part of his good mood, however, may have been due to the lazy up and down stroking of his thickening cock which he was enjoying. Already semi-hard when Terry stepped from the shower, it rapidly grew harder and thicker at the sight of Terry's naked, dripping body, and Mark's smile grew wider and hungry. "Mm, pink and clean," he said happily, advancing on Terry, leaving off his cock stroking to reach out for his muscular tag partner.

To both their surprise, Terry twisted to avoid him. "Yeah, well, you're neither."

Mark's smile flickered, just a little. "Thought you'd like me all sweaty. The smell and taste of victory."

Terry stepped past Mark to sort out his boxers and jeans, pulling them on as quickly as possible. "At the moment I'm just up for the smell and taste of a cup of coffee."

For a second, Mark hesitated, and Terry wondered whether he'd come onto him anyway. And what he'd do if that happened. Then Mark simply shrugged, grabbed his own towel and headed into the shower whistling.

Terry sighed and slumped down onto the changing room bench to complete his dressing, relieved but massively frustrated at the same time. Exactly what he'd been lusting after for days now was being handed to him on a plate, and he was turning it down. Why? Because they'd won a bout? But it was the way they'd won, wasn't it? The way Mark had been in that ring. But did that matter? He shook his head. When did the game get so complicated?

By the time Mark emerged from the shower, Terry was fully dressed and sitting on the bench waiting. Mark said nothing, emerging from a cloud of steam to stand in front of Terry. His grin was gone, the smile replaced by something more knowing, slightly mocking even. He stood, water dripping from his body, his cock less tumescent but still thick and long, hanging heavily between his legs. Slowly, he began to towel himself down, from head to chest, rubbing the towel back and forth across his pecs and chest hairs, then over his belly and down to his crotch, massaging the cock and wiry ball sac before moving down still further to the lightly furry thighs. By the time he reached his calves, Terry was rock hard and leaking pre-come in his jeans. Dick and brain had swapped functions, and miraculously, the questions he'd been wrestling with just a moment previously no longer seemed to matter.

"I'm sorry," said Mark, but that mocking smile was still on his lips.

Terry just wanted that body in bed with him, that cock in his mouth, his cock up that arse, or any combination of the above. He lunged for Mark's kitbag, pulled out his jeans and threw them at him. "What about my underwear?" Mark asked, laughing.

"Waste of time," Terry said. "Now get 'em on and let's get out of here!"

Mark hurried eagerly to comply. It was just as he was pulling on his trainers that there was a knock at the door." Terry, nerves stretched to breaking point by the torment of waiting for Mark to get his clothes on so he could get him back to his hotel room and tear them off again, jumped like a startled hare. "Piss off!" he muttered savagely.

Mark tutted in mock reproof. "*Kommen sie herein.*"

The door opened. It was Stefan Schoenfeld.

The boy was dressed in jeans and tracksuit top. He seemed nervous, looking first at Mark, then Terry, then back again, and then over his shoulder. With a deep breath, as if coming to some kind of decision, he stepped into the changing room and closed the door behind him, then stood, again looking back and forth between the two surprised men regarding him. "*Darf ich mit Ihnen sprechen...?*" he began.

"*Englisch bitte*," Mark said.

Stefan licked his lips, opened his mouth to speak but then stopped. Tried again, but finally shook his head. "*Ich kann Englisch nicht sprechen.*"

"He can't speak English," Mark translated.

"Yeah, I got that. So what does he want?" Terry was worried. Had the lad come to complain, to make some sort of trouble about the roughhouse in the ring? He certainly didn't look angry. Quite the reverse. For the next few seconds, he and Mark exchanged words that Terry couldn't follow in the slightest, relying instead on the expressions on the two men's faces to get some sense of what was passing between them. Stefan was clearly nervous but spoke and acted like someone who had steeled himself to do something and was going to carry it through no matter what. Terry's puzzlement quickly gave way to complete bewilderment as Mark began to grin then smile broadly, as did Stefan, though the heavyset lad still managed to look as nervous as hell while doing it. Terry regarded him closely. There was something else there in Stefan's expression as well, wasn't there? Was that...anticipation? "Would you mind telling me what the fuck he is saying?" Terry exploded finally, feeling like the only guy in the room who hadn't got a joke.

Mark reached past him to get his jacket and picked up his kitbag. "Steffi boy here is up for a little fun tonight, before he heads home to papa." He clapped Stefan on the shoulder and opened the door, leading the boy out with him.

Terry grabbed his own kitbag and followed. "What? You mean he wants to get a drink or something?"

Already a way down the corridor, Mark laughed and called back to him over his shoulder. "You are such a small town boy sometimes, Terence. Don't you know what the German for 'three-way' is?"

"Of course I don't!" Terry yelled after him, stung by the insult.

"It's '*three-way*'! So c'mon!"

☆☆☆

Outside the hall, two men stood in the shadows. They watched as the unmasked Johnny Deuce walked past, his arm draped proprietorially over Stefan Schoenfeld's shoulders. Seconds after they had disappeared in the direction of Johnny's van, Terry appeared hurrying after them. The two men watched as the wrestlers disappeared from sight. Finally one of them spoke. His German was faultless but the accent wasn't quite native. "I was watching you in the ring tonight."

Bernard Schoenfeld nodded but said nothing. His eyes remained fixed in the direction the three young wrestlers had gone.

The man by his side spoke again. "It looked very much as if you were trying to tell young Terry something. Warn him perhaps."

Bernard bit his lip but remained silent. The other man reached up to take him by the chin and turn his face to his own. After a moment, he gave a small smile and let go. "I must have been wrong. After all, they have left. With Stefan."

"He'll be all right?" Bernard stopped, as if angry with himself that he had spoken but unable to keep the words in.

The man at his side laughed softly, a small sound with no real humour to it. "Of course he will. If he does as he is told. He will most probably enjoy himself. You know better than most how Stefan enjoys himself." The older man looked down. "And then he will be returned to you." He turned and left.

Bernard Schoenfeld remained on his own in the shadows. For just a second, it appeared as if he might strike out in the direction Stefan had gone with the two Englishmen, but then, with a look of sadness and bitter resignation on his face, he reluctantly turned and slowly walked off in the opposite direction, back the way he had come.

PART FOUR

Chapter One

Stefan was quiet all the way back to the hotel. Terry couldn't square his supposed eagerness for a three-way with this silence and with Stefan's pale, uncomfortable appearance. He couldn't help wondering if Mark's translation might have had more wish fulfilment than accuracy to it. He'd been about to suggest they all just stop and talk for a few minutes to make sure everyone was on the same wavelength when Mark reached his paw behind his head, pulled him in, and thrust his tongue hard and deep into his mouth. Finally given what it had been craving for so long, Terry's body abandoned his brain's higher feelings, and he submitted completely to the sensation of that thick, wet tongue against his. Dimly, he was aware of Mark reaching for Stefan at the same time, and when he was finally let go to grab a breath, Mark turned immediately to Stefan and kissed him with equal passion. For just a second, the lad looked as if he was going to resist, but then he, too, surrendered to the pleasure of Mark's tongue. For long minutes Mark held both lads in the crook of his arms, turning back and forth, from one to the other, kissing each deeply in turn.

Finally, with a cry of, "Yeah!" Mark let go of them both, kicked off his shoes, tore off his coat, and pulled up his T-shirt. He paused, looking at the two boys who were still standing there with slightly dazed expressions. "Well, what are you waiting for?" Stefan and Terry looked at each other. Terry smiled reassuringly, trying for a 'What can you do?' face. Stefan's expression was unreadable, but when Terry began to remove his clothes, he did the same.

The first to get naked, Mark gave a loud whoop before Terry had removed his socks or the German lad his boxers, and barrelled into the pair of them. knocking them back onto the bed. Leaving Terry to deal with his socks, Mark yanked Stefan's boxers down and threw them across the room. He pinned the burly boy down on top of the duvet and kissed him again, his pumping hips driving his already rock-hard cock

119

into the lad's crotch.

Flinging the last of his socks away, Terry gazed down at Mark's lightly hairy arse as he pistoned away into Stefan, and his own cock shot up, stiff and already oozing. Happily, he dived in, clapping both hands on Mark's arse cheeks, and pushing his face hard into the musky crack. As Terry's tongue met Mark's ring, Mark cried out in pleasure, and his thrusts into Stefan doubled in speed and force, making the German boy cry out something guttural.

After several minutes in this position, Mark broke away, pulled Stefan further down the bed, and plumped his buttock cheeks smack down on his face. He leaned back and pressed down so the lad had no choice but to tongue-mine his arse, already slick with Terry's spit, while Mark grasped his own table leg of a cock with both hands and began wanking himself enthusiastically, eyes closed as he grunted away.

Unceremoniously deprived of Mark's ring, Terry looked for the opportunity that now presented itself, namely Stefan's cock. The boy wasn't long, but he was incredibly thick, his sac and groin completely shaved. To Terry's surprise, though, the boy was still soft. He'd definitely seen more life in Stefan Junior back in the ring. *Probably still nervous. Ah well, Terry to the rescue.* He leaned down to take the flabby tool into his warm, welcoming mouth.

While Mark pumped himself, Terry worked Stefan, first just with his mouth, and then with both hands, easing back the fleshy foreskin as he sucked and licked and teased with the tip of his tongue, cradling and gently squeezing the lad's impressively large ball sac. Inevitably, the blood pumped, and Stefan's cock hardened a little, but it was still not solid and nothing like as eager as it had been earlier. *Maybe he came after the match and just doesn't have much left to give.* Mark was going to be disappointed, and a small part of him was quite pleased at that. No competition there.

"Okay." Mark lifted one leg and swivelled on the German's face, careless of the lad's muffled protests, so that his arse ring was still on Stefan's face but now he was facing down Stefan's pale body. Roughly, he reached out and pulled Terry up so that he was straddling Stefan, and the two Brits were facing each other. Mark leaned in and kissed Terry who cried out as Mark also roughly grabbed his cock and began to pump it. Automatically, he reached for Mark's dick, wrapped his fingers round it and pumped back in turn, the two of them suddenly competing to see who could wank the other the fastest as they kissed deep and hard.

"Gonna make you come, fucker!" Mark gasped between kisses.

"Winner comes second!" Terry laughed before clamping his mouth back on Mark's.

Underneath them, Stefan moaned something incomprehensible, his face still smothered by Mark's buttocks, as he reached up to stroke the arse and sides of first one then the other of the two men riding him.

Only as he broke away for breath did Terry look down and see Stefan's cock again. It had lost even that hint of hardness he had worked it up to. Mark caught the direction of his glance. He looked back over his shoulder and called down to the boy under his arse. "You asleep down there?" Stefan gave a sudden cry and rose up slightly before sinking back down, a happy smile on his face. "No! Mr Tongue is still awake and hard at work down there. Just Mr Dick having trouble getting up. Okay, we'll just have to see what we can do about that."

He got up from Stefan's face, twisted and sat back behind the boy, pulling him up so that his head leaned back against his chest.

"Sweet," said Terry. "But wouldn't you rather he was facing the other way?"

"When I want my dick sucked I'll climb back on your face," Mark replied cheerfully. "This is a little something special for Steffi. Didn't you see him in the ring when I was busting his back in the Boston?" He looked down into Stefan's face and patted it with one hand. "No trouble getting a stiffy then, was there, Steffi?" Uncomprehending, Stefan stared back, unblinking, but there was that look again, that expression of nervous anticipation. Without warning, Mark hooked one of his pumped arms around Stefan's throat and pulled him back and into his body in a tight stranglehold. "You can kiss some guys all night long, but sometimes all they want is to be treated a bit rough."

Instinctively, Stefan grabbed for Mark's wrists and pulled, but the hold was firm. Terry sat back, not sure he really liked this turn of events. "So that's how you're going to get him hard? By knocking him out?"

Mark jerked on his hold a little, just enough to make Stefan squirm and slap his arm but to no avail. "You are such a hick sometimes,

Terence." With his free hand he reached down for one of Stefan's wrists and pulled back and up. There was no doubting the German boy's resistance, but even in a fair struggle Mark would have been stronger. Caught in this position, he had no chance. In seconds, Mark had Stefan's arm pulled up his back in a textbook-perfect backhammer.

Terry winced. Wrestling knockers derided the backhammer. "Look," they said, "it doesn't really hurt," and they'd shove their own arms up their backs and pantomime distress. And they were right. If you stopped with the hand about halfway up the back, which was where most wrestlers did, of course, then it didn't really hurt. But if you pushed it further, forced the hand higher up the back, dragging the arm along with it, the torque on the shoulder very quickly grew more intense, and it wasn't very long at all before the hold grew painful, then very painful, then murderously agonising. And then something would break.

"I think that's enough, man," Terry said quietly. Then with more urgency as Mark completely ignored him, slowly forcing Stefan's arm higher and higher up his back and laughing softly at his futile struggles. "I said that's enough!"

Mark relaxed the hold slightly, looking up from Stefan to grin at Terry then nod downwards. Terry followed the direction of his nod with his eyes, to Stefan's crotch. The German boy's heavy, fleshy cock was undeniably swelling, hardening and rising from his thigh.

"See?" said Mark. "You love it, don't you, Steffi?" Before Terry could protest again or Stefan do anything, he slapped the backhammer on again. Stefan gave a low gurgling sound and thumped the mattress as if in panic. And his cock shot up as solid as wood.

Confused, but faced with undeniable and rapidly growing evidence that Stefan really was turned on by this treatment, Terry felt himself drawn, almost against his will, towards the sizable dick now standing before him. Bowing, literally, to the inevitable, Terry took the beautiful German sausage deep into his mouth. As his tongue pressed against the unyielding cockmeat, Terry felt the boy's whole, beefy body shudder. He could feel the cock growing harder and thicker by the second in his mouth, could taste the first salty spurts of pre-come.

Higher and higher Mark pushed the hammer hold, keeping the boy pinned to his chest by that and the headlock, until Stefan's gasps and cries were continuous, his face twisted in distress. But his cries were inarticulate, no calls for release in either German or English, and his cock grew so ramrod hard and upright that Terry had to shift his position, laying his head sideways on Stefan's body to suck at his dick.

Eyes closed as he wholeheartedly fellated Stefan, Terry only knew that Mark had finally released the German lad when he felt the bed dip and rise as Mark got up from it. Almost immediately after, he felt the first indications that Stefan was losing his hard-on again. Valiantly he pressed on, tonguing the cock and slipping one hand under the boy's plump arse, hoping that a little hole-play with his fingers might renew his flagging enthusiasm. Despite his best efforts, though, he felt Stefan slipping away from him. Then Mark returned to the fray.

Hard as oak and pointing proudly skyward, Mark's cock was now sheathed, his fierce erection stretching the latex to its limits. "Miss me?" he asked as he resumed his position behind Stefan, and Terry felt the cock in his mouth jump and begin to harden once more.

Seemingly too dazed to resist, Stefan allowed Mark to take hold of him as before. But when Stefan cried out more strongly and bucked more frantically than ever, Terry was convinced that, with typical lack of control, Mark had lost the plot and was hurting Stefan to a degree that could well lead to injury. He leaned back, Stefan's wet cock, released from his mouth, slapping back against the German boy's belly, and urgently held out his hands to Mark. "Whoa, whoa there. Slow down, man!"

Mark's eyes were screwed tight and at first Terry thought he was ignoring him. Then he took in the complete picture: Mark was again backhammering Stefan with one arm, holding him round the throat with the other. But now, having pulled the boy onto him, he was also fucking him, driving his blue-steel meat hard into the German's chubby arse cheeks and tight hole with rapid and powerful upward thrusts of his hips. "Hey. Hey!" Terry leaned across to Mark, shouting into his face to bring him out of his fuck frenzy. "Come on! This is too... This is..." He stopped. *Actually, I'm not sure what it is.* "Just lay off, will you!" he yelled.

Mark opened his eyes. "Wha...?"

"You'll break his arm."

Mark looked down at the arm he was twisting so mercilessly, even as he continued to pump the German lad's arse. "No I won't," he said simply.

"Look, sometimes you don't know your own strength, yeah, and that arm is being pushed way past what is safe."

For just a moment Mark stopped his upward thrusts into Stefan, then, "He likes it, Terry," he said simply.

"Don't be..."

Mark leaned over Stefan's head to look into his grimacing, *"Sie wollen mich zu halten?* Want me to stop, Steffi? Do you?"

Stefan groaned, licked his lips. *"Nein. Nein!"* he gasped.

"Yeah! You like it, you little fucker, don't you?" Mark leered and jerked the boy's trapped arm up still further in a movement so fast it made Terry wince.

"Ja! Ja!"

Terry felt a splash of something warm on his thigh and looked down to see Stefan's truncheon of a dick spurting pre-come in time to its rapid drumbeat tattoo against his stomach.

Mark indicated the spasming cock with a nod of his head. "Better get in there before it's too late." And to the accompaniment of a cry of undisguised pleasure from Stefan, he returned to reaming the lad's arse with a ferocity more marked then before.

"Suck me! Suck me!" Stefan cried.

So the sick freak does know some English. And couldn't you guess it would be something like that? Unhappy, but really not knowing what else he could do, Terry bent down to take Stefan's cock back into his mouth. Driven from beneath by Mark's now violent pummelling, the whole of the cock was rammed into Terry's mouth and down his throat in one go. He gagged, even as Stefan finally climaxed and shot thick, creamy and very plentiful gouts of come all the way down his throat. Terry choked and spluttered like a boy giving head for the first time, and had to pull back so that the German's still spurting seed covered his face and chest. He heard Mark's laugh but couldn't see his face as he, in turn, shot his load up the lad's arse.

Their dual climaxes finally finished, Stefan and Mark lay on the bed, Stefan staring fixedly and silently up at the ceiling, breathing as heavily as a man who'd just run a marathon, and Mark with his arm thrown across his face as if to keep the light out of his eyes. Both of them were in their own cosy cocoon of post-come bliss and both apparently oblivious of Terry who still knelt on the bed between their legs, rigid cock at an angle of forty-five degrees, feeling more of a gooseberry than he could ever remember. Disturbed, and not sure if he should be, frustrated but really just not in the mood for release any more, Terry got up off the bed in search of tissue paper or a towel.

When he got back, Mark was urging Stefan up off his cock with a few slaps to his buttocks. The German lad complied, and began to dress. Terry couldn't help noticing how little he used his left arm. It might not be broken, but the muscles and ligaments had been well stretched, and it would take a while for that arm to get back to full working order.

When he was dressed, Stefan turned awkwardly, first to Mark and then to Terry. It was clear that he wanted to say something but simply didn't have the language. Perhaps *suck me* was more or less the extent of his language. "*Danke,*" he said finally, and, "*Gute nacht.*"

Mark, arm still across his face, cock limp and long across his thigh, waved vaguely. Terry wanted to say something but didn't know what, and didn't know how. For long seconds he stared at the young German who looked impassively back at him. "Good night," he said finally. Stefan nodded, as if that was what he had expected Terry to say all along, opened the hotel room door and left.

Terry stood by the bed staring down at the naked Mark. He'd looked forward to his next sexual encounter with this man, thought about it a lot, and pictured how it might go, often in quite graphic detail. Mark's body, given the many opportunities he'd had to see it in trunks and less, was pretty much as he'd pictured it, of course. Everything else, however, had turned out very differently.

Eventually, Mark opened his eyes and looked up at Terry as if awakening from a short sleep, or as if remembering that he wasn't alone. He smiled lazily at the sight of Terry who had momentarily forgotten that he, too, was still naked. "Want a little hand?" he said. "You know..." He mimed a careless wanking motion with one hand.

"No thanks," Terry found himself saying.

Mark smiled sleepily. "Sorry I can't offer you anything

more...personal at the moment—" and he gestured to his recumbent cock "—but if you want to snuggle up and hang around, I dare say later on I could...summon up a bit more enthusiasm."

Terry considered. He had no doubt that Mark would be ready to go again in the not very distant future. The night was still quite young. It would be nice to be held in those strong arms, to wake up in the same bed as someone. Then he thought about Mark hurting Stefan even as he fucked him, remembered the violence of their own first meeting which had just seemed a bit of fun at the time but now seemed somehow...different. "No thanks," he said. "I think I'll head back to my room for the night." He waited for Mark's reply, for the protest, the apology, the request to stay.

Mark yawned and closed his eyes. "Okay," he said. "See you in the morning."

Terry dressed, collected his things, and left. He was pretty sure Mark was asleep before the door closed behind him.

Outside in the corridor he nearly bumped into Baz, returning from his drink with his German opponent of earlier that evening. "Went to the wrong room?" Baz said. He meant it as a joke.

"Too fucking right!" Terry snapped, slamming his own door behind him.

☆☆☆

Baz stood in the corridor looking from Terry's door to Mark's and back again. "I had a nice night, too," he said softly to the empty air. "Couple of beers, bit of chat, bit of a flirt. Nothing else." He looked mournfully at Terry's door. "Thanks for asking."

Chapter Two

The three weeks the POWer crew spent in Germany turned out to be even more successful than their time in France. True, there were some changes in the group dynamic. Terry was as popular as ever, with a noticeably wider male and late teen fan base than had been the case in France. 'Johnny Deuce' got off to a shaky start as Germans seemed rather wary of masked wrestlers. But quite quickly they seemed to 'get him'—most especially, and to Terry and Doug's annoyance—when he played the brawler rather than the technician. Which merely encouraged him to do that for at least half of his bouts. Eric was dismayed that the crowds didn't go for his good-natured clown act, so he tweaked it, becoming the kind of clown kids screamed at in nightmares rather than laughed at in circuses. Mark claimed it was just a reflection of his real mood, but it seemed to work.

The surprise hit in Germany turned out to be Jonesy. In France, he'd taken to calling himself the 'Fifth Beatle' and had begun to supplement his already plentiful diet with comfort eating. The Germans, however, seemed to like their wrestlers on the larger side, which was probably why even an overweight kid like Stefan Schoenfeld could be a crowd pleaser. At first, Jonesy was touchingly bemused by the way the punters took him to their hearts and cheered him on. It even got him thinking about training rather than 'eating to keep his strength up' which had been his mantra up until then. On a couple of occasions, he joined Terry and Baz on early morning runs. "Won't last," grumbled Doug, but Terry saw him taking the Welsh lad to one side on a couple of occasions to give him advice about diet and a healthy carb/protein balance. How much sank in Terry couldn't tell, but the lad had nodded a lot, and that was at least a start.

And Baz...? Well, he was just Baz as always, happily opening the bouts or closing them, sound, reliable, and good-natured as ever.

But although, on the whole, the lads were enjoying this leg of their 'Grand Tour', there was no denying their relief when they reached the hiatus of four whole days without wrestling that Mark had written into their schedule. One gloriously long weekend stretched before them, without their having to get into Lycra and boots for the benefit of others, before they crossed the border into Switzerland and the last leg of what Terry was starting to refer to as their 'first' European tour.

From the start, Terry had had those four days circled, emboldened, and underlined in his mental diary. They'd been days, and nights, he'd intended to spend with Mark. But, after the night with Stefan, and Mark's return thereafter to keeping his distance from him, Terry was no longer so sure that was how those days were going to turn out...or, in fact, if he still wanted them to.

"Four nights off," Mark had said to no one in particular, as the POWer boys enjoyed a lazy breakfast in their latest B and B. "What is a boy supposed to do?"

"I'd have thought you'd have had plenty of ideas," Doug responded tartly. "You're the bookings whizz. Nothing booked for yourself?"

Mark laughed good-naturedly enough, but when Doug walked away to warn Jonesy off a bacon sandwich and to point him in the direction of some muesli, he'd turned to Terry and lowered his voice. "Actually," he whispered, "I have." Checking all the time that Doug wasn't looking, Mark tore a strip of paper from a magazine, and wrote something hastily on it. "My contacts tell me that this is the place to go to in this area," he said as he wrote rapidly.

"What is it, a club?"

"Club, hotel, yeah kinda." He handed the paper over and stood up. "See you there at eight." And he left before Terry could ask whether he should bring the other lads or not.

He sat, holding the piece of paper, trying to decide if he even wanted to go somewhere with Mark. The man was so unpredictable. Terry never knew where he stood with him. As he deliberated, Baz cheerily strolled over to his table. He cocked a finger over his shoulder. "Me and Eric are thinking of going to the Rat House tonight." He tapped his nose as if imparting a great secret. "That's German for town hall. There's films on."

128

"You want to go see a German film?"

"Nah. It's their foreign film night. They're showing three *Carry On* films. They're classics over here, apparently. Should be a laugh. Jonesy'll come as well."

"What about Doug?"

Baz snorted. "He's not really a comedy film guy, now is he?" Baz stooped slightly, the better to catch Terry's eye. "So, you wanna come?"

Terry thought about it, twisting in his fingers the piece of paper with its address that Mark had left with him. "Nah, I'll pass thanks, mate. *Carry On* isn't really my scene, either."

"Okay," Baz said, straightening up again. He looked disappointed, but Terry didn't notice. "Looking forward to a long night cuddling up with Doug, then?"

"It'd make a change," Terry said. He slipped the magazine strip into his back pocket so he'd know where to find it later.

☆☆☆

At eight o'clock promptly, Terry was sitting in the bar of the establishment whose address Mark had given him. It was not a nightclub. As far as he could see it was a hotel, but barely so, far smaller and seedier than the place Mark had actually booked the POWer crew into. It served drinks, but to call it a pub would have implied a sense of hospitality. Most importantly, it was somewhere Mark was not, and that was pissing Terry off, big time. If this turned out to be another of those occasions when Mark was late or simply didn't turn up...

To drown his dark thoughts, Terry went to the bar and ordered a beer, his language skills having grown to the extent, just, that he could do that. His old school language teacher would, he decided, have been proud of him, and probably enormously surprised. The litre successfully ordered, he took it back to a small, rickety table, and carried on waiting for Mark.

An hour later, near the end of his second litre, Terry was still on his own. Back home he'd have been on his mobile, but apart from Mark, the rest of the crew only had one phone between them that worked abroad, and Doug kept hold of it as the man least likely to lose it. Angrily, Terry drained his stein and reached for his coat.

"*Herr Bacchus, ja?*"

Not expecting to hear his *nom de guerre* outside a ring, and slightly tipsy from the unaccustomedly large glasses of beer they served in Germany, it took Terry a second or two to realise that the big man who had approached his table was addressing him. "Er, yes. *Ja.* I mean...yes."

"I am Dieter." The paw that engulfed Terry's hand gave a hard squeeze that made Terry wince. "Can I?"

Dieter pointed to the now empty stein, and for a second Terry thought maybe he was the glass boy and he was asking to take it away. And then the Euro dropped. He was being bought a drink. He hesitated, glanced at the clock. Saw that Mark was now well over an hour late. "Yeah. Why not? *Danke.*"

Dieter gave a small, brisk nod, turned, and walked off to the bar, and Terry took the opportunity to get a proper look at him. About fifteen stone, he guessed, most of it in the right places. Probably mid-to-late thirties. Long, black hair with just a few strands of grey, tied in a ponytail. His frayed jeans were stretched tight across his backside as he leaned across the bar waiting for the drinks to be delivered. The leather jacket he was wearing had some sort of design picked out across its back in studs, though it was so old and so many of the studs had been lost it was hard to see what the original pattern had been. *Not normally my type. If I wasn't miles from home. In a bar on my own. Having been stood up. Again!* Dieter turned and walked back, a large stein in each hand. Nice goatee. Bit of a widow's peak, accentuated by the hair being drawn back tight into its tail. Pale blue eyes. Not handsome. Definitely not ugly. *There'll be ink. Guys like that with the whole biker thing going on always have ink.* He mused in a slightly tipsy way as to just where on Dieter's body the tattoos might be.

Dieter planted himself heavily down next to Terry and handed him a stein. Terry raised it to him. "Cheers," he said.

"*Skol.*" Dieter raised his stein and sank nearly half of it in one go. He put it down, and the two men looked at each other.

Right. Is that the limit of Dieter's English, because we've already gone well past the limit of my German? Is this going to be another Stefan-type situation? Will he know anything more than 'suck me'?

Terry took in the large frame, the broad shoulders, and the eyes, which really were an amazingly pale blue. It occurred to him that Dieter might not need to know how to say anything else. "So. You come here often?" he ventured.

"*Ja.*" Dieter didn't even crack a smile. He'd got the words but probably not the irony.

"With anyone?" Terry fished.

"*Ja.*" There was a pause. "He is...away."

"Ah," said Terry. "Right." The picture was coming into a not unpleasing focus.

Presumably feeling that he had successfully broken the ice, Dieter became a little more fluent, and direct. "We stay here often," he said, his English careful and amusingly sing-song. "We know the owner. We have an...arrangement."

Terry's brow furrowed. "Arrangement?"

Dieter leaned in closer, though when he spoke, his heavily accented voice was at exactly the same volume. "He has a room. He lets us use it."

A room. A special room? Terry's brain, dealing with its third stein, tried to work out all the possible meanings of that.

"You like to see?"

Terry went to laugh, to say *no thanks.* Then he looked again at those very broad shoulders, at the hint of strong black hair at the wrists just visible under the cuffs of his leather jacket, and yeah, sure enough, that glimpse of a tattoo there. He looked again at the clock on the wall, and thought of Baz and the others having a good time with Kenneth Williams and Barbara Windsor. "Yeah," he said, lifting and draining the stein. "Why not? I mean, *ja.* Lead on."

Dieter led the way out of the bar. As he passed the man behind the counter, he gave a nod that the man returned. Terry followed him down a short, sparsely lit corridor. Two turns to the left and they came to a door, shabbily painted, otherwise unmarked, and featureless except for the stout combination padlock on the hasp holding it shut. Dieter bent and twisted the rings of the combination lock with practised ease, unhitched the lock, pushed the door open, and walked in. Terry followed. Dieter turned on a light, and, when he saw what was revealed, a light went on in Terry's head, too. "Ah," he said. "Right." Maybe Dieter had been a little coy when he said the manager of this place had a 'room' he let him and his absent companion use. Or maybe he just didn't know the English word 'dungeon'.

The room was small, maybe only six metres by six, the walls whitewashed brickwork, the floor covered in a slightly spongy black matting. In one corner was what Terry at first thought was a bed, but, looking closer, saw was little more than a framework with no mattress. On the opposite side of the room, fixed to the wall by stout metal brackets, was a cross in the shape of an *X*, each of its two wooden arms well over two metres long. Terry knew plenty of Scots wrestlers who made a big thing of this cross on their ring jackets and trunks, so he knew that it was called a St Andrew's Cross or saltire. He looked more closely at it, at the pallet, noted the buckles and straps at the four corners of both. He looked from them to the racks and hooks on the walls. Chains, ropes, and straps hung in neat ranks the length of each wall. Enough to tie up an army of guys, he reckoned, certainly more than could have been squeezed into that small room at one go. *But then*, he mused, moving along the rows of implements, running his hands along the chains so that they jingled softly, *maybe there are times when a red rope just won't do and you really, really have to have a green one.*

Terry took a minute to slowly walk around the four walls, taking in the variety of gear on display, and using the time to think about just what the hell he'd gotten himself into and what exactly he was going to do. Dieter stood, as expressionless as before, in the doorway, his arms folded across his broad chest. The door was still open. Terry could easily get out if he wanted to. Couldn't he? It wasn't as if Dieter was blocking the door, was he? Although with those shoulders, technically he was.

Terry found his fingers had come into contact with what at first he thought was a black latex club. He lifted it off its hook on the wall, ran his fingers the length of it, over the rounded studs. Unbidden, the image of Dieter straddling him flashed up before his mind's eye. He pictured the big man pressing his legs over his head, teasing his tight arsehole with the end of the sex toy, slowly pushing it past the resistance of his ring, the studs massaging his aching sphincter muscles one by one as they slipped slowly inside him, further and further in. Terry swallowed.

"So," Dieter said. "You want to play?"

Terry turned round. "What the hell? Yeah. Why not?"

Dieter closed the door behind him.

Facing Terry, he pulled off his leather jacket and threw it onto the pallet across the room. Underneath he was wearing some kind of heavy metal T-shirt, cut high and ragged over the arms to show off the curves of his tattooed, hairy delt muscles. *Eagles*, Terry had time to think, *or maybe angels, something with wings.* Then the other man was on him, shoving him up against the wall, careless of the resulting crash and rattle of all the varied equipment hanging there. His mouth fastened on Terry's like an animal's going to tear meat off the bone, and his tongue pushed hard into his mouth. He tasted of cheap beer and cheaper cigarettes, smelled of old leather and sweat, and Terry loved it. Clapping his hands on the man's big, denim-clad arse, he gave himself up to the rough embrace completely.

After days of enforced celibacy this was just the release Terry wanted. Dieter grunted as he kissed, as if already working his way to orgasm, his mouth moving from Terry's mouth to the sides of his neck, nuzzling hard, licking, almost biting, and then moving back to the mouth, leaving the skin wet with saliva, and Terry gasping for breath. Dieter's hips were already grinding frenetically into Terry's crotch and, pinned against the wall as he was, Terry could feel the iron length of the German's already hard cock against his, sending the blood rushing to his dick. It thickened and stiffened swiftly in response to the heavy massage.

Something designed for shoving up an arse was sticking painfully into Terry's back. With a nimble twist that would have sent an opponent in the ring flying, Terry spun them round so that it was now he who had the German pinned up against the wall, and it was now his crotch thrusting again and again into the other man. "Like that, big man?" He laughed as Dieter's widened eyes registered his surprise at Terry's move, and as the increased speed and urgency of Dieter's moans made it clear he liked it a lot.

Without warning Dieter reached up behind Terry, wound his thick fingers in the boy's hair, and pulled back sharply. Terry yelped in surprise and genuine pain, but he had lost his footing, and before he could protest, Dieter had pushed him away from the wall and across the small room until the backs of his legs collided with the wooden pallet.

Unable to help himself, Terry fell backwards. Pinning Terry to the pallet, Dieter clambered up his body till his denim-covered crotch was pressing down onto Terry's face, burying his mouth and nose buried deep in the thick musk of his jeans. Dieter face-fucked him vigorously. The metal teeth of his zipper rasped against Terry's face, but Dieter didn't seem to know or care. Frantically, Terry tore at the zipper, pulling the rough denim down. He wasn't surprised to find that Dieter was going commando. The massive erection released was rubbed red raw along its length by its frot against the zipper, but any pain caused by the rasping didn't seem to have put Dieter off at all. In fact, Terry was guessing he might even have liked it. *What was it*, he wondered, *about Germans and pain?*

With no sign of wanting to stop, Dieter continued to grind his cock into Terry's face, Terry alternately feeling the dry heat of the shaft and the wire wool scratch of his ball sac over his skin. Terry shoved his hands under the German's T-shirt to grab the mounds of hairy pecs underneath. Dieter groaned and yelled as Terry pulled hard on the big tits. He briefly left off fucking Terry's face with his giant dick, tore off the shirt, and with one hand, reached down and under Terry's head. Before he could stop it, or even get a proper look at it, Terry felt his face being pulled deep into the hairy bulk of Dieter's stomach. Mouth and nose covered in hot, furry flesh, unable to breathe, the animal part of Terry's brain panicked. Digging his nails into the bear's pecs, he twisted hard.

Dieter released the boy and stepped back. For a second, Terry lay on the pallet, sucking in lungsful of blessed air. Still breathing heavily, he stood up, one arm stretched out to slow the big man down, ready for him to complain at the rough usage. Dieter was standing, face upturned and eyes closed. His jeans had fallen round his ankles, and he was holding his engorged cock like a flesh crowbar. As Terry watched, the bear spat into one hand and rubbed it up and down the length of his thick shaft, twisting. Dieter wasn't about to protest. He was still plainly very much enjoying himself.

Terry stepped away from the pallet, stretching out his abused back. "Now, look," he said. "You know, I'm not against a bit of the rough stuff now and again, but you know, really...." He stopped. Naked except for his socks and boots, the hairy German stood there, cock raised in fierce salute. He opened his eyes, looked over to his discarded trousers, bent, unthreaded the long, thick leather belt that had circled his waist, and straightened again. The belt hung from one fist, heavy metal buckle swinging from the end. Slowly, he advanced again on Terry.

Terry swallowed hard, torn between strongly conflicting impulses: the very, very strong desire to let that sexy bear gather him up in his tattooed arms and do whatever the hell he wanted to do with his body; and the dawning realisation that the German was possibly into far rougher games than any he was used to. *And that's speaking as a pro wrestler!* "Look, mate. This..." He waved his hand around the makeshift dungeon and then back to the belt and its heavy buckle in the bear's hand. "This is all a bit new to me, y'know? I mean, what do you want...? That is, how far... I mean... Don't you need to have, I don't know...some kind of safe word?"

Dieter stopped. "*Ja?*" he asked.

"So what is it?"

Dieter took hold of the belt with his other hand, brought his hands together and then sharply apart in a rapid tug that made the leather crack. "*Ja?*" And right there and then, Terry nearly gave into that part of his brain that was completely hungry for the monster cock advancing on him. For just one second, he would have been happy to have Dieter mount him again on the pallet and face-fuck his brains out. But then, the saner, less sex-driven part of his brain reminded him he'd been trapped in backbreakers in the ring that had been more comfortable than that position, and he held out his hand again to slow the man down. "Easy, big man. Easy."

To Terry's relief, Dieter stopped, looking puzzled. Slowly, but not so slowly he might lose the bear's attention, Terry began to unbutton the navy-blue polo shirt he was wearing. His eyes were fixed on Dieter, wary of the slightest sign of him charging forward again. Dieter's eyes, he was pleased to see, were fixed on the smooth chest he was, inch by inch, revealing. Terry's cock ached at the thought of his skin pressed tight against the German's furry flesh. All buttons undone, he slipped the shirt up and over his head and dropped it to the floor. Facing Dieter, half naked, he ran his hands over the curves and contours of his toned body, inviting the big man to come closer.

135

Dieter took a step towards him, stopped, and took another step as if fighting something inside himself, his eyes transfixed by the beautiful male body being offered to him.

"That's right," said Terry, like a father encouraging a toddler's first steps. "Let's take our time this time, yeah? Let's both enjoy ourselves?" The belt slipped from Dieter's hand, and fell with a thud and clatter to the floor as the large man advanced, step by step, on the smaller man, until bare skin met bare skin, and Terry was caught up in his arms once again.

This time the kiss was longer, less aggressive. Freed of fear that something horrible was going to happen to him, Terry felt himself melting into the burly man's arms, losing himself in the hairy warmth enfolding him. The scratch of the bigger man's chest and belly hair against his uncovered skin was thrilling, like a thousand tiny static shocks. He ran his hands up and down Dieter's sides and back, over his hairy arse cheeks.

Caught up in the embrace, Terry didn't feel the heavier man moving with him across the floor, didn't realise where in the small room he was until he felt his back pressing up against the wall, and they both stopped. No, he realised a second later, not up against the wall. *Up against the cross.*

Dieter stepped back, looked him square in the eyes, and then slowly he knelt so that his lips were at Terry's side, just above his hip, where he kissed him. The unexpected tenderness of it sent a warm wave of pleasure right through Terry, and banished, for a moment, the nagging worries about this new position. Dieter kissed him again, then dragged his tongue slowly up the side of the lad's body. Terry gasped at the sensation of the slick tongue sliding over his flesh, immediately followed by the rasp of facial stubble. Further and further upwards the German licked and kissed until his nose and mouth reached the light hair of Terry's armpits. Automatically, Terry reached up so Dieter could press his mouth into the pit where he paused, nuzzling and breathing in deeply the scent of Terry's fresh sweat, before pressing on up still further. He pushed his lips and cheeks the length of the arm till he reached Terry's wrist. Where he stopped. He took hold of Terry's wrist with one big hand, pinning it to the board of the cross arm, and stepped back.

"Ah. Right." And now Terry knew he'd been right the first time about just what it was the big man had in mind. He hesitated, looked at the mute appeal in the pale blue eyes regarding him steadily, felt the tingle still thrilling along the length of his body where Dieter's saliva was drying on his skin, and saw that glistening hard cock so close to his body. He nodded once. "Okay. But not... tight. You know. Not actually tied off." Dieter nodded, and Terry hoped that meant he had actually understood what he had said.

Dieter pulled Terry not ungently towards him in a move that made Terry's own now rock-hard cock leap in expectation, then turned him round so he was facing the cross, and pressed him carefully back into it. Terry's cock was shoved up against the wood where the two beams met, and he gasped at the sensation. *Not the kind of wood I was expecting. In fact, not what I was expecting at all.* Dieter reached for the thin leather straps hanging at the end of one of the cross's arms and looped them swiftly around Terry's wrist twice. Taking Terry's other wrist, he raised that arm and did the same with the straps on the other side of the cross. Then he stepped back to survey his work.

Terry stood, spread-eagled, in front of a near-naked German bear. He turned his head to look back over his bare shoulder at his captor. "So, c'mon then. What you going to do to me?"

Dieter stepped in close again, his lips close to Terry's ear so that the lad thought he was going to say something, but instead, he brushed his cheek against the length of his neck, rubbing it up and down, the prickly stubble fretting the flesh and making Terry moan in pleasure. He placed both rough, broad hands on either side of Terry's body just under the armpits and slowly, possessively dragged them down the length of the slender, V-shaped torso. He came to the narrow hips. He reached round Terry's body as if to embrace him, and Terry felt his hands fiddling with his belt. Quickly, it was undone and the trousers pulled, not roughly, down and away, leaving him standing on the cross clad in just pale blue briefs. Dieter cupped both arse cheeks in his broad hands and smoothed them over the curves. Terry gasped again, feeling the thin material slide over his buttocks. A shove down and they were off, too, and now Terry was completely naked, exposed, and helpless on the cross. His arse ring throbbed in time to the pulsing in his rigid cock. He had never felt so vulnerable, so exquisitely ready for a damn good, hard fucking.

There was silence for a moment, and Terry wondered what was happening. He fought the temptation to turn round again and look, getting off on the pretend helplessness of his predicament, on not knowing what was going to happen next. When it did he couldn't help crying out.

At first he thought it was Dieter's finger probing his arse, but the slick, speedy progression followed by the rasp of stubble against his arse cheeks made it clear it was Dieter's tongue. Terry groaned and relaxed totally into the most delicious rimming he had ever experienced in his young life. For a moment, he wondered whether it was the German's technique that was making it so good, or was it the new sensation of playing at being tied up and at a man's mercy that added a new thrill. But pretty soon the sensations of Dieter's tongue thrusting deeper and harder than any tongue he'd had down there banished all rational thought, and he abandoned himself totally to the pleasure of the tongue fuck.

As he rimmed the boy, Dieter slapped the firm buttocks of his arse, a little harder each time, building a fine rhythm of tongue then slap, tongue then slap. Terry couldn't have said how long it went on for, but when it suddenly stopped he couldn't help but give a small moan of disappointment. His head was lolling backwards so that his hair fell across his shoulders, and his long back was arched in pleasure, his stiff cock jammed into the wooden intersection of the saltire's cross-beams. The wood was already slippery with his pre-come, droplets of it glistening on the black matting beneath.

He heard Dieter walk away from the saltire to another part of the room, heard the sound of something on one of the wall racks being removed, and Dieter's walking back to him and stopping. Terry waited. The sudden crack made him jump, and the intense stinging sensation in his left buttock made him cry out involuntarily. "Shit! What the...?" He twisted on the cross, straining over his shoulder to see. Dieter was standing there. In his hand he was holding a long, flexible rod with a flat paddle on the end. As Terry strained to see, Dieter drew the paddle back again and brought it down with a second loud crack across the boy's right buttock. "Fuck!" Craning over his shoulder, Terry could just about make out the scarlet marks now blooming on both arse cheeks. Instinctively he went to unwind his wrists from the leather straps holding them, but in his haste they tangled. "Look, just hold on there," he began. Dieter was standing still, as impassively as ever, watching his captive struggle. He was holding the paddle now so the broad, flexible blade rested on his chest, and moving it slowly from left to right and back again across one of his nipples, occasionally raising it slightly, and letting it fall softly on the puckered nub of his tit. The nipple was visibly swelling and hardening as Terry watched, thrusting up out of the mat of black bear hair. Watching it grow under the gentle teasing, Terry felt an echoing ache in his own nipples, and he was seized with an urge to take that growing nub on the German's chest and chew on it till the bastard cried out as he had just done.

Dieter looked at him steadily, the question in his eyes clear. Terry hesitated. The smacks of that thing on his defenceless arse had stung like hell, but actually... He shifted on the cross, flexed his glutes, and moaned softly at the mingled fading pain of the swats and the jolt of sweetness that shot up his cock as he pressed it into the wood of the cross. Actually...the pain was fading pretty quickly, the worst of it having been its unexpectedness. Now, it was mostly gone, leaving a...warmth that was not unpleasant, and an ache that was all too familiar, and demanding.

Nodding as much to himself as to the German, Terry turned again to face the wall, and squared his shoulders to take what was about to come. "Come on then, you bastard. Do your worst." He flinched instinctively when Dieter placed the small paddle on his shoulder, but he was just resting it there. Slowly, he slid it across the boy's shoulders to the nape of his neck then down, slowly, very slowly, the curved length of his spine and over his arse...and then cracked it down onto the right cheek. Then again, and then once more on the left buttock. A pause, then the welcome return of Dieter's tongue slipping sweetly and easily, deep into the musk of his hole. "Oh yeah," Terry groaned. "Kiss it better, you bastard."

For long minutes the German bear worked the British boy's bare arse, alternating fiery swats of the paddle with the insistent, fierce probing of his thick, wet tongue. At one point he let the paddle fall to the floor and, kneeling behind the bound Terry, seized both of the firm globes of his behind and began kissing them, biting them, rubbing his face and unshaven chin all over them. Terry gasped and squirmed in discomfort and delight as the now highly sensitised flesh of his tight cheeks burned at the rough usage. When the bear finally stopped, Terry could feel his entire arse glowing. And deep inside, a throbbing piece of him was crying out for even more. Letting the straps wound round his wrists take his weight, Terry pushed his behind out from the cross towards his sweet tormentor. With feet placed right at the bases of the two struts, he stood with legs spread wide, arse open and inviting. "C'mon, then, you bastard," he said. "Finish it off."

"*Ja. Danke.* We will."

Chapter Three

Before he had a chance to react to the unexpected new voice behind him, two pairs of hands seized each of his wrists and the dangling ends of the leather strips wound round them were tied off tightly and knotted with speed and expertise. "What the...?" Terry tried to shove his whole body backwards but something heavy hit him hard in the small of the back, driving his chest forward again and into the wooden beams of the cross, knocking the breath out of him. Before he could recover, the two pairs of hands were at his ankles, twisting the so far unused leather straps there around them, binding them tightly to the base of the saltire. In well under twenty seconds, Terry's play bondage on the St Andrew's Cross became all too real. He yanked at the straps, twisted, turned and swore, but it was useless. He stopped, realising he was only wasting his strength and, if anything, making the restraints at wrists and ankles tighter. He twisted his head as far as he could to the right. Dieter stood, arms folded across his bare chest, for once a small smile on his lips. And twisting his head to the left... "Yeah. Right." This had to be the guy who used this room with Dieter. The one who was 'away'.

The new arrival's leather waistcoat was wide open revealing a hairy chest, even broader than his partner's, with more than a touch of grey to the black, and a tattooed blazing skull glaring out balefully at the world from beneath the fur. His leather chaps were crotchless, the black cotton jockstrap they revealed already bulging, already damp. The metal buckles on his biker boots gleamed dully in the dim light of the makeshift dungeon, as did the studs in the armbands wrapped tight around both biceps. A good fifteen years older than Dieter, shorter, balding—with what hair remained white and cropped close—he was nodding and smiling to himself as if at some private joke as he pulled on a pair of soft black leather gloves. That done, he stood, hands on hips, and looked slowly up and down, possessively, at the defenceless, trussed wrestle-boy he and his partner had landed. *"Guten Abend,"* he said. *"Ich heisse Kurt."*

Terry took an uncertain breath. "Okay..." he began. Kurt shook his head slowly, stepped forward, and reached up and placed one gloved finger on Terry's lips. He spoke again, a soft stream of German, none of which Terry understood. When the boy stayed silent, Kurt nodded again as if pleased, took his finger off Terry's lips and placed both of his hands on the bound boy's shoulders. As his partner before him had, he slowly smoothed both hands down the length of Terry's body, bringing them to meet on his arse, cupping the firm curves and stroking them gently. Terry shivered at the softness of the leather on the skin that Dieter had made so tender. He couldn't help a soft moan as the older man gently rubbed the cool leather over his tight butt, letting one finger trace the line of his arse crack. *Okay, the start was rough, and two on one wasn't what I expected, but maybe...maybe.*

Kurt dug his fingers in hard and began to slowly prise the cheeks apart, as if trying to split the boy open like some ripe peach. "What the fuck? Stop it! Stop it! *Shit!"*

Kurt let go and stepped back. Craning over his shoulder again and looking down the length of his own body, Terry could clearly see the pale marks of the older German's cruel fingers on his reddened buttocks. "C'mon! Too much!" he shouted. But Kurt wasn't listening. He and his partner were too busy getting ready for the next stage of their fun and games.

Kurt raised his arms and held then out in front of himself. Silently, almost ritualistically, Dieter stepped up to him. First, he removed the leather waistcoat, laying it carefully down on the wooden pallet to one side of the room. Then, he knelt to one side of Kurt and started to unlace the chaps. Terry watched, twisting back and forth on the cross to see clearly as, with fetishistic precision, Dieter removed the leggings, revealing Kurt's hairy tree-trunk thighs, folded them, and placed them on the pallet along with the waistcoat. Finally, Dieter knelt in front of his master, his face level with the black jock. He reached up to the waistband, but Kurt took his boy behind the head and pulled his face into the heavy, cotton-covered lump at his crotch. With his eyes fixed on

Terry's lean, hanging body, Kurt pumped his hips and leisurely face-fucked his partner. Dieter moaned happily, showing more emotion than any Terry had seen from him so far that evening. Blindly, he stretched his arms to reach for the heavy silver rings hanging from Kurt's dark brown nipples, pulling on them with a force Terry was amazed didn't rip them from the older man's skin. Fascinated in spite of himself, Terry couldn't tear his eyes from the soaked fabric of the older man's black cotton jock as the cock within speedily forced its glistening purple head way above the waistband of the strap.

With a sudden grunt, Kurt pushed Dieter backwards. The younger bear went sprawling but got up quickly, kneeling once again in front of his master, waiting for his instructions. Kurt stood still, eyes closed, calming his breathing, bringing himself back from the brink of climax he had clearly so quickly reached. When he was in control again, he opened his eyes and nodded sharply once. Dieter leaned in again and, slowly and very carefully, pulled down the jockstrap. Kurt stepped out of it, fully naked apart from his long biker boots and the circlets of studded leather around his biceps. "Fuck!" Terry whispered.

Kurt's cock stood thick and proud over the heaviest ball sac Terry had ever seen hanging between a man's legs. The head was fat and purple, pre-come flowing freely over the chunky silver Prince Albert piercing. Even in the dungeon's dim light, Terry could make out the lines of twisting tattoo work all the way up the length of the penis. Snakes, by the look of it. *That had to have hurt,* he thought with a sympathetic wince and twitch of his own pulsing cock. *And I bet he loved it!*

Kurt took a step towards him. Terry's arse instinctively clenched, the muscular action only making his hard glutes look even more fuckable, sending a sweet thrill through his groin that made his own cock jerk and let loose yet another spurt of pre-come. "Okay," he said quickly, "now look. I'm not saying no." He couldn't help but look down again at that magnificent cock advancing on him. *God no,* he was not saying no. "But... But I'm gonna need a little help here, you know. I mean, it's not gonna be easy and, like, this—" he pulled futilely at the straps holding him to the cross "—doesn't make it any easier. It's not really my kind of thing, you know! I mean, I think it could be my kind of thing, but I'm gonna have to be eased into it."

The pierced cock stood now only inches away from his twitching arsehole, and Terry could tell it was the only thing Kurt was thinking of easing anywhere. At least, he hoped he was thinking of easing it in. The bear's only response to his desperate attempt at plea bargaining was to grasp his swollen tool with one paw and slowly pump, making the pre-come flow even more hot and free over his cockhead and its silver ring. Too late, Terry understood that his pleading and struggling were exactly what Kurt was looking for. He forced himself to relax, achingly aware of how completely vulnerable and defenceless he was.

Forgotten for a moment, Dieter was momentarily out of Terry's restricted field of vision, but now he heard the bear taking something from one of the racks of implements around the small room. When he moved back into sight, Terry was dismayed to see what he had retrieved and was handing to Kurt. All thoughts of trying not to struggle and protest went out the window as, once again, he yanked and kicked at the restraints holding him. "Now just you hang on a fucking minute there! No fucking way!" His renewed struggles made the grizzled older man smile as he stepped closer, holding the long leather whip that Dieter had just handed him.

The whip was coiled in Kurt's hands like an oiled black snake. As he stopped right next to Terry, so close the boy could feel the man's breath on his skin, he let it unroll so that its length fell heavily to the floor. He moved in, his bulging belly pressing against Terry's bare back, the coarse body hair scratching his skin. Unable to stop himself, Terry gasped as something hard pressed into his arse crack. Was he ever going to be able to relax enough to accommodate that pierced monster without it hurting...a lot? Quickly, though, he realised his mistake: it was the pommel head of the whip. Smooth and rounded, Kurt was working it into Terry's arse, pressing it in, harder and harder, past the automatic resistance of his muscles. Right next to his ears, Terry heard the harsh, short breaths of the older man, the grunted, staccato words that he couldn't understand but whose blunt meaning he could easily guess. Was that it? Was that all he was going to do with the whip, fuck him with its handle? Terry could probably take that up his arse more easily than the donkey dick between Kurt's legs. But did he really want to?

Slowly, inexorably the smooth whip handle slid in, stretching the ring muscles of Terry's arse painfully. Terry gritted his teeth, denying the German the expressions of pain he just knew he would have liked. "Fuck you," he said, low and clear.

Kurt stopped, the whip handle half-buried in Terry's arse. Then, with an abruptness that hurt, he pulled it back out. Terry gasped with relief, unable to believe it had been that easy. So he was completely unprepared when Dieter stepped up again, reached round his head, and pulled a ball gag into his mouth. The gag was in and being tied off behind his head before he could do or say a thing.

Craning his head over his shoulder, Terry watched in enforced silence as Dieter sank to his knees in front of Kurt again and ran his tongue up and down his master's tattooed shaft. All the while, Kurt stared fixedly and hungrily at Terry's body, weighing the weight of the whip in one hand.

"*Genug!*" At the barked word from Kurt, Dieter left off the fellatio and stood respectfully to one side. His own cock was full now, its skin stretched tight, and he took it in both hands and started pumping and wringing it slowly, all set to really enjoy what was coming next. Kurt gave a small flick of the whip, sending a ripple down the length of the oiled leather lash. Then he raised his arm.

Unable to look, Terry turned swiftly to face the wall, head down, eyes screwed tightly closed. *Back or arse? Back or arse?* Crazily, the question was the only thing he could consider as he waited for the first stinging touch of the whip. He thought of Dieter, the work he had done on his buttocks earlier. The bastard had just been setting him up for the main event. *Arse it is, then.* Terry gritted his teeth so tightly he thought they might crack, forced his body as tightly into the cross as he could, as if being a fraction of an inch further away from the whip was going to help any, and waited for the German bear to begin.

When the sudden crack split the air, Terry jerked reflexively, pulling hard on his bonds, crying out inarticulately into the ball gag. He waited for the pain to sear through his screaming nerves. It didn't. Incredulous, he opened his eyes a fraction, and forced his head round to see what games the German pair were playing with him now. The sight that met his eyes was as unexpected as it was completely welcome.

The crack he'd heard had not been that of leather in the air. It had been the crack of splintering wood as the door of the makeshift dungeon was smashed open by someone on the other side hurling his weight against it and barging his way in. That someone was a very, very angry Doug. And behind him, an anxious-looking Mark.

"Fucking let him fucking go! Fucking now!" Doug bawled.

Dieter dropped his cock and looked to Kurt. Kurt stood solid, the whip in his hand still ready to start its work on Terry's body. There was something else in his expression, something at the corners of his mouth. Terry strained to see what it was. *Shit! It's a smile!* Kurt said something in German, and to Terry's surprise Doug answered. The exchange continued for another minute, the words harsh, guttural nonsense to Terry's ears. Doug's answers were brief, staccato, maybe because his knowledge of the language was limited, maybe because he was being characteristically terse. To his left and behind him, still in the doorway, Mark looked from one man to another. He appeared as surprised as Terry.

"Get him down." Mark blinked at the sudden brief burst of English, seeming to almost not take in its meaning for a moment. Doug was nodding towards Terry. "Get him the fuck down!"

Glancing from Dieter to Kurt, wary of the slightest move from either of them, Mark stepped up to the saltire and, as quickly as he could, undid the bonds at Terry's wrists and ankles. As soon as his hands were his own again, Terry tore at the gag in his mouth. "Shit!" was his first word when restored to the power of speech.

"Get out!" Doug jerked his head at the door. Dieter and Kurt were standing still, the former looking nervous, Kurt as stolid as ever, eyes fixed unblinkingly on Doug who returned his stare with equal intensity. "I said, fuck off!" Doug barked. "Now!"

"C'mon." Mark took Terry by the shoulder. Pausing only to grab the clothes still piled on the pallet, he half-pulled, half-shoved the naked young man to the door.

Still bewildered by the speed of events, Terry let himself be led as far as the doorway where he stopped and looked back to his friend and rescuer. "Come on, then," he said to Doug.

Doug glanced at Terry before returning his burning, level gaze to the massive German. "Later."

"But…"

"I'm finishing up here."

"Finishing… What the fuck do you mean?"

"It's a deal. Me and him." Doug indicated the impassive Kurt. "And him," he added, taking in Dieter, too.

"But, you…"

Kurt said something in German and laughed softly. "Yeah, right." Doug spat. "Now will you," he said to Mark, "fucking get him the fuck out of here!"

"C'mon!" Mark took Terry again by the shoulder.

More confused than ever, Terry let himself be led from the room and out into the corridors beyond. Two corners on, he finally stopped and pulled his shoulder free of Mark's insistent grip. "We can't just leave him in there."

Mark shrugged. "Why not? It's not like he needs us."

"Did you see what they were going to do to me?"

"Are you kidding? It's not like there was much left to the imagination, was there?" Mark reached out and cupped one of Terry's arse cheeks with his hand, squeezing the firm flesh playfully. "I didn't know you were into scenes like that."

Terry knocked the hand off hotly. "I'm not!"

"Right." Mark frowned exaggeratedly. "So tell me then, how'd you manage to get yourself naked and tied to a cross?"

Terry went to answer, stopped, tried again. "I thought it was a game."

"Right."

"Like role-play, yeah? Look, I didn't know it was going to go that far, okay?"

"Well, didn't you have a safe word?"

Terry shuffled his feet uncomfortably. "Of course." Mark waited. "*Ja.*"

Mark waited some more. "So, what was it?"

"*Ja,*" said Terry again.

Mark's laugh was a snort of incredulity. "*Ja!* Your safe word was *ja?* Why not use 'More please,' or 'Harder, faster, big man!' No wonder you ended up trussed like a chicken."

"Whatever! Look, while you're joking away out here, God knows what they're doing to Doug in there."

Mark snorted. "Nothing he doesn't want them to, I'm guessing."

"What the fuck does that mean?"

"I mean, Terence," Mark said with a sigh, like a teacher addressing a small child, "it very much looked to me like Doug wasn't at all uncomfortable with that whole scene in there. If you know what I mean."

Terry struggled to take this in. "You mean...?" Mark nodded. Only once had Terry ever tried to talk to Doug about what actually floated his boat. Doug had pretty quickly made it clear that whatever it was, it was none of Terry's damn business. "So what was he saying to them back there?"

Mark's good humour momentarily wavered. "I'm not sure. I mean, I got the gist. Mostly."

"I thought you were the linguist."

"Yeah, well, I'm more a getting-you-into-hotels kind of guy. Not so much a getting-you-out-of-dungeons kind of guy. The language tends to be a bit more specialised."

"From where I was, it pretty much looked like it was Doug who was doing all the breaking out."

"Or was he just breaking in? For all we know, he's in there now, hopping up onto that cross and letting King Kong and Cheetah shove a whole wardrobe of kinky stuff up his arse."

Terry grappled with the idea. And then tried not to. "I'm going back."

"Fuck that!"

"Why not?"

"Because...because it's stupid. And because Doug wouldn't want you to. And...."

"What?"

"You're naked."

Terry glanced down, taking in the all too obvious truth of that statement. "Right." He snatched at his clothes that Mark was still holding.

Mark rolled his eyes as the young man pulled on top and trousers. "This is mad," he muttered." Terry just glared at him. "All right, all right.

If you've got to do this, just...just hang on, will you?"

"What for?"

"I'll be back."

"You going to get help?"

"Kind of. Just wait."

"All right," said Terry, hopping in his hurry to get back into his jeans. "But move it!"

Mark was as quick as his word, but even so, Terry had hauled his clothes on and was pacing the corridor with impatience by the time he got back. "What?" he said incredulously when he saw him. "Really? Now?"

Mark was wearing his Johnny Deuce mask. "It helps," he said simply.

With a disbelieving shake of his head, Terry turned and ran back down the corridor. When they got back to the door of the dungeon it was once again closed.

"Right," hissed Terry, rolling his shoulders and eying the door. He took a couple of steps back.

"Hold it!" Mark laid a hand on his shoulder, holding him back. "Before you get all Seventies Cop." He indicated the rickety plasterboard wall that stretched to one side of the door, and to the small holes easily visible in its surface.

"Handy," said Terry.

"What? You think Mein Host upstairs isn't above charging for peeping Toms to get a peek at what goes on in there? Now shut up and look."

Chapter Four

The two young men stood, faces pressed to the plasterboard. Gradually, their eyes adjusted to the gloom of the room inside. "Fucking hell!" breathed Terry at last.

"Yeah!" agreed Mark.

Things had moved on in the short space of time since the lads had been in there. Dieter now hung from the cross, stripped to all but his boots. He was breathing heavily, sweat running down the ridges of his back, matting the hair there and making the tattooed angel that spread its wings across his shoulder blades glisten. Crossing the hairy mounds of his arse cheeks were three long, angry red weals. The whip that had undoubtedly created them lay thrown to one side on the floor. It was the sight of the other two men in the room, though, that had drawn the cries of surprise from the spying pair. Surprise mixed with lustful approval and frank envy.

Kurt was bent forward over the pallet, arms stretched out in front of him, his face twisted in a grimace that could have been pain or pleasure, and he was grunting loudly and rhythmically in time to the powerful pounding of his arse. The pounder was Doug. Stripped down to socks and boots, the bald-headed rescuer had both hands on Kurt's broad hips and was piston-fucking the German like a machine. Eyes closed, face twisted into a snarl that literally showed his teeth, he was thrusting over and over into Kurt's arse, so hard it was shaking the solid pallet and making the rows of sex toys hanging from the hooks behind it jingle against the wall. Both men were drenched in the sweat of their exertions. From time to time, Kurt would try to shift his position, probably to ease the brutal reaming he was taking. But Doug would deny him with a swift blow around the head or an extra brutal thrust of his hips that made the big bear gasp and submit to however the Englishman wanted to shaft him.

The two young men outside the dungeon stayed glued to their spyholes. As the minutes ticked by, Terry whispered again, "When's he going to stop?"

Mark shook his head. "Not any time soon," he whispered, a note of perceptible awe in his voice. "Man!"

"Hey!" Terry pointed to himself. "Still here, you know?"

Mark pulled back from the spyhole, momentarily nonplussed. "What?"

"He's like my dad, y'know?"

"Yeah, okay... I mean, I know but... like, I mean... Just...look at him!" Mark pressed his face back up to the hole in the wall to get another eyeful of the brutal screwing taking place just the other side of the thin plasterboard. "I mean, fuck!" he breathed.

"Where the hell were you?"

Mark dragged himself back from the spyhole. "What do you mean?"

"You said you'd meet me here at eight. You didn't turn up. That's how I got into this mess." Under the mask, Terry could see Mark frowning. "Where were you?" he insisted. "And, come to think of it, how come you knew where to find me? And how come you turn up with Doug, of all people, just in the nick of time?"

"You'd rather I hadn't?"

"You're not answering the question."

"Maybe the question is how you were so stupid as to get yourself into such a mess in the first place. I mean, how old *are* you?"

"Mark, I..."

Terry broke off as from within the dungeon there came an animalistic howl. As one, both young men rushed back to their spyholes. In the room, Kurt was still bent over the pallet. Doug's arse-hammering had stopped, but he was still deep in the German, both of them soaked in sweat and panting heavily as if they had run marathons. Down the side of the pallet, pooling thickly on the black dungeon floor, was the gallon of come Kurt had finally shot from those massive, swinging balls of his. "Damn! Missed the money shot," Mark whispered.

As they watched, Doug collected himself and unceremoniously pulled out of Kurt, making the German leatherman whimper in a way

Terry couldn't help enjoying.

"Then again..." Mark added, seeing the still rock-hard state of Doug's sheathed erection. "Bloody hell! How do you even get a condom around that?" Terry had no idea. "Did you know he had a cock like that?"

Terry shook his head mutely. *I didn't know anyone had a cock like that!*

As they watched, Doug carefully removed the two condoms he had used, tossing the stretched latex contemptuously at the still bound Dieter, before reaching over, dragging Kurt up by the shoulder from the pallet, and pushing him back down to the floor. Fucked into submission, the dom-turned-sub lay passively, looking up at Doug as the shaven-headed ex-wrestler straddled him, feet planted firmly on either side of his hips, and began wanking himself off with the vigour and power he had put into his fucking. Beneath him, Kurt shook his head from side to side weakly and said something which Doug apparently ignored, looking down on him with a sneer as he pushed himself rapidly towards a spectacular come shot. His thick jism shot over the prone bear's face, into his eyes and mouth. Behind them there was the rattle of restraints as Dieter strained to break free of the cross he was bound to—whether to prevent Doug's humiliation of Kurt, or to get a better view wasn't clear.

When he'd finished, Doug gave one quick flick of the wrist to shake the last drops of come off his dick and into Kurt's face. He stood there, breathing slowly and deeply, looking upwards as if staring into something that no one else could see. Terry narrowed the one eye he had pressed to the peephole, trying to make out the expression of this man he'd thought he knew so well. Doug looked...what? Satisfied? Relieved? Pained? Terry just couldn't read the complicated mix of feelings written on his lined, craggy face. He'd never seen such a brutal, dark side to Doug, and yet, inexplicably, he found what he wanted to do right then was walk into that room, heavy with the smell of sweat, come and testosterone, and throw his arms around the man.

Next to him, Mark was strangely silent as he, too, looked at the man who had given him so much grief. *Perhaps he's beginning to see just how much grief Doug could give him if he ever got* really *annoyed!*

Terry jumped when Mark touched him on the shoulder. "We've got to go."

Terry nodded reluctantly. He didn't imagine that Doug was going to stick around for a little post-fuck pillow talk with these two, and he didn't think his mentor would be too pleased to know he'd been watched through the wall. He turned and followed Mark as the other man made his way quickly along the corridor. "I still want to know..."

"Later," Mark hissed back.

But by the time Terry reached the bar, Mark was well ahead of him, and by the time he made it outside, Mark had gone. Alone, Terry made his way back to the hotel. He was disappointed to find that none of the other lads were back from their *Carry On* trip.

Body exhausted, mind whirling, Terry threw himself into bed and sank immediately into a night of bizarre, disturbing dreams. He was running along endless corridors, desperately trying to escape Dieter and Kurt's grasping hands that seemed to shoot out of every shadow. Mark was there, too, also running, though whether he was chasing Terry or leading him on, Terry couldn't tell. And it didn't matter which way Terry ran, which way he turned; all the corridors led back to that small black room and the monstrous, terrifying figure inside.

With a strangled cry, Terry shot up in his bed, sweat pouring off his body. It was Doug!

Terry sat in bed, hugging his knees, waiting for his heart and breathing to slow to normal. *What the fuck is going on?*

PART FIVE

Chapter One

Terry and Doug spent the best part of the following morning not talking about what had happened in the dungeon. Mark had gone on ahead in his camper van to cross the border into Switzerland and secure their next booking. With Baz, Jonesy, and Eric chatting blithely about everything and nothing as the rest of the posse drove to meet him in their mini coach, the older man and the younger sat in uncomfortable silence. When they stopped at a service station and the guys hopped out, Terry and Doug pointedly remained behind, the moment to talk having obviously arrived. Even so, a couple of minutes passed before either of them could bring himself to speak, and just as Terry had decided it was ridiculous and he was going to open the conversation, Baz leaped back into the bus and the moment was lost. It was only when they came to the second service station after having crossed the border and stopped for lunch that Terry and Doug finally found themselves seated at a small table in a café. Baz had gone in search of the video games he loved, and Eric and Jonesy haunted vainly for what they called a 'proper English breakfast'.

This time, it was Doug who went first. "You're a twat!" he said.

Terry opened his mouth to instantly rebuff the comment and closed it again. He *had* been a twat. "Thanks," he said at last. It could have been sarcasm; it could have been genuine gratitude for Doug's having got him out of a messy situation.

"Do you have any idea what those two could have done to you?"

Terry shifted on his seat. Sitting for too long was literally an uncomfortable reminder of Dieter's handiwork.

"Those two are into some serious deep shit. It's a nasty scene."

"You seemed to be enjoying it right enough." The words were spoken before he had thought them through, and Terry regretted them instantly. But they were out now, and his pride was too stung for him to take Doug's haranguing without some comeback, deserved though it was.

Doug went very quiet. That was never a good sign. "What do you mean?" he asked eventually.

"We...I...saw you. Afterwards. I thought you might have needed...rescuing."

Doug sat, staring into the cup of milky coffee in front of him. "It had to be...sorted," he said finally.

"Yeah, they both looked well and truly 'sorted' by the time you'd finished with them. Especially Kurt. Don't think I've ever seen anyone so 'sorted' in my life." Terry leaned in closer to the man he'd thought he'd known so well. "So, are you into that scene? Y'know, dungeons and..."

"Don't! Just...don't go there, Terry." Doug picked up the coffee cup, clasping it as if for warmth, and Terry was astonished to see that his hands were actually shaking. "In the past, I got...involved with things I wish to hell I hadn't. That's how I knew what those two last night were like. That's how I knew what had to be done."

You could have walked away. You didn't have to fuck them. Showing unusual wisdom, Terry stayed silent.

"But it's not me. Not any more. And it's dangerous." Doug drew a deep, shuddering breath. "Keep away from it, Terry."

Something was nagging at the back of Terry's mind, something he couldn't ignore. "Involved, you say? Was that like, when you were in Europe before, all those years ago?"

"Leave it, Terry!"

"Was that why you never wanted to go back? Why you didn't want us to come here?"

"I said..."

An awful suspicion bloomed in Terry's mind. "Was it... Was my dad 'involved', too?"

With a sharp scrape of metal on tile, Doug pushed his chair back and rose from the table. "We'll be late," he snapped.

"No wait, tell me. Was Dad...?"

But Doug had left him and was already striding towards the exit. He nearly collided with Eric who was coming back in, proudly carrying a plate piled high with bacon, eggs, and beans. "C'mon," he snarled.

"But I..." Eric began to protest.

"I said come on!" And Doug was gone, leaving a dismayed Eric looking helplessly at Terry.

☆☆☆

"So where the hell were you?" Terry snapped.

"What do you mean?"

"Don't act dumb, Mark. You know what I mean."

Terry was already in gear for that night's wrestling: a burgundy-red tracksuit, top and trunks, and black patent leather boots with a matching red stripe down the side. Jonesy and Eric had opened. Terry was up, next followed by Mark, with Baz to close. Mark, of course, had turned up late in his van. But it wasn't this latest tardy arrival Terry was referring to. It was the previous night's near-disastrous no-show.

"I got...held up."

"Right. And what was his name?"

Mark grinned. "Jealous?"

"Gimme a break. And how come when you did turn up you were with Doug?"

Mark spread his hands. "I was late, yeah? I'm sorry. You know me. I just happened to bump into Doug, and the next thing I knew he's grilling me about did I know where you were, who you were with, etc., etc. When I told him where we were meeting he got kind of...angry. More angry than normal, I mean. And he just charged over there ahead of me."

Something about Mark's story didn't ring true. Hell, most of it didn't seem to ring true, and the truth behind it was almost certainly some other guy that Mark had met and just as certainly fucked. But, for the moment at least, that wasn't Terry's main concern. Oddly enough, Doug was. "Angry you say? Doug? When you told him where we were going to meet?"

"Yeah."

Almost like he already knew what sort of things went on there.

"Get your arse into gear!"

"Talk of the devil," Mark said with an easy grin as Doug stalked into the changing room.

"Terry, get out there. You'll be up in five." And Doug stomped back out.

"He is such a prick!" Mark said when the changing room door was safely closed.

"Thought that's what you liked about him."

"What do you mean?"

"Last night you were practically dribbling over the size of his cock. Knowing you, I thought you might actually have made a play for it today." Part of Terry hated the queeny baiting he could hear himself spitting out, but part of him thought it was Mark who was the prick, and as such he deserved it.

"Was I?" Mark sounded faintly incredulous. Then he laughed. "One of those heat of the moment things. I mean, really. Me and Doug. Can you imagine it?"

For a second, Terry did just that: imagined Doug's massive stanchion of a cock pounding into Mark's hot, sturdy arse with the implacable ferocity he'd shown when fucking the German. That'd wipe the smile off Mark's face pretty damn quickly. He shook his head to clear it of the image. It was oddly disturbing being turned on thinking about Doug having sex.

"You're up." A sweating, panting Jonesy, still garbed in his green ring trunks and boots, burst into the changing room. "Cute guy for you in the front row, left-hand side. Ask the guy you're up against nicely, he might throw you in his lap."

"Cheers," Terry replied without too much enthusiasm, his head too full of conflicting thoughts to find room for the prospect of pretty punters. He turned and headed moodily for the ring.

Jonesy, however, had been right about just how cute the guy in the front row was, and in spite of himself, Terry couldn't help feeling a certain distraction whenever he caught sight of him. Probably a year or two younger than Terry, he was dressed in skinhead fashions that would have been quite tame in a UK setting but were actually rather outrageous by the conservative standards of this German backwater. His hands rarely left his crotch, and whenever Terry contrived to get his body twisted into a position of especially appealing suffering, the lad leaned forward so much in his attempts to get as close to the groaning grapplers as he could that he was in real danger of falling from his seat.

But for all that, Terry didn't manage to get himself thrown into his lap. For the one thing, his opponent that night, a po-faced doughboy whose untrained body no amount of lurid Lycra could disguise, was far too lumpen a wrestler to manage so exciting and energetic a move. Most of Terry's energy had to go into making him look good lest the audience die of boredom. And for another thing, Terry found himself just too preoccupied with thoughts of Mark and Doug and even of what had happened to his dad all those years ago, to get excited at the prospect of some skinhead lad, no matter how cute and willing.

He dutifully waltzed the German grappler around the ring for five rounds before pulling off the one fall required for victory. Even as the referee raised his arm, Terry felt guilty for having turned in undoubtedly the worst bout of the tour so far. Without any real enthusiasm, he glanced to the front row to see how the young skinhead was taking it. He wasn't at all surprised to see the lad pressing hard into his lap, his eyes fixed on the ring and oblivious of all else. A distant, slightly pained expression on his face suggested the climax of the bout might have already taken place in the ring, but was only just about to take place in his pants. What completely wiped the start of the smile off Terry's face was the realisation of just where the boy's eyes were fixed. On Doughboy, the lump of German lard who'd managed to make even Terry look bad. With a barely restrained "Fuck!", Terry rolled his eyes to the heavens that seemed to be persecuting him so mercilessly. It was when he looked down again that he caught sight of the man who sat behind the teasing, tasteless tit of a skinhead, and everything changed yet again.

While the rest of the crowd cheered and applauded in the way Germans responded to even mediocre shows, Yves Montaigne sat with his head slightly to one side and met Terry's eyes with a look of wry amusement that made it plain he knew exactly what kind of bout that had been. Then, with just a small upturn of the lips and the raising of an eyebrow, his whole expression changed, and Terry knew Yves was thinking of something completely different. Something he liked...a lot!

Happy days are here again!

☆☆☆

161

"*Quelle coïncidence.*"

"What are the odds?"

"*En effet.*"

"Yeah. Right."

Yves smiled and stepped in closely to Terry who was still in his wrestling gear after his bout. He put both arms round his waist, slid them down to the trunks-clad butt, pulled him in and kissed him deeply, his hands firm on the hard curves of Terry's pert arse. Even through the cut of Yves's expensive trousers, Terry could feel the long, solid ridge of his hard cock against his own.

"You'll spoil your clothes," he said breathlessly when Yves finally pulled back a little. "I'm all sweaty."

Yves leaned in close to his neck, breathing in deeply as if savouring the bouquet of a wine. "*Eh bien,*" he said softly. "It smells good." He ran his tongue the length of Terry's neck, and the boy thought he might possibly come on the spot. "And it tastes *divine!*"

Terry went to kiss again, but with a soft laugh, Yves held him off. "But perhaps you are right. These clothes are *un peu cher*. And besides—" he let his hand fall to the front of Terry's tenting trunks and pressed, drawing an involuntary sound from Terry midway between a sigh and a groan "—I would rather not be wearing anything at all when next we kiss." He picked up a towel from a nearby bench and tossed it to Terry. "Shower, *mon brave*. And then I am taking you to dinner."

"Dinner?" Terry couldn't keep the note of disappointment from his voice. He was sure a meal with Yves would be fabulous. But it wasn't the kind of refreshment his body was crying out for right at that moment.

"*Mais oui,*" said Yves, and he gave Terry that look again, the one he'd given from ringside, only minutes earlier, that had set Terry's nerve ends tingling. "After we have fucked, *bien sûr.*"

Chapter Two

"Mark! Wait there a minute!" Doug strode over and stood next to the wrestler. For a moment he just stood there, staring at the man in front of him who stared back, expression concealed beneath the Johnny Deuce mask, eyes unreadable, to Doug at least. Then the words came out of him in a rush. "You saw what went down the other night." It wasn't a question.

"What?"

Doug gritted his teeth. "You came back to that room, and you saw what happened. With the krauts."

"I don't think we're supposed to call them krauts any more, Doug."

"It's that or a lot worse," Doug said sourly. He stared at the other man, as if trying to physically drill words into his head without actually speaking them. "It happened, right?" He waited. "Right?"

"Er, right."

"Right." Doug shot him one last angry glance, turned on his heel, and stalked off.

The victim of his verbal assault watched him go. From around the corner, where he had been watching, unseen, a third man approached. "That was... interesting," he said.

"The guy's a dick! I don't see what..."

"You never do."

The two men stood, looking off in the direction Doug had gone. "I've got to go," said Mark.

"You're making a mistake."

"Won't be the first time, probably not the last. But it's got to be done."

"No. I mean you *are* making a mistake."

"What do you...? Ah, I see."

The mistake rectified, a quick exchange of information about where next to meet, a brief, awkward embrace, and the unmasked figure watched the man in the wrestler's mask walk away purposefully in the same direction as Doug. Not for the first time that night, he shook his head. "Dicks," he muttered to himself.

☆☆☆

"Oh, fuck! Yes! Yes!"

"*Tu l'aime?* You like it?"

"Oh, fuck, yes! Don't stop!"

Terry had no idea how long he had been in the hotel bedroom, face down on silk sheets with Yves's piston of a cock pounding tirelessly again and again into his sweetly aching arse. He only knew he never wanted it to end, though he also knew he couldn't hold back for much longer the bollock-busting explosion that had been building in his balls for God knew how long.

In some ways, their second rendezvous had played out like a repeat of their first. A journey in Yves's swanky wheels to a posh hotel, and a more or less immediate start to their lovemaking. In others, it had been...different. Excitingly, *violently* different.

Yves had been on him like a tiger, tearing his clothes off and flinging him onto the bed. Not expecting quite such rapid exuberance, and having just been through six rounds with one wrestler, Terry had been quickly overpowered. There was no doubting what Yves wanted to do to him that night. First, the Frenchman's tongue was up his arse so swiftly and forcefully the unprepared lad nearly came then and there. Then a finger, in fast and strong, and Terry's hole so well lubed by the tongue and so eager for the penetration that the Frenchman was quickly able to slip in another. Then a third finger with almost no pain, skilfully stretching the tight ring muscle, working it, preparing it, even as he massaged the throbbing, pulsing sweet spot beyond.

After five minutes of the delicious massage, Yves withdrew, rolled a condom the length of his curved erection, lubed Terry with some more gel, and entered him again, sliding in deep and easy. Terry gasped as he hungrily took in the implacable length, thrilling to the unyielding curve as it worked into him. Yves fucked him hard with an unstoppable, insatiable rhythm, all the time his lips next to Terry's ear, sometimes nipping at his lobe, at his neck, sometimes whispering to him in a stream of strangely guttural French that made no sense to Terry at all.

Then Yves slipped his arm round his throat.

Terry slapped at the biceps pressed against his Adam's apple, relishing its taut muscularity.

Yves tightened the hold.

Terry tried to swallow but found he couldn't. He slapped again at the arm, more insistently this time, and brought his other hand round to pull on it, to relieve the pressure round his throat.

Yves tightened the hold still further.

Instinctively, Terry tugged at the arm throttling him, but Yves had locked the hold off by bringing his other hand round to clasp his own wrist. And, unbelievably, considering the force of it before, the pace of his fucking actually increased, his curved boner driving into Terry's arse faster and harder. Terry tried to speak, but all he could manage were inarticulate gurgles, and now a yellow fog was beginning to creep in from the edges of his vision.

Yves relaxed the hold.

Terry gasped, drawing in lungsful of air. Yves still held him, wiry arm wrapped around his throat, but the pressure was gone, and his remorseless reaming had, for the moment, stopped. The Frenchman held himself deep inside the gasping lad. "*Tu l'aime*," he whispered into his ear, stroking Terry's chest with one hand. "You like it."

"I couldn't...breathe."

Yves kissed him tenderly on the tip of his ear. "You are safe, *mon brave*," he whispered. "You don't think I am going to hurt you, do you? It's all about the control. The power. You are a wrestler. You know what I mean, *non*? You know how good it feels to control another man. To dominate him?" He kissed the ear again, then licked it lightly, the tip of his tongue tracing the whorls. Pinned to the mattress with one of the horniest men he knew hard inside him, heart hammering in his chest, Terry struggled to take in what was being said, what was happening to him. Somewhere in the back of his mind a memory flickered. *Mark*. Why was he thinking about Mark now, of all times? But not just Mark. Mark and Stefan. Mark with his arm round Stefan's throat. Mark forcing Stefan's arm up his back. Stefan growing harder and harder.

On top of him, Yves shifted, withdrew, then slowly thrust back into him, withdrew and thrust, varying the angle just enough each time to knead the hot, demanding nub deep in Terry's arse. All those vague memories were swept away in the waves of white-hot sensation washing through him, and all Terry could gasp out into the pillow was, "Yes, yes."

"*C'est bon*," said Yves as he fucked his boy, faster and faster. He reapplied the chokehold.

Twice more he brought Terry to the brink of unconsciousness. After the third time, when he took his arms away from Terry's throat he fully withdrew, leaving Terry on the bed as he rose to dispose of the condom. Terry lay on the cool, expensive sheets, trying to gather his thoughts. Had Yves come? He didn't think so, but he'd been so close to being out of it he couldn't tell for sure. *That had been truly fucked up. And yet...* His cock was harder than he could ever remember. Yves's fucking had aroused him more deeply than any he could recall. *And yet...* Terry rubbed his throat.

Yves returned to the bed and lay down next to Terry, face down. Terry turned to gaze at the beautiful lines of his trim body. He leaned over, unable to help himself, to trace the length of Yves's back with one finger, drawing it slowly over the swell of his pale buttocks. Yves closed his eyes, smoothed one hand over his own arse cheeks, and lifted his head. He looked Terry straight in the eye and smiled. "*Et maintenant*, I want you to do the same to me."

☆☆☆

"About last night."

Doug stopped in his tracks and turned to face the man who'd addressed him in the street. "You again! I told you. It happened. End of." He grimaced. "And take that mask off."

"Some guys say it makes me look hot."

"I say it makes you look like a wanker."

"That's the last thing I want to be."

Doug narrowed his eyes, scrutinised the figure standing in front of him. "Mark. What are you...?"

Mark stepped forward so that he was more fully in the light cast from the nearest shop window. "When I saw you last night, when I was with Terry." He held up a hand when Doug went to speak. "No. Listen. When I saw you, you...were hot. I mean, you were *really* fucking hot!" Doug grimaced and went to turn on his heel. "But that wasn't what got to me about it." Doug came to an abrupt halt, back turned to the speaker, but he was listening. "That's not what made me want...to talk to you."

Slowly, Doug turned. "Mark, I..."

The masked figure held up his hand again, speaking quickly before he could be interrupted. "You didn't have to stay after we'd got Terry out of there. You stayed because you wanted to. Because you *needed* to. That's what I saw as I was watching you. I think I've known it for weeks now on some level, but I hadn't really understood it until I saw it in your face that night." He hesitated, as if nervous that what he was about to say would spark a violent reaction in the other man. But he had gone too far to turn back now. "It's been a long time, hasn't it, Doug?" The shaven-headed man remained silent, but the outburst Mark had feared didn't come. Instead there was...something else. "How long has it been?"

Speaking slowly, as if from a long way away and through a lot of pain, Doug spoke. "You're like him. Like Terry. You're young and you don't understand."

"Understand what?"

"I... None of your fucking business."

The masked figure reached out a hand tentatively, took it back, then reached out again and rested it gently on Doug's shoulder. The stocky man flinched but did nothing to dislodge it, almost as if, for some reason, he simply could not.

"Then show me," the man in the mask said.

☆☆☆

Terry lay on the bed, staring up at the ceiling. Yves lay next to him, not touching him, eyes closed. Terry felt more exhausted than if he'd gone ten rounds solo against a world champion. He felt great. He felt...worried.

He'd just fucked the most incredible sexual athlete he had yet met. He'd been on top. He, at Yves's insistence, had slipped his muscular arm round the Frenchman's throat and slowly squeezed, strangling him as they screwed. Yet it was Terry who had felt out of control. Somehow, it had been Yves, with his arse muscles tight around Terry's cock, who had driven the pace, dictated the fucking. It had been exciting, thrilling. *Hot!* But Terry felt... used.

"You are awake?"

Terry jumped slightly. He'd thought Yves was asleep. "Yeah."

Yves smiled and rolled over, letting his arm fall across Terry's upper body, still without opening his eyes. "Did you...enjoy yourself?"

"Yeah. Of course. It was... great."

Yves opened his eyes and looked directly at him. "You enjoyed possessing me, *oui*? Not just fucking me, but holding my life in your hands."

"Yeah. I mean, no. I didn't... I wouldn't have..."

"But you could have. You could have choked me, even as we fucked, squeezed the life out of me, even as you came." Yves eyes burned as he spoke with obvious passion about what they had just done.

"I..."

Yves put his finger on Terry's lips, silencing him as one would a small child. "Just as you could break a man's arm in the wrestling ring, snap his back, or splinter his legs. That is what the crowds urge us to do, *non*?"

Terry pushed the finger away. "But that's different. That's..."

"Play?"

"I was going to say 'acting'. It's all...show," said Terry, uncomfortable at this betrayal of the 'sport' he loved—even to someone who knew as well as he did exactly how professional wrestling worked. "Mostly show."

Yves laughed softly. "We are all actors, *mon cher*. All the time. Even when we fuck. *Especially* when we fuck! Reality! Fantasy!" He gestured at each word as if it was as worthless as the other. "It is we who decide which is which. Be honest with me, *mon brave*. Have you never wanted to fuck the men you are wrestling?"

Memories of Phil and Mark rose unbidden in Terry's mind. "Yeah.

'Course I have," he said uncertainly, feeling lost in the face of the Frenchman's bewildering intensity and twisting train of thought.

Yves sat up, his eyes bright. "I don't mean after the bouts, Terry. I mean *during* them, while you have total control of a man's body, once you have shown your mastery of him, your physical superiority. While the crowd are baying for you to show you are the—how do you say it in English? The *alpha male!*"

"Yeah. I mean, yes. I mean... I suppose so." Terry waited for Yves to show his contempt for the uneducated Englishman's failure to understand, for his insipidity.

But Yves just laughed softly, and stroked his face. "You are very young, Terry," he said, "but you are learning." Something in Yves's words struck a chord, revived another memory, but it was faint, and he couldn't recall which exactly. Before he could think about it any more, Yves leaned in and seized him by the shoulders, pulling him up off the pillows. "Terry, I have a confession to make. And an offer."

Terry sat on the damp silk sheets, feeling the strength of the naked man at his side as he gripped his shoulders, caught in his intensity that was almost palpable. His head spun even more than it had when Yves had been literally choking the life out of him. Could the evening get any more confusing?

Chapter Three

In the cramped confines of Mark's camper van, the two men faced each other, their discarded clothes at their feet. They had undressed mechanically, deliberately, as if reluctant to admit what it was leading to. Each matched the other, a shirt for a shirt, socks, trousers, briefs, each garment placed to one side, eyes fixed on each other, only the obvious and undeniable thickening and rising of their cocks giving a lie to the neutrality of their expressions. Finally they stood, like reluctant wrestlers waiting for the bell to signal the start of a round, both stripped naked, both with erections as solid as rocks. It was Doug who eventually grunted and said, "For fuck's sake, get rid of this," as he went to untie the mask the other man was still wearing.

His companion raised a hand to ward him off. "Let's leave it on," he said.

"What?"

"I...like it."

"Mark, I..."

"Please. It...works for me."

Reluctantly, Doug let his hand fall to his side. "Okay."

The masked man took Doug in his arms. He gently pulled him in close, holding the stickily-built man to his body, warm skin against skin. For a moment Doug stood rigid, unresponsive, then gradually he relaxed into the embrace. His thick arms that had wrung many a submission out of men with crushing bear hugs wrapped tenderly around the taller man's torso as Doug rested his shaven head on the other's chest. And finally, inevitably, cock pressed up against cock, both steel, bolt upright, the pressure of one on the other a thrilling surge in their blood. "Mark!" The whispered name came out with the urgency of a cry for help.

"Call me Johnny."

"Fuck."

"Please. I…"

"I know. You like it." The other man shifted his hips just slightly, and his stiff cock slid over Doug's, making him gasp, "Johnny!"

For long minutes the two men just stood there, fighters, gently stroking each other—down backs, flanks, over buttocks, chest and stomach, and the inside of thighs—as they nuzzled and kissed, at the centre of a whorl of erotic sensations, the focus point the demanding solidity of their erections. Older than his masked lover, Doug's skin was more weathered by the years, his face craggier, more lined, but his muscles had lost none of their iron. His stomach was ridged with muscle, not fat; his arms were pumped and hard from years of training, and his buttocks were as meaty and firm as a man's half his age. Johnny's head tilted backwards, and he groaned at the sensuality of having a rough, hard man like Doug tenderly kiss his neck and nipples, the habitual gruff hostility melted away completely. It was he who finally pulled them backwards and down onto the converted sofa bed, Doug landing on top of him, between his splayed legs. The collision of their throbbing boners made both men cry out as helplessly as teenagers making love for the first time.

Only when he saw the other man reaching for the box of condoms on the small shelf under the window did Doug pull away slightly. "You don't…you don't have to."

The other man looked up at him through the eyeholes in his mask. "I want to," he said.

Doug sat back. "There's not many guys—" he began awkwardly. "Look, I'm not just bragging here. Guys find it hard to…to take this." And he nodded down to the already dripping cock thrusting up from his grizzled crotch hair.

He regarded the mammoth tool steadily, then reached out and cupped its heavy length with one hand, smoothing his palm very gently along its taut skin. The cock leaped involuntarily at the touch, landing back in his hand with a soft smack, and Doug made a sound almost like a whimper and screwed his eyes shut tight as he fought for mastery of himself. "I want it," he said. "I want you." He handed him the foil packet.

Doug opened his eyes, blinking at the small silver square as if he couldn't quite believe it. He quickly tore it open, took out the rubber and began to work it over his cock. It was tight, very tight, and Doug had to take care that the act of rolling it over the fiercely throbbing length wouldn't be enough in itself to push him over the edge. At last, with a shuddering breath, he was sheathed, and he lay there for a moment to collect himself. He gasped when the younger man leaned in to slowly smooth cool lube all along the latex. "Use a lot!" he whispered.

The lubing done, the masked man threw the empty tube to one side, turned over on the narrow bed, and lay on his belly, waiting. With his face turned to Doug's, only the eyes through the expressionless mask showed the depth of his need, of his yearning for this.

Slowly, Doug lowered himself onto the supine, muscular body, resting his broad cockhead on the lightly hairy arse crack, feeling the involuntary twitch of the buttock muscles through the latex. A second to collect himself, then he pressed in, slowly, gently parting the cheeks with his cock, resting its crown on the puckered sphincter which spasmed excitedly at this first, teasing pressure. Another second, and Doug pressed in further, holding his breath as the thick length of veined meat slid in deeper and deeper, the tight muscle parting yet pressing, tightening then relaxing, tightening again until...

"There. Just...there!" gasped the man under him. "Fuck! Hold it! Hold it there!"

"Is it... okay? Is it...? Is it hurting? Do you want me to...?"

"No, don't stop! For fuck's sake, don't stop. Just give me a second. Just to...to take it. Yeah. Oh fuck, yeah!"

Eyes screwed shut again, his face twisted, Doug held back. He fought the primitive instinct crying out in every fibre of his body to drive his cock into that magnificent, willing arse again then again, deeper and faster, to fuck this muscular young body harder than it had ever been fucked, in more ways than it had ever been fucked. He fought to obliterate all thought, all sense, all feeling in one sensational, never-before-achieved climax. It was the hardest fight of his life, harder than any he'd ever had in any ring, but he did it, he held on, until...

The man impaled on his cock turned his head to look round at him over his shoulder. The eyes behind the holes in the mask were wide, wondering. "Yes!" he whispered, and Doug felt the relaxation of the muscles gripping his cock, letting him in, completely, utterly, all the way into the willing body. Slowly at first, then faster and faster, Doug fucked the sweet tight arse beneath him, as hard if not harder than he had reamed Kurt, but with a tenderness he had shown none of to the German. He always allowed the boy time to adjust to each new thrust, wary of hurting him with his club of a dick, a joyous relief sweeping through him as he realised that this man wanted him, *really* wanted him. Mark's need to take was as strong as Doug's to give. There could be no pain, no hurt, only the inexpressible and total loss of two men, each in the other. Fucking Kurt had been about punishment, possession. This...this was completely different.

The small camper van filled with the breathless gasps of the two men, their grunts and groans and wordless cries, and the alarming creak of the cheap wooden bed frame as the entire van rocked in mimicry of their increasingly abandoned motion.

All too quickly, in spite of the desperate resistance of both men, they came together, Doug bellowing on the release of a volcanic orgasm, his hands clawing at the sheets of the bed so tightly they tore under his nails. Just as he thought he'd peaked, his lover thrust his arse up at him one last time, and Doug felt the unbelievable but uncontrollable contractions of a second orgasm rip through him, making him cry out helplessly again.

When the last drop of come had finally spasmed from his aching balls he collapsed on top of the man who had drained him more thoroughly than any other he could remember, and lay there as if poleaxed, his hairy arms and legs wrapped lovingly and protectively around the other.

He had no idea how long he lay there, drifting in and out of consciousness, listening to the breathing beneath him growing deeper and slower. When he eventually tried to move, he was surprised to find his cock still semi-swollen, and as careful as he was, his gentle withdrawal made the other man moan and rouse from his own blissful sleep. When he peeled the condom from his dick, Doug's thick come spurted over both their bodies, released at last from the pressured confinement of the overstretched latex.

"Fuck," breathed Doug.

"Yeah. And no whips needed."

For a moment, the softness in Doug's face faded, replaced by the more usual severity. "Don't even joke about things like that."

"Hey. I'm sorry. Relax." The masked man sat up and kissed Doug full on the lips. Doug hesitated before returning the kiss unrestrainedly. "Shit. I don't believe this." He nodded down to his lap, at the cock that had just shot its load like come was going out of style. "You've got me going again."

"You're surprised?" Doug said in a growl that somehow had none of its normal bitterness. "That's the trouble with kids. No stamina." He kissed his lover again, deeper, taking one of Mark's hands and pulling it gently down into the warm fur of his crotch and the cock that was also already rising and hardening again. "Me? I can go all night. And I want you again." He reached up. "And this time without the fucking mask."

"Not yet!"

Doug stopped his advance, surprised by the vehemence of the rejection. "Okay. Like I said, no stamina. I can wait a few minutes. We've got all night."

"No, I mean, not without the mask. Not yet."

Doug frowned. "Aw, c'mon, Mark. Why not? I don't need that shit any more."

"I told you. It...it just works for me."

Doug looked at the younger man closely. "Is there...?" he began, then stopped. "Aw shit, Mark. You're not... Is that really what you're into? Fuck!" He sat up fully, looking down, and the man next to him waited. Then, "No," he said, and he got up from the bed. "I made a decision a long time ago." Doug reached for his clothes and began to dress, talking all the time but not looking back at the man on the bed. "I didn't want shit like...like that place last night, the kind of scene those two fuckers had going. What happened back there was a mistake, a...a lapse. It's over for me now, and I don't want it in my life any more. And that includes masks and 'games' and crap like that. I..." He stopped, one arm through the sleeve of his jacket, and finally looked back at his erstwhile lover. "I thought you got that." The masked man in front of him looked back, expression concealed, eyes unreadable. "All right, then," Doug said quietly. He turned to leave the van.

"Wait!"

Doug turned back. The two men regarded each other. Doug felt his heart pounding as hard as it had when he'd climaxed inside the masked man. When Mark's hands rose to the ties of his mask, Doug's breath actually caught in his throat. Three sharp tugs of the laces, and the mask fell away. Doug's pent-up breath came out in a sigh. He knelt down on the bed and leaned in closely to look long and hard at the unmasked features of the naked young man he had just fucked. "You look different," he said at last.

"Different?" An anxious expression clouded the other man's eyes.

"Yeah." Doug leaned in and kissed him softly on the lips. "Less of a prick."

With a choked laugh of relief, the other man reached out for him and pulled him back down onto the bed. For long minutes both were lost again in the passion of their kisses. When they finally broke apart, the naked man's eagerly renewed erection was clear to see, while his now clothed lover's hard-on was no less obvious. Hands reached out for Doug's zipper. With some difficulty, the hardened meat was manoeuvred once more into the open, but as the smiling younger man bent down to take it into his mouth, a frown crossed Doug's features, and he held him back with one hand. "You going to tell him, then?"

"Who?"

"Terry, of course. And the others, I suppose."

"Tell them what?"

"That we're... That things are different between the two of us. I mean, don't get me wrong, I'm not rushing anything here, and I don't know what the fuck it is that we've got, if we've got anything at all, but..." Doug paused, the words obviously harder for him than any physical conflict might have been. "We've got *something*, Mark. Haven't we? I haven't felt this way in a very long time. And the others are bound to notice that things have changed." He waited, the need in his eyes as plain as it had been when they'd first stood naked in front of each other. When the answer came, he had to strain to hear it.

"I... I don't think we should say anything to anyone for a while."

Doug flinched. He waited for the other man to say more, to explain himself, perhaps even to change what he had said. But he didn't, and slowly, the new warmth and softness in his face drained away. Looking down, he saw his cock jutting hopelessly out of his jeans. Gritting his teeth, he forced it back in, carefully pulling up the zipper before rising from the bed. "Guess I'd better go, then," he said. His voice sounded hoarse.

"I... Look, Doug, it's not that I don't want to... exactly. It's just..."

Doug nodded grimly. "Someone else?"

"No! That is... Yeah. Yeah, I guess there is."

"Right. There always is, isn't there? There always will be. My mistake."

Doug pulled his jacket on without further words. He left the van without looking back once.

Chapter Four

"Television."

"What?"

"Well, the Internet to begin with anyway, leading into downloads, DVDs, and then television."

"What, and then wide-screen fucking 3D movies?"

"I knew you'd be like this."

"Yeah, well, I never thought you'd be like this! Again!"

"Like what?"

"Stupid!"

Terry and Doug glared at each other from either end of the B and B's breakfast table. To the side of the table, between them, sat Mark, leaning back on his chair with his mask off, unusually enough. Though from the inscrutability of his expression, he might just as well have left it on.

"So, just let me get this straight," Doug said, visibly struggling to contain his rage. "This fucking frog..."

"Frenchman."

"Yves La-di-da..."

"Montaigne."

"Who you've met once in a wrestling ring..."

"Three times, actually. And not just in the ring."

Doug's diatribe wavered for a fraction of a second as he mentally reviewed that last statement before pressing on. "...is going to make you a film star."

"He's going to make me a wrestling star, over here in Europe. And these days, that means more than just traipsing around from hall to rotten hall. For a start, it means putting yourself out there on the Net."

"S'right," said Mark. Doug glared at him ferociously, and Mark quickly looked back down at the table in front of him and shut up.

"And he chooses you."

"Yeah, why not?"

"Why?"

"Maybe I made a good impression."

"I'll bet you did!"

"I'm a fucking great wrestler, Doug!"

"You're a fucking stupid one!"

Terry gave a strangled roar of frustration and ran his fingers sharply through his hair. It was like being a teenager again, for real, and being told by Doug and/or Mae that he couldn't stay out late on a school night. "Look, I'm not the only one! It's not like he's been stalking me and only me across the continent. He's the owner of one of the largest promotions in Europe."

"*The* largest," Mark said. Doug growled in his direction, and Mark quickly added, "Probably," before dropping his gaze a second time.

"He's been recruiting guys like this for years. I was headhunted."

"You need to be head-*examined*."

Terry thumped the table with both fists in exasperation. "Why can't you just be happy for once in your life when something goes right?"

"Because it's all too damn convenient, Terry!" Doug exploded. "You meet this guy in a bout because the man you're supposed to be wrestling doesn't turn up, but Monsieur Swanky Promoter and Champion Wrestler just happens to be there and jumps in to take his place. Then, he's coincidentally in the audience of a bout in another country. Now, you tell me we just happen to find ourselves not so far from his base of operations—in, might I add, yet another fucking country—and he wants to whisk you off and record you in some show and make you an internet sensation."

"Actually..." Mark raised his hand like a small child in a classroom, and the two feuding members of the Ryan family stopped and turned to face him, Terry with hope, Doug with undisguised hostility. "I think I might have had something to do with some of that."

Doug's glare would have killed a basilisk. "You?" he said, quietly but very dangerously.

Mark carefully settled all four legs of his chair back on the floor and leaned forward on the table as he went on to explain. "Yves—" Doug gave a contemptuous snort at the use of the first name, but Mark ignored him "—was one of the contacts I made when I was over here last year. Well, actually he was *the* contact. I mean, he is big, man! If you haven't got him on your side, you might as well forget it. Practically all of the venues we've used have been under his control. He started out in France, worked his way through Germany, and then across the border into Switzerland for pretty tasty tax reasons. All we've been doing, more or less, is following his chain of venues. See?" He spread his hands as if all would now be well. When Doug's baleful expression changed not one whit, Mark cleared his throat and pressed on. "Anyway, while I was setting things up, I may have mentioned this hot young wrestler I'd met. I mean 'hot' as in good...at wrestling... Really good at wrestling." Doug's glare could have split rocks. "Needless to say, as he is a headhunter, he was interested and said he'd maybe go along to the first bout to see for himself. The rest, as they say, is history. He liked Terry. He liked him a lot."

There was an awkward silence, then, "See!" Terry exclaimed, as if saying that enthusiastically would be enough to win Doug completely over.

"Bull. Shit!"

Terry threw his hands in the air. "Oh, for pity's sake!"

"You're not doing it, Terry, and that's that."

There was a second, icier silence.

"I'm sorry?"

Doug actually blinked. Terry's question had been quiet and slow, not delivered in the petulant whine he was used to. And suddenly Doug knew. Things had changed. He pressed on, but even Mark could sense the lack of conviction in his tone. "I said you're not getting involved with this Montaigne guy. It's... It could be *dangerous.*"

Terry gave a bitter laugh. "Again with the *danger.*" He waved his hands about in childish imitation of a ghost, mocking Doug's word. "You know what you are, Doug? You're paranoid, that's what you are."

"Yeah? So was I being paranoid when I came looking for you back in Germany and found you strung up like a Christmas turkey about to get the shit whipped out of you?"

"Okay, right! There, I made a mistake."

"I'll say!"

"But everyone gets to make mistakes. That's what people do. Didn't you ever make mistakes?" Abruptly, Terry leaned forward as a new idea seized him. "You did, didn't you? That's why you've always been so against touring in Europe. You made a mistake when you were over here, didn't you?" Then another idea, even more stunning than the last, struck him. "And Dad was involved, too? Wasn't he? Wasn't he, Doug?"

For long seconds the three men around the table sat in tense silence. Terry's gaze was riveted unwaveringly on Doug as he waited for an answer. Mark looked from one to the other. Doug stared at the table before them. When he looked up, it was Mark's eyes he looked straight into. "This isn't the right time..." he began.

Terry exploded to his feet. "No. It's never the right time, is it, Doug? You've been telling me that since I was a kid. Well, you know what? I'm not a kid any more. I've listened to you, and Mae, all my life, tried to do what you want, tried to keep our company going, but all you've ever done is hold me back. I came here for all of us, but now I've got a chance to do something for myself, and I'm going to take it. Yves is recording a show tonight for streaming on his website. I'm going to do it. And I'm going to do more. And if I can make a go of it, who knows? Perhaps I'll live over here. That way, I doubt I'll ever have to see you and your frowning, moaning face ever again." He stormed for the door and threw it open. "I mean...have you seen the car Yves drives?" Then he was gone, the reverberations from the slammed door taking several minutes to die down.

"It's a Lamborghini," Mark said softly.

"Shut the fuck up!"

"Shutting the fuck up."

Mark rose from his chair, and Doug assumed he was going to follow after Terry. Instead, he walked round to where Doug was sitting, stood behind him, and reached out with both hands. He placed them on Doug's shoulders as if about to massage the mounds of knotted muscle standing out clearly under the black T-shirt.

"Don't."

Mark waited for a second but left his hands where they had been on either side of Doug's thickly corded neck, and gripped more firmly than before.

"I said don't!" And Doug shrugged them off violently, surging to his feet to face the other man.

"You need to chill out, man."

"Don't talk to me like..."

Mark ignored him, stepping in closer until their bodies were practically touching. "I think we both know what helps you to relax." He slid both arms around the stocky, smaller man and kissed him hard on the mouth, his tongue forcing itself past the instinctive resistance. When they finally broke apart it was hard to tell whether it was because Mark had withdrawn or Doug had pushed him off. Mark was smiling broadly. Doug was breathing heavily, his face distorted by a confusion of emotions.

"Don't ever..." Doug began, but for a second time, his words were cut off, this time by Mark swiftly reaching out to grab the crotch of his jeans. He squeezed gently and grinned, showing his teeth. "You are one huge little guy, you know?" He squeezed again, not so gently. "And getting huger! C'mon." He leaned in, looking to kiss Doug again. "We both know you want it."

"Not...not like this."

Mark laughed. "Listen to yourself, man. You're sounding like some nervous schoolgirl. We both know you're definitely not that."

He stepped forward, and Doug automatically stepped back. Behind him, a chair caught Doug in the back of his legs, and he fell back into it. Mark was instantly on top of him, sitting on his lap, looking down into his face. "Nice," he murmured as he ground his arse down hard into Doug's crotch. The older man cried out helplessly at the pressure on his hardening cock, and Mark whistled in pleasure at the sensation of the swelling member under his buttocks. He leaned down and fastened his mouth again on Doug's, silencing the cries, working the man's mouth with his tongue. Pinned to the chair, Doug struggled at first. But as Mark mined his mouth and slowly gyrated his arse on Doug's stiff cock, Doug's struggles gradually slowed then stopped, and he was returning the kiss as passionately as it was being given. His hips strained up under the younger man's weight as if they could thrust his already painfully full erection up through both sets of jeans and directly into Mark's eager, hot fuck hole.

With a gasp, Mark drew his head back to look down at the man he was straddling. Slowly, he dragged his arse heavily from side to side on Doug's lap, frotting the pinioned cock beneath him, making Doug moan uncontrollably. When the pitch of Doug's wordless exclamations changed, abruptly rising as the man was pushed closer and closer to his climax, Mark jumped up, looking down at him and massaging his own iron erection. Both men breathed as heavily as if they had run a race.

With another of his wolfish grins, Mark knelt, pushing the seated man's thighs apart roughly. His fingers went for the zipper of the jeans that were standing out under Doug's massive excitement. "No," Doug gasped. Mark laughed softly and ignored him, pulling the zipper all the way down, teasing apart first the denim of the jeans, then the vent in Doug's boxers, his fingers seeking their stiff prize. Working against both the narrowness of the trouser opening and the thickness and rigid resistance of the cock, Mark finally drew Doug's swollen meat out into the open. Doug watched wordlessly with horrid fascination, as if unable to do anything to stop what was happening to him. Mark leaned down and nuzzled the cock, dragging the stubble of his chin across its exquisitely sensitive, purple head, and making Doug hiss sharply before licking it gently. "No," Doug whispered again, his hands clenched into tight fists. Still paying no heed, Mark leaned in still further, opened his lips, and took the full length of Doug's thick, hard dick deep into his mouth.

Instinctively, Doug's hips rose, but Mark used both hands to shove him back down, square onto the chair, even as he pressed his face harder into Doug's lap. He deep-throated the seated man, working him with tongue and lips as Doug squirmed and moaned. Up against such a determined erotic assault, it was only seconds before Doug was brought again to the brink of climax. His head thrown back, his mouth open in a silent bellow of release, Doug's whole body tensed as he prepared to spectacularly shoot his load.

"Hey, you guys. Anyone know where Terry...? Oh, shit! Sorry! I... I... Shit! Sorry!"

His focus momentarily broken, Mark's head bobbed in too far.

Doug's mushroom cockhead banged into the back of his throat and he reflexively gagged on the thick shaft. Coughing and spluttering, he pulled back, leaving Doug sitting open-mouthed, eyes shut tight, and his dripping cock punching the air way out beyond his lap for the world to see. Or at least, in this case, for Baz to see. The boy stood rooted to the spot just inside the doorway, mouth wide open, and eyes, unfortunately for Doug, likewise.

"I..." said Baz. Then, "I..." again, before he turned and fled the room.

Mark laughed out loud then turned and made as if to kneel back down beside Doug and complete his work. Doug shakily stood up, his cock still jutting out from the gap in his jeans, and roughly pushed Mark back. Mark laughed again. "Oh, come on! You can't tell me you don't want me to finish you." He pointed to the still practically perpendicular evidence.

"I don't know you," Doug said, the words seeming to come out only with an effort. "I thought maybe you and I... I thought you were different. I was wrong. Again. You are a complete and utter...."

Mark raised a hand. "Save it, baldy! I was just trying to make a point."

Doug's eyes narrowed in bewilderment. "A point?"

"Not to you. To...me, maybe." He laughed again, as if at a private joke. "Yeah, to me." Then he also narrowed his eyes. "Funny thing is, I'm not sure now if I have made it or not." He walked over to the door, poked his head out and called out, ironically, "Thanks, Baz!" Leaning against the lintel, he looked back into the room at Doug, first at his face, then down to his still magnificent and still very visible hard-on. With an effort, he returned his gaze to Doug's face. He sighed. "Love to stay and finish the job, but I think my work here is done. Anytime you want me to lather the trouser snake, you just let me know, all right?" And with a blown kiss, he was gone.

Doug stood staring at the door, his mind a raging confusion. "Bastard! Shit! Fucker!" he spat under his breath while forcing his treacherous erection back into his jeans. His dick under control once more, or at least out of sight, Doug went in search of Baz.

He found him sitting outside the pension. For a moment, Doug simply looked down at him, but when the lad continued to stare fixedly at the wall of a house across the way, as if the plain brickwork was one of the most fascinating things he had ever seen, he forced himself to sit down by Baz's side. Immediately, Baz went to get up and leave with some muttered apology.

"No! Don't go!" Doug hesitated. He was aware that, even for him, his tone had been sharp, much sharper than it had any right to be at that moment. "Please," he added with no small effort. With obvious reluctance, but with a trained response to doing whatever Doug told him to do, Baz sat back down on the bench.

The two men sat there as the minutes ticked by, both now staring at the masonry across the way.

"Look, it happened," said Doug abruptly.

"Look, I'm sorry I barged in like that," Baz said, at exactly the same time.

They stopped. Baz gave a short laugh. Doug didn't. "Go on," he said gruffly.

"No, it's okay. After you."

Doug took a deep breath and repeated what it had cost him a huge effort to say the first time. "It happened, right?"

"Right!" said Baz, giving an appreciative whistle. "Oh yeah, it really happened all right. No doubt about that. Large as life and twice as ugly, as they say. It was really..." He tailed off, Doug's sour expression making it clear that no further comment was needed. "Right."

"Right."

They resumed their inspection of the brickwork.

"I suppose," Baz continued, "I just hadn't expected it, y'know? I mean, not that I often do expect to walk into a room and see two guys giving... doing... y'know. What it was you were doing." In the corner of Doug's mouth a small muscle was twitching, the only outward sign of just how hard he was gritting his teeth. "I just hadn't expected to see *you* doing it." Doug turned his head to glare at him and Baz flinched, a reaction that would only have seemed disproportionate to someone who didn't know Doug. "I mean, not that I don't assume you *do* do it. I'm sure you do, all the time. Right? I mean, you're only human, right? Right? It's just..." Desperately aware he was digging a hole for himself that he soon might have no hope of escaping from, Baz struggled to salvage some sense from his nervous babbling. "I suppose I just hadn't expected you to be doing it with *him*." He stopped, nervously searching Doug's face for signs that he wasn't actually going to be chewed up and spat out. "I mean, it was Mark, wasn't it?"

"Of course it was Mark. You going blind or daft?"

"Yeah, right. Mark. 'Course it was. I couldn't really see from that...angle."

Doug harrumphed disbelievingly.

"It's just that I thought..."

"What?"

Momentarily, Baz looked as if he were considering something, but then he shook his head. "Never mind."

He looked strangely crestfallen, almost sad, and very unexpectedly, Doug felt a pang of regret that he'd felt so harshly about the boy. Baz had done nothing wrong. It had been he, Doug, who'd been acting like a teenager in heat. "Look..." It was his turn now to struggle for the right words. Apologies were not something that had ever come easy to him. "It's not your fault. You're young. You don't know how these things go."

To his amazement, the words that had been meant to placate Baz seemed to ignite a sudden anger in him. "I don't know how these things go? I'm too young?" he said incredulously, his face flushing an indignant scarlet. "Of course I know how they go. I'm not a bloody kid. For Pete's sake, what is wrong with you guys?"

For a moment, Doug struggled, torn between amusement at the mildness of Baz's swearing and puzzlement at that reference to 'guys'. But there had been genuine distress there, too, in Baz's outburst, though Doug had no idea where it had come from or why it had erupted now. "You're... right," he said awkwardly. "You're not a kid."

"And neither's Terry," Baz snapped.

Doug was completely lost again. How had Terry got dragged into this? "I...know?" he said uncertainly.

"Then why do you keep treating him like he is?"

"Because... Because...." *Why am I even answering him? I don't owe him any explanations. It's none of his business. Tell him to fuck off and stop barging into rooms without knocking. Tear him a new hole and tell him to shove his head up it. Tell him...* "Because I want to protect him," he found himself saying out loud. "Because… he's like a son to me."

"Okay," said Baz, as if between them they'd just discovered the answer to one of the world's most difficult mathematical puzzles.

"Okay what?" Doug demanded, completely at sea.

"What do you want to protect him from?"

How to explain? How to explain? "Everything!" he said, throwing his hands up.

"And have you any idea how crazy that makes you sound?"

Doug felt like he had in his wrestling days when, on very rare occasions, he'd been caught off guard by a forearm smash or drop kick in the ring that had left him stunned and reeling against the ropes. How the fuck did this boy, this *boy,* get off calling him crazy? Where did he get the balls? But all too quickly his own admission of only a minute previously came back to him. Baz wasn't a boy, was he? And…he was right. It did sound crazy. To anyone who didn't know. "You…don't understand," he said, and it sounded lame even to him.

"Of course I don't." The anger in Baz's voice was already fading so that he was now talking almost gently to this scary man. "And neither does Terry. That's the problem." Just for a second, it looked as if Baz was about to rest a hand on Doug's arm but, clearly thinking better of it, he forced both of his hands into his lap and held them there as if worried they might try such a foolish manoeuvre a second time. He took a deep breath. "It's all to do with what happened with you and Terry's dad, isn't it?" he asked, the words coming quickly as if he were forcing them out before he could think better of speaking them.

"How did you…?"

Baz waved a hand in the air. "Honestly, if you guys spent more time with your eyes looking up, instead of down at other guys' cocks, you'd have a better idea of what is going on around you."

"What are you…?"

With completely uncharacteristic impatience, Baz waved Doug's mutterings to one side. "I'm right, aren't I? Nod once for yes, twice for no." Doug dumbly nodded once. "At last. Good. So, tell. What happened?"

"I'm not going to tell…"

"Tell me! You won't tell Terry, but you need to tell someone." Baz shrugged his shoulders. "Might as well be me."

Doug stared at the face of the young man he'd known for almost three years now, with whom he'd been travelling in close company for weeks, and realised that he didn't know him at all. He was a cheeky, upstart, know-it-all, brash, nosy, son-of-a-bitch bastard. And...he was right. Everything was spinning out of control. Terry had gone off the rails, and some cocky fucker he hardly knew had ripped Doug's heart out of its hiding place and was kicking it around like a football. If there were anyone he could have talked to, asked for help, it would have been Mae. But she wasn't there. There was only...Baz.

Wondering how it had come to this, but knowing that finally it had, Doug gathered his thoughts and reached for this unlikeliest of lifelines. "It...it was about twenty years ago," he began, uncertainly. And even as he started, he could feel again the appalling, familiar tightness deep in his soul where he had so long ago buried his past, hoping that he would never have to face it again, but knowing one day he would.

It looked like that day had finally arrived.

PART SIX

Chapter One

It had been the biggest adventure of their lives.

And if Doug wondered why Geoff wanted to have it then, less than two months after the birth of his son, Terry, he didn't ask.

They'd both already been wrestling for years. Doug had started after he'd left the merchant navy, which, in turn, he'd joined as soon as he could legally leave his last foster home. Geoff, of course, had been brought up wrestling, the sport having been in his family for literally generations. Grandparents had wrestled in fairground booths, and parents had been wrestlers or promoters under a variety of names. When Doug signed up with the Ryan family their company had simply been known as Power Promotions, without the extra capital letters. (Terry would add those later in an unfamiliar and all too rare burst of creativity.) Mae Ryan and her husband, a former 'world champion', ran it though there was some uncertainty as to which weight division. (Mae would sometimes joke that they weren't sure which world, either.) The then quite sizable roster of wrestlers included one of Doug's uncles plus two cousins from another aunty who were shaping up nicely, as well as a handful of other regular and semi-regular grapplers.

The only non-wrestler in the entire set up had been Geoff's young wife, Liz. Doug never found out for sure just where Geoff and Liz had first met. It definitely hadn't been at a wrestling show—that much he could be sure of. She was a pretty thing, he supposed, which must have been important given that she and Geoff had so little else in common. She seemed to love her husband, and he her, but she had never quite fit in with the rest of the wrestling clan. Although she was never horrid to Liz, Doug could sense that Mae Ryan had reservations about the girl. Natural enough, he supposed, given that she was the first person in decades to come into the family without a wrestling background. However, she very quickly provided the Ryans with the heir to the company they all wanted, and everything seemed good. Power

Promotions had its young prince, pro wrestling in Britain was booming, and, much to his surprise, Doug discovered he'd found the home he had been looking for all of his life.

Yet, one day, Geoff had proposed that they tour Europe. Just he and Doug. Mae certainly hadn't been happy about it, but Geoff wouldn't listen to any arguments. It was almost as if he felt he *had* to get away for a while, to put space between him and the family he'd lived and worked with for all of his life. Even his young wife and their newborn son. And if there was another thing Doug really didn't understand, it was why Liz hadn't protested more. But she hadn't. Geoff had his way, as he usually did, and the two of them left, simply packing their kit and the bare essentials into two holdalls, hopping onto the ferry, and beginning to work their way through the wrestling halls of France and Germany, as years later Terry and his crew would.

At first, it worked. Doug picked up a good deal of useful French and German in the merchant navy and was a natural communicator, or at least, he always managed to get what he wanted using words and a forceful physical presence. To begin with, they'd slept rough quite often, gone hungry a lot of the time, and had to do their share of menial physical labour when the money was really tight and the bouts were few and far between. But slowly the bouts had come. They started in the smallest halls with the poorest promotions, but gradually Geoff and Doug worked their way up the pro wrestling ladder as their reputation spread.

Wrestling individually, but most especially wrestling as the tag team they'd established back home, The Bacchus Brothers, they quickly won over their audiences and began to establish themselves on the European scene. Thanks largely to Geoff's youthful good looks, they mainly played good guys—'blue eyes'. Geoff certainly was the charming, charismatic one who would bound through a hall and up to the ring, shaking hands with all and sundry, and even kissing some of the women who were bold enough to put themselves forward. Doug played the quieter, older 'brother', the one whose dark nature had to be held in check, and who was kept to the path of righteousness and virtue by his good, younger brother, while in turn protecting him from the vicious onslaughts of the various 'heels' they encountered. Yet, as they left the halls after each bout, there were always at least as many 'autograph hunters', sometimes more, who were as eager to press up close to Doug as to Geoff. The requests that were whispered, pressed into hands, or sometimes even shouted were often for a great deal more than a simple name on a piece of paper. It seemed the lure of barely supressed violence that Doug offered was strong, for both men and women.

For the most part, Geoff resisted the approaches of the 'fans', but just occasionally he would leave Doug alone for the night as he went off with one or other of the more insistent young ladies. He never asked Doug what he thought about this lack of fidelity to Liz, and Doug never presumed to comment. If Doug ever noticed that those few girls Geoff did follow home were the ones who bore the strongest resemblance to Liz, he never said.

Doug never went home with any of the fans. His and Geoff's trip abroad had made one thing absolutely clear to him. He was completely and utterly in love with Geoff.

Doug had known and accepted from an early age it was men he was attracted to. That had never been a problem for him. The problem had been intimacy. Throughout his childhood and adolescence, a succession of homes and foster homes, foster parents and foster siblings—here for a while then gone forever—taught him that attachments were fleeting, and their ending always caused pain. So, he learned to avoid them. A roaming life in the merchant navy had been chosen specifically to keep him on the move, to keep him from forming 'relationships' with people that could only ever collapse and cause everyone hurt and misery. And it had provided easy sex, the kind of sex men looked for when they were cooped up on board a ship for months at a time, and it was understood that what happened at sea stayed at sea and would mean nothing to their lives back on land. The fucking then had been rough, casual, unthinking, and it had met his needs and got him through the days and most of the long nights.

When he left the sea, he'd fallen into the life of a wrestler mostly by accident. Drawn by the memories of TV bouts he'd seen that had first made him realise what truly turned him on, he'd started to frequent the halls and other venues where wrestling was put on. His physique and attitude set him apart from the usual punters and drew the attention of a promoter who'd always been on the lookout for burly, brutal men, for his rings and for his bed. Doug started wrestling and quickly found the life of an itinerant grappler a reasonable substitute for a life at sea. It was a life of travelling from town to town, city to city, with plenty of sex and little risk of being asked to share a bed for more than one night.

But then, he signed up for a series of bouts with Power Promotions, and the hard shell he'd built around his heart was cracked with a speed and ease he would never have thought possible. In the Ryans, he found the family he'd never known he'd been looking for. And in Geoff, he found the man to love he'd never known he needed.

Needless to say, Doug had been able to do absolutely nothing about it. Indeed, when Geoff first suggested they tour abroad, just the two of them, even as his heart leaped at the prospect, Doug's head said no. Being alone with Geoff for so long was just asking for trouble.

But he had said yes.

Like most people, but with far more reason, he could refuse Geoff nothing, and the tour had been a personal roller coaster of joy and heartache as the two men worked and wrestled their way through first France and then on into Germany. The early nights when, strapped for cash, they were forced to share not just rooms but a bed were the sweetest and the most painful Doug had ever known. He often lay awake all night, sometimes less than an inch from the man he desired so badly, his back turned to Geoff, terrified of turning over and brushing his partner's side with his uncontrollable erection, listening to his breathing, feeling the warmth of him, but never daring to touch him. Until *that* night.

It had been a swelteringly hot day and a close, sultry evening. Doug and Geoff had wrestled top of the bill as the Bacchus Brothers in a crowded, muggy hall in a small German town. All four wrestlers had so quickly become slick with sweat it was hard for them to grip and hold each other, resulting in several chains of moves failing with almost comic, pantomime-like results. Years later, Doug could still vividly recall standing in that ring next to Geoff, both of them in the Bacchus Brothers trademark gold trunks and boots, and with sweat dripping onto the soiled canvas, raising their clasped hands to the crowd's applause, although whether it was to acknowledge their victory or graciously accept defeat he couldn't remember.

As they were signing autographs at the backstage door, a young woman with large, grey eyes propositioned Geoff, and he quickly went off with her. Doug had been approached by a shrilly eager blonde girl whom he'd pretended not to understand. His attention had been caught by the nervous young lad hanging back from the small crowd of fans, obviously wanting to approach but not having the courage. Doug knew he could have the boy for the asking. All he'd have to do was smile at him. No, all he'd have to do was *look* at him, and the boy would have come to him. But Doug's eyes were drawn to Geoff, the sight of him walking off with the voluble *Mädchen*'s arm round his waist, and when he finally looked round for the boy again, he had gone.

Doug had gone back to their hotel room. They were sharing a room, but with mercifully separate beds. He'd torn his clothes off moodily and dropped naked on top of his bed, sweating again in the night's high humidity. He closed his eyes, exhausted by the heat, by the wrestling, by the constant struggle against his burning desire for Geoff. He wanted to sleep but was tormented by thoughts of Geoff and what he would be doing to that girl. He tried to imagine what it would be like to be her, to be held by Geoff, kissed by him, taken by him. He stretched out on the bed, arms above his head, picturing Geoff standing naked over him, his beautiful long cock that Doug had only ever snatched glances at in the showers, gloriously, unashamedly up, and hard. In his mind, Geoff was climbing onto the bed with him, climbing onto him, the feel of his naked skin on his, not as he knew it in the wrestling ring, but caressing, caring, intimate. Geoff's lips were on his, his tongue in his mouth. Doug moaned, thrusting his hips up into his imagined lover's body, his erect cock thick and hard against his damp belly, wanting the feel of Geoff's hands on his arse, in his arse, working him, readying him for the longed-for cock that he would take deep, deep into himself. "Geoff!"

He opened his eyes, and Geoff was standing over him. He'd been dreaming. Hadn't he? And wasn't this still a dream? But Geoff was clothed now, wearing the jeans and jacket he'd last seen him in when he left with that girl. The bedroom light was off when Doug was sure he'd left it on, and Geoff was lit only by the pale orange light coming through the window from a street lamp outside. He was holding an open bottle of some kind and was looking down at him. The orange-hued shadows made his expression unreadable, but Doug could see his eyes, fixed on his body, unblinking, unwavering. Doug's head swam. He didn't know if this was dream or reality. He didn't know if he cared. He should have been moving, getting up, throwing a cover over himself. Something! Not lying there, his almost painful hard-on in plain sight for Geoff to see at last. He'd never been so hard, or so vulnerable. Doug waited. For Geoff to turn away. For Geoff to shout at him, accuse him. For...what? He didn't know.

But Geoff wasn't moving or saying or doing anything, and if Doug had moved or spoken it would have broken this dream, made it real, and he didn't want that. So he lay, looking up at Geoff looking down.

Without taking his eyes off Doug, Geoff put down the bottle, and began to take off his clothes.

Doug had seen him undress countless times before in numerous changing rooms, but it had never made his cock ache so fiercely, never made his stomach twist into such tight knots. Each item of clothing was removed like a promise, or a threat, until Geoff stood as naked by the side of the bed as Doug had imagined him—only many times more *real*, more desirable—and Doug couldn't help himself. At last, he could gaze long and unashamedly at the cock rising up powerfully from the scrub of honey-blond hair at Geoff's crotch. It was...the most perfect thing he had ever seen. It made him feel strong and weak at the same time. He wanted it.

Hesitantly, as if the distance were miles not metres, Geoff approached the bed. Doug watched, not daring to move, hardly daring to breathe, hardly able to, his heart hammering so rapidly in his chest. At the side of the bed, Geoff stopped momentarily then climbed onto it, throwing one leg over Doug's body, lowering himself onto Doug as smoothly as if they were in the ring and he was going for a pin. Throwing his arms round Doug's shoulders, he buried his head deep into the pillow by the side of Doug's head. At last, his stiffened cock was pressed hard into Doug's. Like a drowning man grabbing for the salvation of driftwood, Doug wrapped his arms tightly around Geoff, burying his face into the other man's brawny shoulder and shoulder-length blond hair to stifle the cry that would have otherwise been torn out of him.

For what seemed to Doug like an eternity, they lay there, each gripping the other tightly, desperately, hardly moving, while between them, like burning iron bars, their aching cocks pressed harder and harder against each other. The sensation shot through their nerves, building to a white-hot intensity that was all but unbearable.

When they could hold back no longer and began fiercely, blindly to thrust into each other's bodies, they came almost together. Streams of hot, white come spasmed from their balls into the dark, hot space between their bellies, running down their sides, and pooling on the mattress under them. Doug smothered his cry of release in Geoff's corded neck, his mouth filled with the other man's hair and flesh and the taste of his sweat. He heard Geoff as he climaxed again and again, pumping his seed into Doug's body. It sounded like sobbing.

Doug had no idea how long they lay there afterwards, still wrapped in each other's arms, while the come slid from their bodies and cooled against their skin. Doug sensed that any movement would spell the end of this moment. The dream would be over; reality would have to return. He never, ever wanted that to happen, but he knew that it must. Then what would happen? Where would he and Geoff go from here? Where could they possibly go?

At long last Geoff stirred. Doug never knew whether he had been sleeping or whether he, too, had lain there, his head a maelstrom of thoughts as Doug's had been. Geoff unwound his arms from around Doug, and pushed himself up from the bed. He padded over to the room's washbasin, and Doug heard the sound of running water as Geoff cleaned himself. He padded back to his own bed, and Doug heard the sound of springs creaking as Geoff lay down on it. Then silence. Doug listened, trying to tell from the sound of Geoff's breathing whether he was falling asleep, but he could hear nothing.

Doug lay there, his come and Geoff's now chilled on his belly, and he watched as the black of night gave way to the grey of dawn. The streetlamp outside turned off, making way for the pale light of a new day. He closed his eyes when Geoff stirred, heard him rise from his bed, pull on his clothes.

"Morning," Geoff said. "Breakfast." And he left the room.

Doug opened his eyes and lay there staring up at the ceiling. He knew then that they would never talk about what had happened.

In the days and weeks that followed, their wrestling successes continued. They moved from town to town, hall to hall. They wrestled together and as a tag team, laughed, joked, talked about everything under the sun as they always had…except for that one night. It had eaten Doug alive.

He still didn't pick up the guys who hung around the halls after bouts. But if Geoff picked up a girl, which he seemed to do more often than ever after that night, Doug would doggedly seek out that town's roughest gay bar or club and screw the brains out of anyone who'd have him. And just as the Bacchus Brothers' wrestling reputation grew, so Doug's reputation as, literally, one mean fucker, spread from town to town. He wasn't looking for love. He shunned closeness that might lead to anything 'meaningful'. The obliteration of thrust and climax was all he looked for. It was an escape, a release in more than the normal sense, and like any drug, the more he used it, the more he needed, and the rougher and harder it had to be. The BDSM scene, so much more visible and accessible here than in stuffy old England, opened its leather-scented arms and welcomed him in. It wasn't the fetishism as such that drew him, though as someone who made his living displaying his body in boots and tight Lycra, he was hardly unaware of its power. And many a young man had breathlessly and hopefully told him that wrestling was 'just bondage without the ropes'. More than that, it was the sheer anonymity and impersonality of the scene he craved. All too quickly, though, even that failed to ease the pain in his heart.

Then he met Jean-Michel Colline.

Chapter Two

Looking back, it was easy to see how inevitable the meeting had been. Doug was a hard wrestler looking for rough sex. Colline was a promoter, but the fights he organised didn't take place in public places. Colline catered for men with special tastes, men who enjoyed watching other men fight, really fight. Men who were turned on by the primal struggle of wrestling...but who had no time for the artificial niceties of rules and safeguards. Men who would pay good money to watch one man ruthlessly bend and twist and rack an opponent until he begged for mercy, then fuck him savagely until he begged again. And men who would pay more for the fighters to go even further.

Colline had 'recruited' Doug himself, challenging the dour Brit in a seedy club specialising in rough sex that Doug wound up in one night. Doug eyed up the comparatively slight man with the mocking smile, reckoned he'd be not much of a challenge but that he would be an easy fuck. Weeks of heartless screwing in the boltholes and backrooms of the towns they had been travelling through had blunted any finer feelings he might once have had, so Doug hardly baulked at all when Colline suggested they wrestle there in just their briefs, in front of the drunken bar crowd.

"I'm not wearing any briefs," Doug growled.

"Then neither shall I," said Colline, and he stripped off there to the raucous approval of the audience. Doug took in the long, quite slender cock that was swelling in anticipation, and the neat, tight little arse that he was going to rip open with his own massive member. He shrugged and pulled down his own trousers.

They wrestled for over an hour in that poky back room on a sticky mat with no ropes, no corner posts, no seconds, and no rounds. Men stood round with litre glasses in one hand and their cocks in the other, pumping frantically as the two wrestlers on the mat thrashed, writhed, sweated, and wrung submission after submission out of each other, even as come from the cheering, whooping wankers around them rained down on their steaming bodies. There was no 'showmanship' there that night. Holds were applied to hurt, and if they didn't at first then they were wrenched and yanked and jerked until they did. Legs were twisted until they felt as if they were coming out of sockets, arms pushed so far up backs that tendons nearly tore, and forearm smashes and throws and drop kicks were delivered with such force they sounded like mallets being smashed into steaks. Doug had no idea what was going through the head of the other man, but for him, finally, he had found what he craved. Here at last in this stinking little glory hole of a 'club' all his heartache and pain could be sublimated in this vicious, savage, no-holds-barred fight for a fuck. Because there was no doubt the loser was going to get fucked right there and then on that grubby mat for all to see. And it was going to be brutal.

Afterwards, Doug would claim Colline had done it because he knew he was finally losing. He was almost certainly right. Doug had trapped the smaller man between his powerful thighs in a killing body scissors and was bearing down on him with all his strength, gasping with the effort of trying to crush the crap out of him and secure the winning submission. It had looked over for Colline, his twisted features making it all too clear how much real pain he was in, how little air he was able to draw into his tortured lungs, and how much real danger there was of his snapping a rib. But with one last heroic effort, he suddenly twisted. Soaked with sweat as they both were, Colline's slickened body slipped round so that with one lightning jab of his hand he was able to shove his fingers right up and into Doug's hairy arse. Lubed by the sweat pouring from both of them, Colline's fingers went deep into his man, jabbing straight and with unforgiving force, smack into Doug's pulsing hot prostate. Doug howled, all thought of crushing his opponent driven out of his head by the wave of primitive sensation. Taking advantage of the fleeting respite, Colline reached round, grabbed Doug's dick with his other hand and pumped hard.

Doug howled again, and in an instant it was all over. Both men were covered with the ropes of come pumped from Doug's cock as Colline wanked his opponent with one hand and thrust through the tightness of Doug's rarely reamed arse with the other. Almost always the top, the unfamiliarity of the sensations ripping through him made Doug howl even louder, so that even the cheering, booing uproar of the greedily watching crowd couldn't completely drown him out.

When it was finally done, the two spent men lay exhausted on the mat, Colline still tangled up in Doug's legs though there was no pressure brought to bear now. They stayed there as the men watching concluded their business, zipped up their trousers, and left, some of them throwing money to the wrestlers who had entertained them so viscerally, the notes falling unheeded onto the sweat- and come-soaked mat.

Colline was the first to rise. He gathered the notes and the coins up, split the money in two and gave one half to Doug. The shithole they were in did not boast showers, and after they'd dressed, Colline bought them a simple meal of meat and potatoes, and he told Doug all about his 'special' fights. Doug ate, drank, and listened. When Colline invited him to join his roster, he agreed without hesitation.

So began the new and final phase of Doug's first European tour. It quickly settled into a regular pattern. He and Geoff would journey to that day's wrestling venue. In the evening they'd wrestle. Afterwards, most often, Geoff would leave with some girl he had picked up. Once a week on average, Doug would go to some dive Colline directed him to, work some guy over until he couldn't take it any more, and then fuck him hard while small, 'exclusive' groups of men watched and threw money and come at them in roughly equal quantities.

At first, Doug had been surprised that Colline was able to fix so many of these matches. The audiences were small, but the men paid well for their extreme entertainment. Doug couldn't really have cared less whether there were people watching him or not, but even he gradually began to recognise some of the faces in the shadows beyond whatever mat he was wrestling on. He came to understand that though some of the watchers might change, there was a core amongst them who were not only prepared to pay good money for their 'entertainment', they were prepared to travel a very long way to get it. As the bouts went on, the opponents grew tougher, and the fighting harder. The money went up, too. One night, Doug broke a man's arm. He still fucked him afterwards, and the prize money that night was twice what he usually got. He didn't care. It wasn't about the cash. By that stage he didn't know what it was about any more. He just knew he needed to do it. The fighting and the fucking, they kept him from thinking about Geoff. Most of the time.

Then the Bacchus Brothers' tour finally brought them to Switzerland, the land of peace and plenty. Colline assured him that his underground fighting network was at its strongest there. Now, his new English friend would have his greatest fights, earn the biggest pay cheques, and become the biggest star in his organisation. "And they are powerful people, my friend," he whispered in Doug's ear, "the men who will come to see you fight here. Make no mistake. The tastes I cater to do not come cheap, but then the men who come to my 'entertainments' do not come poor. It is all one, *non*? Great men do not ascend to positions of power in this world without great...appetites, and a ruthless determination to satisfy them. They are not bothered with petty moralities and concerns about the pain of others. They live to rule, to dominate, to own. And that is why they come to me. The fights I put on embody the way they see the world. They want to see opponents beaten, humiliated, crushed. Fucked! And who doesn't?" Here, he put his arms round Doug's shoulders while he breathlessly went on. "Don't you feel it when you are out there, *mon brave*? The primal rush, not simply of winning, but of *beating* the other man, forcing him to admit your mastery through the strength of your muscles, over and over again, making him scream out his utter submission to your will, owning him in every way one man can own another, and showing it to the world. Doesn't it make you hard as steel, *mon cher*, being the *alpha male*?"

Doug looked at him, insensible to the arm around him or the passion in the other man's voice. "To be honest," he said, "I don't give a shit."

Colline laughed. "*Eh bien! C'est bon. C'est très bon!*" He leaned forward then, lowered his voice, and as he spoke, Doug at long last caught the first sight of the abyss into which he had willingly sleepwalked in his determination to blot out the pain of his life. "Tonight will be your greatest fight yet, *mon brave*. Your opponent is a young man, Ramon, very fast, very...beautiful. He is skilled, yes, but that will mean nothing against your strength and experience. You will beat him."

Doug frowned. He'd never gone into any fight in his life thinking that he would lose. But Colline's certainty here was different. It smacked of the show business of the professional ring, something that had been refreshingly different from the underground fights he'd fallen into, and a world away from the savage philosophy Colline had been spouting so enthusiastically only seconds before.

Seeing Doug's uncertainty, Colline laughed again and put one finger on Doug's lips to silence him before he could speak. "It is not enough that you beat Ramon," he said softly. "You will *crush* him. Completely. The men watching this match do not believe in...half measures. They want to see only one man walk away. *Tu comprends?*"

Finally, Doug felt something pierce the ice wall he had built up around his feelings. With a dawning sense of horror, he regarded the man who was whispering his vicious, sick thoughts and requests into his ear. "I... I don't..." He struggled to articulate his thoughts. "You mean...you want me to..."

Colline gently stroked the side of Doug's face. "My clients would be disappointed if they did not get to see the...'sport' they enjoy. Very disappointed." Colline's hand stopped stroking and stayed where it was, possessively, on the side of Doug's face as he looked in his eyes. Doug had never appreciated how cold those eyes were, and didn't know how on earth he had never noticed it before. "And so would I," Colline concluded, and he slapped the side of Doug's face lightly and laughed. "Until tonight." And he kissed Doug on the cheek.

Dazed and sickened, Doug stumbled back to the *pension* he and Geoff were staying in that night. Geoff wasn't there, so he drew the curtains and lay on the bed, his thoughts a dark storm in his head. Colline's threat had been clear, and Doug had seen enough of the men Colline worked with to know he could carry it out. Hell, he'd become one of those men! And that was what really devastated Doug. What struck him to the core of his being was that, for at least one moment, he had seriously considered doing what Colline asked. Why not? Life was pain and suffering, fuck or be fucked. Colline was right: fighting for him was just a reflection of that. This Ramon knew what he was letting himself in for, didn't he? He presumably thought he had a chance of winning, of being the *alpha male*, the man who would actually walk away from the fight. Even though Colline clearly didn't want him to.

Feverish, Doug got up from the bed and went to the washstand to splash cold water on his face. Standing there, thinking about what it would mean to 'crush' this young lad in front of a baying, ejaculating audience, he looked deeply into his eyes in the mirror over the basin. Had they always been like that, he wondered. Had his eyes always looked like Colline's?

When Geoff returned, he found Doug completing his packing. "I'm leaving," he said.

Geoff closed the door and stood with his back to it. "Not until you finally tell me what's been going on," he said calmly.

Doug gaped at him. "Me! Tell you! *Finally?*" Geoff stood impassive in the face of his fury. His defences shattering all around him, Doug looked at this man he adored, for whom he would have done anything, because of whom he had nearly lost everything, and he knew it was all over. "I love you!" he gasped. "I...I love you!" He stumbled forward, one step, two, and then he fell into Geoff's arms. Geoff hugged him, took him back to the bed, and cradled him as Doug told him everything. For only the second time in his life, he cried like a baby.

When he was done, Geoff just held him silently for long minutes, a time that Doug would forever cherish as the most precious in his life, more precious even than that other time when they had made love because now Geoff *knew*. Finally, Geoff spoke. "Guess we'd better go, then." And he rose to look for his bag.

Doug gazed at him. "But, the tour... I mean, I know I've screwed up, but you... It's going so well. You don't have to..."

Geoff looked at him, sighed, and shook his head. "You're such an idiot, y'know? We're brothers, yeah? We're the Bacchus Brothers."

Doug shook his head. "But that's not real. It's...it's a lie."

Geoff knelt in front of him and took both of his hands in his. For one wild second Doug thought he was going to kiss him, but he didn't. "Not to me it isn't," he said, and went back to his bag.

They'd nearly made it.

Colline caught up with them just outside Calais. Five men, two of them guys Doug had wrestled for Colline, ambushed them as they left their hotel to catch their ferry. Doug never knew what their intentions were: maybe if they'd just taken their licks Colline would have been happy to leave them in hospital. They might even have still been able to wrestle afterwards. Maybe. But Doug had listened to his impassioned, poisoned words, and more importantly, he had looked into his eyes. He didn't believe that. He believed that he and Geoff were fighting for their lives. So they did. And that was how Geoff had died, with his head open and bleeding, cradled in Doug's lap, as Doug wept openly for the third and very last time in his life, and swore he would kill Colline for what he had done.

Chapter Three

"Shit!" Baz held up his hand in hurried apology as Doug brought the story of his disastrous European trip to an end. "Sorry, man! That wasn't what I meant to say. It's just that I never had any idea! I mean…"

"Shit," agreed Doug dourly.

Baz looked around him dazedly as if trying to bring their surroundings back into focus after the tale he had heard. He clearly wanted to ask for more, eager to know the details of that terrible fight, to know…what had happened after that. He stopped when he saw Doug's face. Telling this tale had been like tearing out something rooted deeply inside him. But Baz had to know. "What…what happened? In the end? Did you…go to the police?"

"What do you think?"

"Right. So, no police?"

"No."

"So, did you…?"

"Did I see Colline again? Yes."

There was a long pause. "And?"

Doug looked at him, straight in the eye. Baz could hold the stare for only a few seconds before looking away. Doug nodded once to himself as if getting the response he expected.

They sat as the morning gave way to midday. People came and went, and the world went on as if there weren't people like Colline or even Doug in it.

"You should have told Terry this," Baz said finally.

"I don't know why I've told you, let alone him!"

"You *needed* to tell someone."

"Who died and made you fucking Oprah Winfrey?"

"That would have to be Oprah Winfrey, wouldn't it? But she hasn't, and I'm not. Though I am a lot smarter than everybody around here gives me credit for!"

"Yeah," said Doug, "I guess you are." Then he mumbled something so quietly Baz couldn't quite catch it.

"You what?"

"I said thank you," Doug barked with a volume that made Baz jump back. "What, you want me to shout it from the fucking rooftops? I think...I think you were right. Just talking...about things... Getting it out of myself after all this time, it feels...better. I've been letting what happened to me and Geoff affect the way I've thought about things. Terry's...been right all along. That was a long time ago. A different world. I've got to let it go. I've got to let...Terry go." He drew himself up on the bench and attempted what was for him a smile. "He's a grown man. He knows what he's doing. He's not going to get himself into the kind of trouble I did."

"Yeah," said Baz thoughtfully. "Right."

He didn't look as if he believed a word of it.

☆☆☆

Terry hurt.

Carefully he took a deep breath in and then let it out slowly. He looked up and to the left, the right, and to the handcuffs still locked around both wrists. He took another breath. Yeah, still hurting.

But fuck! It was a *good* hurt.

"I think you can get these off me now," he said.

Looking down at him from where he was standing next to the bed, as naked as he was, Yves smiled. "*D'accord. Pardon.* I shouldn't have kept you like that for so long. I was just, shall we say, transfixed by the sight of you." He leaned down to unlock the cuffs at Terry's wrists. As he bent over Terry's face, Terry raised his head and kissed his nipple. Yves gave a throaty chuckle.

"That," said Terry, rubbing his wrist, "feels better." He wasn't just referring to the freedom from bondage.

He'd arrived at Yves's place incandescent after his argument with Doug. It had taken a good ten minutes before Yves could talk him down enough to be able to coherently share his outrage. Yves had sympathised with him, but also tried to put forward Doug's point of view, tried to make the lad see that the older man was only looking out for him. Still enraged, Terry had resisted and raged on about his surrogate father's pig-headedness and narrow-mindedness until Yves sighed and gave up and leaned in and kissed the lad, stopping his stream of invective with his tongue. Terry's response very quickly drove all further rational, and irrational, thoughts from his head.

In Yves's bedroom, Terry was surprised neither by the sumptuousness nor by the handcuffs dangling so obviously from the bedposts. Given what they'd done that first meeting it was hardly a revelation. He was surprised when Yves held them out with an arch smile and an obvious invitation for him to wear them. He hesitated only a moment. *Why not?* Yves had allowed himself to be tied up on their first meeting, and hadn't he let himself be lashed to a cross in a German dungeon only fairly recently? Terry winced slightly and moved on from that memory. "Okay," he said, lying back on the bed and stretching his arms out and up. "*Bon,*" he added, and Yves laughed as he bent over him and cuffed him to the bedposts before running his mouth and tongue all over his bare, exposed skin, making Terry arch and moan in expectant pleasure.

Left to his own devices, Terry would have galloped headlong to a much needed, stress-relieving climax just as quickly as he could have. As ever, and this time with much more justification, Yves was in control, and he made it clear that he was in no hurry with his handsome young 'captive'. First, he took his time kissing and licking, what seemed to Terry, every inch of his skin until his whole body was tingling with desire. Then, he teased Terry with his cock, ball sac and arse, frotting them over his body and face, sliding down the boy's body. Teasing Terry's raging erection and twitching arsehole with skilful use of tongue and fingers quickly had him crying out lustily and bucking energetically on the bed, pulling helplessly at the implacable handcuffs.

"Fuck!" Terry gasped. "You're giving me blue balls, man!"

For just a second Yves stopped, giving Terry a startled look before glancing down at the golden, hairy cobs he had been massaging with his tongue. "*Comment?*"

Terry laughed. "It means I want to come!" He yanked on his cuffs. The huge wooden bed was so solid it didn't even shake.

Yves grinned. "Ah." He returned to his work. "Not yet," he said, his voice coming muffled from deep in Terry's crotch.

When the dangerous tightness at the base of Terry's sac and the shortness of Terry's breathing became all too obvious, Yves finally sat back up and away from the boy. He squatted there between Terry's open legs, rubbing his hands up and down the subtle hairiness of the lad's inner thighs, gazing at his chiselled body, his handsome young face, his muscular arms stretched up and cuffed over his head. With a crooked smile, he took hold of both Terry's ankles, lifted his legs up, and moved in. Terry didn't try to resist as his ankles were pushed easily up to his wrists, and Yves was straddling his open arse. One thing you had to be as a pro wrestler was flexible. "Yeah," he breathed heavily. "Do it!"

But still Yves teased him, sliding his pre-come-lubed cockhead over and over Terry's tight fuck hole, ramming its crown into the pulsing softness beneath the ball sac, but never piercing the aching sphincter ring. "Do it! Fucking do it!" Terry cried out over and over again, begging the man to ream him hard and fast and end the screaming demand in his arse.

"*Non!*" Yves said. And just at the very minute, when Terry had known that, even without being fucked, even without any more physical contact from Yves, he was going to blow his load right up into the fucking prick-tease's devilishly handsome features, Yves sat back once again.

For long moments, he gazed at the vision of bound beauty before him: the beautifully erect cock, its head practically touching the tight little whorl of a navel on the taut stomach heaving up and down to the rhythm of Terry's rapid breathing; Terry's eyes, screwed shut tightly as he fought the muscular spasms sweetly tormenting his pulsing perineum; Terry's blond hair, sweat-plastered across his forehead; the circlets of metal around Terry's wrists.

Finally, Terry knew he had beaten back the climax he wanted so very, very badly, and he could let out, in one go, the huge lungful of air he had been holding. He opened his eyes to look up at Yves who was laughing silently down at him. "Why...?" Terry began, and then stopped. His mouth was dry as sand. He swallowed and tried again, "Why didn't you fuck me? Why didn't you let me come?"

Yves went to lean forward and stroke him but then pulled up as if all too aware of what that could lead to. "Because we need you full of...how shall we say...vim and vigour for tonight."

"Tonight?" Terry frowned, finding it hard to concentrate on anything other than the lithe man sitting on his muscular haunches between his legs, so close and yet so untouchable because of the handcuffs. *Every fucking inch of him looks so fucking fuckable.* All too quickly, he felt his ball sac pulling up again into his crotch, and he forced himself to focus on Yves's words.

Yves leaned forward and whispered dramatically, "For the fight." He reclined on one elbow, reached out and touched, with the very tip of one finger, just one curl of the honey blond hair that curled at Terry's crotch. Terry hissed and shifted on the bed. Edged to the very brink of climax, even this slight teasing was almost unbearable. "Actually, *sur ce sujet,* talking about that, I have a small surprise for you, Terry."

"Yeah?" Terry gasped, less than half his mind on Yves's words, most fixed firmly on what Yves was doing with his finger, trying not to think about what he wanted that finger to do.

"*Oui.* Well, two, actually. One—" and he gave the smallest tug on the blond curl that drew a cry from the teased boy "—there will be an audience."

Terry lifted his head slightly. "An audience?" He wasn't sure if he had heard correctly.

"*Oui.*"

"But I thought you said we were filming this, for streaming on the Internet."

"*Oui, c'est vrai.* You are right. But that does not mean we should not invite an audience. They add *ambiance, n'est-ce pas?* Atmosphere. And I have many loyal...followers who will be very, very interested in seeing new young talent like you. And besides—" and he gave another tug of the coarse hair "—they were particularly interested when they found out who your opponent was going to be."

Terry blinked, longing with every atom of his body for Yves to take his hand to his cock and vigorously pump out, there and then, the gargantuan spunk load he could feel filling his balls to the point of explosion. "Who?" he made himself ask.

"C'est moi!" Yves took his hand away from Terry's crotch and held both arms out as if displaying for one last time his beautiful body: sharply defined pecs and abs, tapered waist, sinewy arms. "Me!"

Chapter Four

It was early evening when Doug came across Mark in the *pension* hallway. "Thought you'd be with Terry filming his star bout," he growled.

Mark shook his head. He didn't look too pleased. "Nah. Yves said he didn't need me for this shoot."

Doug snorted. "I'll bet," he muttered under his breath.

The two men stood in the sparsely decorated hallway. It was Mark who made the first move. "Look, I've got to..." he said, making as if to walk past Doug.

"Wait!" Doug held his hand up to stop the other man. But he almost immediately dropped it, and said, "Wait," again, moderating his tone so that it sounded less like a command, almost like a request.

Mark stopped and looked at him, not bothering to disguise his impatience.

"I've been doing some thinking lately," Doug said slowly, "and some talking." The words were hard for him to say, but not as hard as they would have been before his unexpected session with Baz. As he had said, it was time to move on. Maybe even to move on with someone else. "I'd like to talk...with you."

Mark stared at him, saw the naked need in his eyes, the difficult reaching out that was costing this man so much. And he laughed. "Thanks, Dougie boy," he said, "but no thanks."

The pain of the rejection was much worse than Doug had expected. *This is what happens when you leave yourself exposed,* a small voice cried out in his head. *This is what happens when you let someone in.* But another part of him, less vocal but somehow all the stronger for that, was pushing against the pain, driving him on. "I don't understand..." he began.

"Right! You don't understand," Mark snapped, cutting through his words and holding up his hand to forestall any more. "And maybe one day you will, and maybe one day you won't, but d'you know what? I don't give a shit. This tour's nearly over now. Everyone's got what they came for. Everyone's happy. If you're not then that's just your damn problem, and you've got to live with it."

Doug's shoulders slumped. "You're a cold bastard!" he said in a low voice.

Mark opened his mouth to reply to the accusation but abruptly stopped, paused as if considering. "No I'm not," he said at last, his words measured, careful. "You're the one who treats everyone as if they're squaddies and you're some kind of sergeant major. You're the one who gripes and moans and makes everyone tiptoe around you as if they're walking on eggshells in case you get one on you. You're the one who treats Terry like a kid when it's fucking obvious he's a grown man. No." Mark jabbed a finger at Doug to punctuate his words. "You're the one who's cold, man. And when this is all over, I want you to keep well away from...me."

Doug stood, struggling to take in the words. "How... how can you...? After..."

"After what? After I watched you treat everyone like shit for gone two months? Or after I watched you bugger a pair of German leather queens in a backroom dungeon?"

Doug slowly shook his head. He literally couldn't understand. Something was wrong and he couldn't work out what, and his head seemed actually to be ringing.

"Aren't you going to answer that?" Mark asked sourly.

Belatedly, Doug realised that the ringing was real. It was his mobile. But only members of the POWer posse had this number, and they wouldn't ring unless... He pulled it out of his pocket. "Hello?" He held the phone out in front of him and frowned. "They rang off." It was then he noticed the text message that had been sent earlier. He hadn't noticed the notification sound. Hurriedly he accessed the text.

Mark shook his head in disgust and turned to leave. He halted dead in his tracks at the strangled sound from Doug.

Doug was looking in alarm at the small screen of the phone. When he looked up at Mark, his face was ashen. "It's Terry," he said. "He's in trouble."

☆☆☆

"Nervous?"

Terry jumped slightly. He hadn't noticed Yves creep up behind him until he'd felt his breath on his neck and heard his words in his ear. "Funny enough, yeah, I am." He turned back to the small gap at the side of the curtain covering the entrance to the mat room.

Yves gave a small laugh and a small lick of Terry's neck that sent the boy's skin tingling. "Good."

Terry pulled himself back from the covered door to face Yves. Both of them were ready to wrestle. At Yves's insistence, Terry was wearing sheer white trunks and matching boots. In the absence of a matching ring top, he wore a simple white T-shirt cut high over the shoulders to show his developed delts to their best advantage. Yves was in black: black tights, long, black, shiny patent leather boots, and an old-school black dressing gown.

Yves reached out, wrapping his arms around Terry's taut waist and pulling him in. Kissing him deeply, he swayed slightly from side to side so the thick towelling of his dressing gown rubbed across the front of Terry's trunks and roused the slumbering snake within. Terry pushed back half-heartedly. "Hey," he protested reluctantly, "don't want to make my enthusiasm too obvious too soon. Don't want to shock the punters."

Yves gave a low chuckle. "There is very little we could do that would shock these...punters."

Terry glanced back at the covered door, already beginning to suspect that was true. There was something...odd about the crowd gathering out there, though 'crowd' was hardly the right word. *A select, invited audience*, Yves had said, which was fair enough. Terry had played to practically microscopic audiences in chilly English halls during winter, and Yves's private studio was only a small set–up. But, that wasn't all.

"They're so quiet," he whispered, automatically lowering his voice to match. Normally, punters at wrestling venues weren't known for their respectful attendance on wrestlers. Conversations, good-natured discussions, even out and out arguments were often conducted at full volume right across halls, sometimes even during wrestling matches. But this lot... If he strained, Terry thought he could occasionally catch a murmured word, a cough, a slight rustle of movement. Otherwise...nothing. And they weren't waiting for the wrestlers. It was as if the wrestlers were waiting for them. Or for something.

"Anticipation!" Yves said. "They are looking forward to something special." He kept his hands on Terry's narrow hips but stepped back to look at him. "We must oblige them, *non*? We must not let them down."

Terry gave a short, nervous laugh. "I'll try to do my best."

Yves's smile faded as he continued to look at Terry, his expression harder, colder. "*Non,* Terry. You must do more than *try*. Tonight you will fight as you have never fought before. Tonight will be a true test of man versus man. There will be no 'sportsmanship', no play-acting. No limits!"

Terry stepped back so that Yves's hands fell to his sides. "What, like, are you saying this is going to be NHB or something? That's not something we talked about. I'm not sure I'm up for that."

Yves laughed again. A small, hard sound. "I think you are up for what we will do tonight, *mon brave*. Little by little, step by step, you have been, how shall we say, prepared." He reached out. "Mark. Stefan. Dieter. Kurt. *Et moi*." As he listed the names he rested a finger for each one on Terry's shoulder so that with the last he had his whole hand resting possessively on the boy.

"What...what do you mean?" Terry tried to make sense of what Yves was saying. Yves knew Mark, of course he did. Mark had told them that. But how did he know about Stefan? And how the hell did he know about Dieter and Kurt? And what did he mean, *prepared?* "I don't think..." he began, but his words were cut off by one of the men Yves had introduced as 'technicians' entering the room, walking up to Yves and whispering something in his ear.

Yves nodded once, and the man scuttled away again. "*Bon.* We are ready." He squeezed the shoulder his hand was resting on. It was a sudden, hard pressure with little of comfort or reassurance in it. He was smiling, but his teeth were showing, and his eyes glittered. He extended a hand towards the entrance to the fighting area. "Shall we? After you?"

☆☆☆

They'd expected the concierge to make more of a protest, at least to ask just why two men, one of them so obviously angry, were demanding access to one of his grubby little rooms. But at Doug's demand, the man handed over the key with suspicious ease, and Doug and Mark wasted no time in asking him why. They barrelled through the dingy, underlit corridors of the fleapit Terry's text had directed them to, and without knocking, unlocked and barged into the room he had identified. It was empty.

Doug stood in the doorway, scanning the room anxiously. From behind him, Mark shoved his way in to stop and look around: a bed, a bedside table, a washstand that looked as if anyone using it might come away grubbier than when they had started. "You sure this is the right place?"

Wordlessly, Doug shoved the mobile into his hands as he continued to look around the room, as if he could somehow force Terry out of hiding through the pressure of his eyes alone. Mark scrolled to the most recent message:

Done it again. Big time. Help!!!

The address and room number that followed were undoubtedly those of the room they were now in. "Okay. So what...?" Mark stopped, suddenly noticing the direction of Doug's gaze. The bedside table.

Doug was on it before Mark could move. The slim, expensive laptop was completely out of place in this cheap room. It was still warm to his touch as he picked it up, and it sprang into immediate life the instant his finger touched the touchpad. A picture bloomed on the screen. A POWer publicity photo from a couple of years ago: Terry looking absurdly young in his wrestler's gear, red speedos, and white leather boots with red flashes, his arms out as if inviting the viewer to lock up with him even as his roguish grin at the camera suggested he wouldn't really hurt anyone. Doug sat on the bed, the computer in his lap, and clicked on, finding more pictures. Mark stood on the other side of the bed, leaning forward so that he could see over Doug's shoulder.

219

More photos of Terry. A few publicity shots, the later ones from the last shoot they had done. Then shots from bouts back in England. Doug recognised the first lot: they were shots POWer fans, such as Duncan, had taken and posted on the infrequently updated POWer website. But then followed a series from that bout against 'Nasty' Nick Norris, the last one before Nick had supposedly left the wrestling game. All of them showed Terry on the receiving end of Nick's moves, grimacing in pain from backhammers, leglocks, and backbreakers, his hot young body stretched and spread and splayed for the audience's pleasure.

Doug's stomach clenched as those photos came to an end, and there followed a series of shots of Terry taken since their arrival in Europe. Most were of Terry in action, usually selling the anguish of some opponent's hold. But one or two had been taken outside the ring: Terry smiling as he got out of their minibus, saying something to Baz as they sat at a café table, miming a huge belly as he pointed to Jonesy tucking into yet another Big Mac. They were not, Doug realised with a sick feeling, random. They were in a very specific order. They traced their journey from their arrival in France, through Germany, and on into Switzerland. Doug stopped. The picture on the screen now was from that morning. It showed him and Terry arguing. He saw again the anger on the young man's face, so like Geoff in that moment of pig-headedness, and he saw his own face. He blinked. He looked so... brutal. So thuggish. So... old. Was that what he looked like to Terry? When had he become that person? Caught between dismay at the image in front of him and fear of what was to follow, Doug hesitated with his finger over the touch pad. With a deep breath, he tapped it.

Terry and Yves. A couple of pictures of the two of them wrestling together in that first bout after their arrival. And then two more, close-ups of that series of bear hugs, the pictures framed so that at the centre of each were the wrestlers' solid erections straining the Lycra as they ground their hips into each other.

Then Terry and Yves in bed, from two different occasions at least. Yves choking Terry. Terry choking Yves. Terry handcuffed, his handsome face twisted in a grimace as Yves apparently fucked his tight arse.

Terry on the St Andrews Cross. Doug flicked through those quickly, heart racing. There were none of him and Dieter and Kurt, none showing what he had done after Terry had been rescued. But what followed wiped away any slight feeling of relief he might have had about that.

Terry and Mark. And Stefan.

From behind him there was an odd sound, like a yelp of surprise bitten off. Doug ignored it as he grimly clicked through the pictures of the German three-way. "I... I didn't know," said Mark from behind him. Doug ignored him and clicked on until he came to one picture where he stopped and sat, staring. "I mean," Mark said, his voice strangely hoarse, "I didn't know they'd be used...like this." The picture Doug had stopped on showed Terry, tight arse in the air towards the camera, sucking off Stefan while Mark twisted the German boy's arm up way behind his back in a cruel backhammer. Mark was looking straight at the camera, grinning like a loon, and with his free hand he was making a thumbs-up gesture to the lens.

With cold, forced calmness, Doug put the laptop down, slowly rose from the bed, and turned to face Mark. Mark raised his hands, holding them out in front of him in a defensive gesture. "Now look. Just hang on there a minute!"

"You...didn't...know?" On the screen, the picture of Terry fellating Stefan gave the lie to Mark's words.

"Yeah, yeah, of course I knew. He said he wanted pictures. I thought it was like a kink thing, y'know. A private thing. I didn't know he was going to do something like this! I don't know what the fuck this is all about!"

"I don't believe you," Doug said, and he lunged across the bed, grabbing a handful of Mark's T-shirt in one huge hand and pulling him towards him, the other hand pulled back into the imminent threat of a devastating fist.

"No wait! He's right. He didn't know!" Both men turned in the direction of the shout that came from the door. Baz was standing there. He walked in carefully, hands out, as if wary that a sudden move from him might trigger Doug.

"Told you," said Mark, glaring defiantly at Doug even as the man held him.

"Not all of it, anyway," said Baz, coming to a stop opposite Doug and staring angrily at Mark. "He is, however, a complete tosser who's been dicking us around since day one."

"How did you know we were here?" Doug demanded.

"We followed you. I've...found out some stuff I think you need to know and came back to the B and B just in time to see you tearing off. We followed."

"We?" Doug looked over Baz's shoulder, expecting to see signs of Jonesy or Eric.

"And how did you follow us?" Mark asked suspiciously. "We used the minibus. Did you...?"

From Doug's pocket came the sound of a text message notification. He yanked out the mobile and opened the message. His forehead creased. "I don't get it."

"Give it here." With an assurance that would once have seemed uncharacteristic but now appeared to be par for the course, Baz snatched the phone from Doug. "It's a website address. Why's someone sending you a website address? You've not got internet on this piece of crap, have you?"

"No."

There was a small ironic cough from Mark's direction. When the two men looked up from the phone at him he was pointing at the laptop.

Baz grabbed the computer and dropped down to the bed. "'S got a connection," he muttered as he rapidly opened the search engine and entered the address Doug had been sent. "It's some kind of live feed," he said, replacing it on the bedside table and turning it so they could all see what was on the screen.

"It's a ring."

Baz regarded Mark sourly. "No shit, Sherlock."

The ring they were looking at nearly filled the screen. The camera filming it had been positioned so that they were looking slightly down on it, the classic TV point of view to cover standing and ground work. The only illumination was coming from a bank of lights directly over the matted square that made the space within the ropes as clear as day but threw the audience sitting on the four sides outside into deep shadow. Four rows of featureless black silhouettes, sitting. Waiting.

"Any sound on this thing?"

Baz checked the settings. "It's turned right up." He cocked an ear at the laptop. "If you listen you can hear coughs and movements. It's just...they're so quiet. Doug? Doug!"

In the reflected light of the computer screen, Doug's face had taken on a shocking pallor, his expression drawn. "I know what this is." He looked, stricken, at Baz.

Baz nodded reluctantly. "Yes. Yes, I think it is."

"Would one of you care to tell me what the fuck you are talking about?" Mark demanded. The two men ignored him.

"Colline," Doug said, almost in a whisper.

Baz regarded him levelly. "We both know it can't be Colline. Don't we, Doug?" He held the older man's eyes until Doug looked away. "Right." Baz took a deep breath. "Though, in a way, it is."

"Who...?" Mark began.

Baz ignored him, talking over him to Doug. "It didn't take much research. You or Terry could have found out as much if you'd taken the time to pull your heads out of your arses. Or knew how to use a search engine," he added in a quieter tone. "Yves Montaigne isn't his real name. I mean, c'mon. Hardly a surprise in this game, is it? The surprise is what he's really called. It's Colline. Ricard Colline."

Doug looked physically stunned. "His son?"

Baz shrugged. "Nephew maybe, even cousin possibly, but yes, I'm guessing son. His family's been into wrestling almost as long as the Ryans. Though not exactly in the same way."

With a physical effort Doug tore his eyes away from the laptop screen and faced Mark again. "Did you know this?"

"Know what?" Mark exploded. "I don't know what the hell you people are talking about." Doug moved towards him menacingly, and Mark held his hands up quickly to placate him. "Okay, look. What I told you was true. I contacted Montaigne first. He didn't seem very keen, to be honest. I mean, why should he bother with some two-bit Brit operation?" Doug growled softly and took another step closer. Mark went on hurriedly, "But when I told him it was Chris Bacchus he got interested, very interested. I figured it was because he wanted to get into the kid's trunks." He gave a forced laugh. "I mean, hey, who wouldn't, eh? Who hasn't?"

Doug took another step towards him, but Baz put a hand on his shoulder. "You've been used," he said bluntly to Mark. "Oh, and you're a shit."

"He's been after Terry all along," Doug said almost to himself. "He wants to get him mixed up in the same nasty, vicious scene Colline got me into."

Baz looked miserably thoughtful. "I don't think so, Doug. I don't think this is about Terry. However much Terry might think it is." He looked levelly into the tormented man's face. "I think this is about you. I think it's always been about you."

Doug looked back at this boy who seemed suddenly to be so much wiser than any of them, and gradually, the full import of what he was saying sank in. His mind flew back to that penultimate meeting with Colline, when the insidious 'promoter' had made clear to him just what he wanted him to do to his opponent for his 'special' clients. *It is not enough that you beat him. You will crush him. The men watching want to see you assert your complete and utter mastery of him. And you know there is only one way you can do this.* He snapped back to the present. *Terry!* "We've got to find Terry. Where is that place?"

"I'm assuming it's Montaigne's place. He's got a small farmhouse about three miles from here. Very secluded."

"Come on, then." He jabbed a finger at the screen. "No time to find Eric or Jonesy. It looks like they could start at any minute."

"Whoa there!" Mark demanded. "Hold it right there, short, bald and angry. We're going to go charging in there, just the three of us?" He looked from Doug to Baz and back again. "What? You think I don't care? Okay, I don't get half of what you two are talking about, but it sounds heavy. And...okay, I might have been...misled about one or two things..."

"Bastard!"

"Shithead!"

"Yeah. Right. Okay, topic for another day. But if Terry is in trouble, then I want to help. Right?"

Doug looked at the apparently contrite man as if he could have happily beaten him to a pulp then and there, but finally, he gave a short, sharp nod of his head. "Okay," he said. "The three of us."

"Actually," said a new voice from the doorway, "it's the four of us.

Sorry I've been so long. Got held up by *monsieur le concierge* downstairs. I think he got a bit upset about people dashing around in his charming establishment. Especially ones dressed like me."

Baz, Doug, and Mark turned to face the new arrival.

"Thought you'd got lost," Baz said.

"What the...?" exclaimed Doug.

"Ah shit!" sighed Mark.

"Explanations later," said the man in jeans, T-shirt, and white mask. "Let's go get Terry."

And with no further explanation, Johnny Deuce turned and ran from the room, followed seconds later by the other three men.

PART SEVEN

Chapter One

Yves Montaigne climbed through the ropes and took his position in one corner of the ring, back to the turnbuckle, looking across the illuminated canvas to watch the arrival of his very special opponent. He glanced once up into the shadows. He couldn't see it, but he knew the camera he had set up was there, not simply recording but streaming this fight, sending it specifically to one very particular laptop. The men gathered around had paid the usual exorbitant fees for their specialised entertainment, but as far as Montaigne was concerned, there was only one really important spectator that night, and he was miles away, watching, helpless to do anything. In his tights, Yves' already rock-hard erection ached and oozed pre-come. In an ordinary pro ring he would have been forced to ignore it—not that the anticipation there would have been anywhere near as intense as this, but here... Yves leisurely massaged the long curve of his eager cock, smiling to himself at the drawn-out sigh of pleasure the move drew from several of the men around all sides of the ring.

He watched as Terry threw aside the dressing area curtain and strode through the door into the room, the wrestler's traditional entrance bravado evaporating as the crowd remained eerily silent, focused with a fierce, voiceless intensity unlike anything Terry probably had ever known in his wrestling career. *You should run,* Yves thought, *run now as fast and far as you can.* He smiled again. *But you will not. You are a fool. Like your father.* He shoved down hard on his crotch, his smile growing cold. *Like your 'uncle'.*

Terry walked the short way to the ring and leaped up onto its apron. Yves could see him staring uselessly at the shadowy seated figures at ringside, trying but failing to make out faces. Yves guessed he considered his famed Chris Bacchus leap over the top rope but decided against it. Somehow, this didn't seem the place for such showbiz antics. Yves nodded slightly to himself. The boy was learning. But too little. Much too late.

Terry took his position in the opposite corner, facing Yves. Arms wide, gripping the ropes behind him, he leaned forward in a series of half-hearted stretching exercises, and Yves saw his eyes casting around the ring. *Non, mon brave. No seconds. And definitely no referee. Just you. And me.* He stepped forward, leisurely unlacing the belt of his dressing gown, opening it, letting it fall from his shoulders, swinging it round and folding it before placing it to one side in his corner, behind the turnbuckle, to let the audience appreciate the slow unveiling of his honed body.

☆☆☆

After looking around one last time for any late-arriving official to supervise their match, Terry pulled his white T-shirt up and off quickly and threw it without much thought out of the ring where it was swallowed by the shadows. Now he could feel the heat of the overhead bank of lights on the skin of his body but even so he shivered. He raised and let fall his muscular shoulders a couple of times, and swung his arms, as much to generate a little heat as to flex and stretch. Maybe this was what it was like when you filmed a show. Maybe the audience just couldn't make the kinds of noises a regular audience would make. *Something to do with sound levels?* From somewhere in the darkness he heard a small, appreciative moan as he did his brief warm-up. Normally, Terry liked the feeling of the punters drinking in the sight of his young, trained body. But this felt...different. Uncomfortable. He shivered as he admitted to himself: this felt *wrong*.

Yves strode to the centre of the ring and stood, looking at him, waiting. Terry braced himself and walked forward to meet him there. Time to get it on. Perhaps when they were wrestling, he could lose himself in the activity. Perhaps then it would seem more normal.

☆

The two men stood face-to-face, belly and pecs almost touching. Yves smiled again, seeing how lost the young man in front of him looked, used as he was to some third man outlining the 'rules' and 'penalties' for breaking them. Time for him to learn there were no rules in this ring. No penalties. Or at least, just one. Yves took a last, lingering look at the young man in trunks and boots standing there before him. His gaze travelled possessively up from the boots, the thick thighs with the dusting of golden hair, the tight stomach ridged with abdominal muscles, the round curves of the pecs, and the bunched muscles of the neck and shoulders, to the clear, unblemished face, with its earnest blue eyes, and the classic blond hair. "*Comme tu es beau,*" he breathed. "You are beautiful." Terry glanced quickly to either side, trying to see if the men close to the ring had caught these unorthodox words, straining to see their reaction but unable to. Yves smiled, teeth flashing in the lights from above. "I shall enjoy breaking you!" He reached out with both hands and shoved Terry hard in the stomach.

Caught completely off guard, Terry fell backwards, only just preventing himself from stumbling and falling on his arse. Before he could protest, from somewhere unseen a bell rang, as if Yves' action had been a signal, and his opponent began to circle him. No time now for thinking about anything but the fight. The bout had begun. Terry adopted a traditional wrestler's stance—half crouched, arms reaching out ready to take hold—and began, too, to circle his challenger.

☆☆☆

"Terry!"

"Terry!"

Doug crashed through the rooms in Yves Montaigne's elegant country house with little care for any potential damage. With equal concern but slightly more caution, Baz, Mark, and Johnny Deuce followed. Mark paused to regard the broken front door hanging loose on its hinges. "Y'know, even abroad that's got to be illegal."

"*Introduction par effraction,*" muttered the man in the Johnny Deuce mask. "Or *Einbruch,* if you prefer. Typical German conciseness."

Mark grimaced. "Typical!"

"There's no one here!" Doug declared.

"The outhouses," Baz shouted. "He's not going to stage wrestling bouts actually in his house, is he?"

"That's right," Mark said slowly. "I remember him saying how he'd got a set-up in a converted barn or something. Like POWer's. Only classy."

Doug clenched his fist. "C'mon!" He charged through the battered door and out in search of Montaigne's wrestling space, the others dashing to follow his lead. A ten-minute search revealed two capacious outhouses, one of them indeed fitted with mats, weights, and other training equipment. But both were empty.

"Where is he?" Doug raged. "Where the fuck is he!" He smashed his fist into the rickety wooden panelling of the last outhouse they had searched, and then stood, back to the others, hunched over, evidently struggling to control the fury and fear raging through him.

"I've no idea, mate," Mark declared finally. Baz glared at him ferociously, but Doug seemed not to have heard, sunk as he was in his misery.

Jonny Deuce stood regarding the broken man. Hesitantly he reached out, took a step forward, and then another, closing the gap between Doug and himself, reaching out as if to comfort him. A sudden cry stopped him in his tracks.

"Johnny Deuce! *Fantastich!*"

Mark groaned.

Chapter Two

Terry threw his head back and groaned. Around his waist Yves' sinewy thighs constricted like steel bands, squeezing the air out of his body and bending his ribs until he was seriously afraid they might break.

He no longer knew how long they had been wrestling. Timed rounds, like referees and seconds, seemed not to be a part of this bizarre set-up. Yves had been on him like a tiger, ferociously battering his younger opponent, throwing him around the ring and slapping on a variety of vicious holds one after the other. Disorientated both by the abandonment of even a pretence of rules, and by this hitherto unseen side of Yves, Terry was completely dominated for at least the first ten minutes, his body stretched, bent and pummelled more than he might have expected from a score of matches. And Yves showed no sign of slowing down. The man had become some kind of driven machine, working Terry's body, displaying it in a variety of ingenious contortions for the sadistic pleasure of the audience. But no matter how hard Yves wrenched or jerked or punched his body, no matter how loud and genuine Terry's gasps and cries, the men on all four sides sat in unnaturally absorbed silence. Once, as Terry was arched in agony in a cruel backbreaker over Yves' knee, scrabbling to dislodge either the hand pushing at his throat or the one pulling at his boot, he thought he heard soft moans punctuated by muffled cries of "*Ja! Ja!*" But then Yves sharply upped the torque on his tormented back, and the bolt of agony through his spine drove all else from his mind.

Now he felt as if the man in black was literally cutting him in two with his scissors hold, and Terry finally accepted there was no way he was going either to escape the hold or to win against a man as driven as Yves Montaigne seemed to be that night. If this was what working for him meant, he could stuff it and welcome. "I give!" he cried with what breath he could summon. "I give! I submit! I fucking submit!"

For a second the killing pressure lessened, allowing Terry to draw in a desperate breath, and then Yves snapped the hold on again even more savagely than before. Terry clawed impotently at his thighs, yelling in protest, "I gave! You won! For fuck's sake, stop!"

Yves propped himself up on one elbow as he poured all of his strength into the crushing hold, leaning in so that his face was close to Terry's contorted, sweating features. "You submit to me?" he hissed.

"Yes! Yes! I just said I did."

Yves nodded as if in acceptance and then jerked his legs together in another even tighter convulsive squeeze. "So what?"

Unable to escape and unable to get Yves to stop, Terry clenched his eyes and teeth and struggled to endure. Yves couldn't keep this pressure up for much longer, no one could! Briefly he considered calling out to the audience, getting one of them to climb into the ring and drag this berserker off him. But he knew they wouldn't. Finally, he admitted to himself what he had known at some level all along and had been too stupid to accept until it was too late. This audience wanted to see him struggle, in pain. Punters always liked seeing the 'face', the 'blue eye', suffer a bit at the hands of the heel—before he turned the table and won. But this audience was more honest than that. They wanted Terry to suffer. But they wanted him to *really* suffer. They liked that. They had paid for that.

At last Yves dropped the pressure slightly but still didn't release the boy between his thighs. Instead he twisted his body, dragging Terry round so he was facing in one particular direction. Leaning forward, he wound his fingers in Terry's golden hair and pulled sharply, making him gasp. "See this?" he hissed. "Do you see your boy?"

Dazed by pain and lack of air, Terry couldn't understand what Yves was asking, until he realised that Yves wasn't talking to him, but to some hidden camera—or rather, to whomever he thought was watching via the camera. Yves spoke again, and this time Terry knew he was addressing him. "Smile for him, boy! Smile to show how much you enjoy being my toy!" He viciously clamped down on Terry's waist again with his merciless legs, making the lad cry out.

"Who? Smile for who!"

234

Yves grinned hungrily. "*Ton oncle*. Your uncle. That's what you call him, isn't it? Or is it *Papa?* Daddy? Sir?" With each word Yves cruelly jerked his thighs tighter around the tormented lad, making him cry out, each cry more strangled than the last as his lungs grew more and more starved of air. "And what do you call him when he fucks you, eh, Terry? He does fuck you, doesn't he? How could he resist your tight, young arse? I couldn't. And what about that cock of his, eh? Oh yes, I've heard all about that cock. Did it take him long to break you to it? Did it take long nights of him pressing himself on you, in you, until you could take it? But you're such a hot boy, aren't you? Always so hungry for cock. I'll bet you took it all in one go the very first time. I'll bet you let him plough you every night." Terry shook his head weakly. The words Yves was pouring unceasingly into his ears made no sense, and now they seemed to be coming from far away, even though he was so close Terry could feel the flecks of spit from his mouth as he rattled off his madness. With a shove from both his arms, Yves raised his upper body right up off the mat so that he could bear down even more strongly on the tormented boy, and Terry held on to consciousness for grim death. As if through thick walls, he heard Yves shrieking one last question. "And when he fucks you, does he call you *Geoff?*"

Geoff? Dad? Terry was floating now in a sea of blackness. Strangely, he felt quite calm, the pain and madness of his fight against Yves like something far outside himself. Someone was standing over him, but he couldn't see his face because of the bright ring lights over both of them, couldn't get his eyes to focus. "Dad?" he said weakly.

Yves laughed, released his killing hold, stood, and reached down to pull the near-unconscious boy back up to his feet. "*Non, mon brave,*" he said. "Not your 'dad'. I am no 'dad' and I have no 'dad'. Thanks to him, to your uncle. I have lived with that absence, that *pain*, almost all of my life. Tonight, I pay it back. To you. And to him!" And with the final word, Yves spun and rammed his elbow back hard into Terry's stomach.

Already starved of breath, Terry dropped, utterly winded, to the mat, unable to defend himself as his opponent followed him down. Yves pinned him belly-down to the mat, straddling him and pulling back on his head, arching his spine to a near-impossible degree. Terry gasped out his submission in anguish, but Yves maintained his hold. "*Non,*

non," he crooned. "You must not give up so quickly. You must entertain them—" and he indicated the audience on all four sides of them with a sweep of his hand. "And you must entertain him!" He jabbed venomously in the direction of the camera somewhere out in the darkness. "He is watching you, *mon brave.* I have arranged for him to have a ringside seat. Or at least the next best thing. I want him to see when I take the thing he loves most in the world. The way he took the thing I most loved."

Abruptly, Yves left off pulling on Terry's head, shoving it sharply down so that his forehead impacted with the unyielding canvas, and Terry lay there beneath him, stunned. Sitting on Terry's back, Yves unwound the sash from around his waist, winding first one end and then the other around his two hands. From all around them came a sound like a breeze running through the stuffy, dark hall— the sound of men drawing their breaths in shivering anticipation of what was to come. Yves raised his arms and twisted first one way and then the other as he sat on his young victim's broad back, displaying the taut length of silk held out between his fists. Then, almost gently, he leaned forward, slipped the silk under Terry's head, and pulled back, his sash an unforgiving garrotte around his downed opponent's muscular neck.

Too late, Terry clawed at the tightening sash. Laughing, Yves caught first one of the thrashing wrestler's powerful arms and then the other, hooking each in turn behind his knees so that to dislodge them the boy would have had to dislocate his own shoulders. "Camel clutch," he said. "That is what you call this in English. Such an ugly name for such a beautiful hold, *non?*" And with Terry now completely unable to do anything to prevent him, Yves looped the sash once more around the lad's thickly corded neck and very slowly pulled his fists apart. The silk noose tightened centimetre by centimetre, the men at the sides of the ring shifting and craning forward to get the best view of Terry's bulging eyes, his mouth open and gasping for denied breath. Just as Terry's head nodded forward, indicating his slide into unconsciousness, Yves left off, loosening the sash. He waited until Terry's eyes flickered, until he showed signs of regaining consciousness, before slowly pulling his hands apart again and once more tightening the noose. "I taught you this game, *mon pauvre,*" he whispered into Terry's ear as the lad struggled vainly for breath. "How do you like it now we're playing it properly?"

☆☆☆

Three times Yves brought Terry to the brink of complete unconsciousness, three times relaxing the noose at the very last moment. After the third time, he roughly pulled the silken length all the way from Terry's neck, threw it to one side and stood, looking down at his fallen foe, both booted feet planted either side of his body. He held the pose, letting the watchers take in his dominance, his power, and then he viciously stomped twice on the boy's back. Terry lay, helpless to protect himself, as he struggled to climb back into full consciousness.

Yves nodded as if satisfied that his opponent was exactly where he wanted him, leaned down, and hooked fingers in either side of Terry's trunks at the waist. Slowly he pulled them down, over his arse, down his thighs, past the boots, and completely off his body, bringing them up to his face where he buried his nose in them and breathed in deeply before flinging them, in the way his audience expected, out into the darkness. There was a flurry, as of raptors for meat, as men scrambled to take the trunks for themselves and drink in their scent of young male musk.

Still straddling the prone young wrestler, Yves dropped to his knees, slamming his arse down onto the boy's already abused spine. He ran both his hands over Terry's shoulders and back, displaying beyond doubt his total ownership of the young Brit. Keeping his weight on his victim, he span round as he sat and slid his hands down to Terry's arse, squeezing the two bubble-buttocks so tightly that when he moved on he left white finger marks in the flesh. When he reached the thighs, he paused. With a sudden, vicious movement, Yves pulled the prone boy's legs wide apart, opening up the arsecrack over his tight and completely defenceless fuck hole. His eyes fixed on Terry's vulnerability, Yves held up two fingers pressed close together for all the surrounding men to see, then jabbed them down swiftly and without remorse through the constricted muscle ring and deep into the boy. Terry jerked and cried out as his arse was roughly fucked by Montaigne's fingers. Pulling out and standing, Yves spread his arms wide, inviting applause for his abuse from the watchers. He basked in their approbation, in their jealousy, in their almost palpable desire to do what he was doing to the downed golden boy at his feet.

Hooking his fingers into his own waistband now, Yves slowly drew his tights down his thighs and off past his boots. They were left to one side. No one dared to scrabble for them as they had for Terry's trunks. Naked except for his boots, Yves stood over Terry, his curved cock a rigid scimitar, the thin skin drawn tight over the veined shaft, the wide head dripping pre-come onto Terry's battered back. He cupped the curve of his cock, running his palm gently back and forth under its length, his head thrown back and teeth gritted in silent pleasure. Bending, he leaned forward, planting both hands either side of Terry's blond head, and taking his weight on his arms as if about to launch into a series of press-ups. Very slowly he lowered himself until his cock just touched the line of the crack bisecting Terry's arse. Even more slowly, he rocked his body forwards then backwards, forwards then backwards, teasing himself with the sensation of his self-lubed dick sliding along the arsecrack, teasing the audience. One man openly gave a long, helpless groan, and Yves smiled at the sound, knowing exactly what it meant.

Abruptly he stopped, hips pulled up, taking his cock away from the buttocks, lips drawn back in what might have been a snarl or the tight control of a man fighting to prevent his climax. For long moments, he held himself over Terry, his cock beating a rapid tattoo up onto his own tight stomach in a protest of denied release. Pre-come oozed in a plentiful milky stream from his cock into Terry's musky cleft.

With a nod and a deep breath, Yves finally sat back, master of himself once more. He looked out into the darkness to where he knew the camera was. He stared into it and through it—into the eyes of the man he hated above all others. The smile was gone. His eyes glittered. "*Enfin*," he said.

He leaned in one last time, hooked an arm under the lad's waist, and pulled so that Terry's arse was raised and presented to him. The boy protested weakly, unclearly, still not fully aware of what was about to be done to him. In his other hand, Yves took his cock, angling it, guiding it till its tip rested in the fuzzy line dividing the boy's buttocks. He pressed it in just enough so that the firm flesh dimpled prior to parting completely and allowing full entry. One hard thrust and the lad would be skewered on his unforgiving cock. And that, Yves thought - fire racing through his veins, body trembling with a desire that was not simply lust - was only going to be the beginning.

Chapter Three

"Get your fucking cock off that boy's arse!"

As one, every head in the hall whipped round to the source of the bellowed words, as startling in their effect as the shattering of plate glass windows. The curtain covering the entrance from the changing rooms had once again been thrown back, and standing in the rectangle of light was the squat silhouette of a man. The features were invisible with the light coming from behind him, but the stance and that terrible voice made his mood all too clear. This man was furiously angry. This man was dangerous!

"I said, get off him!" The figure stepped out into the hall revealing the shaven head and snarling features of Doug. From behind him more figures followed. A ripple of alarmed muttering swept around the seated audience as the new arrivals stormed down the short aisle and leaped up into the ring.

Yves rose quickly and stepped back from Terry to face Doug, hands raised as if ready to lock up with a wrestler, cock still curving out hard in front of him like a threat.

Doug stood glaring at Yves who met the blistering look without blinking. Johnny Deuce positioned himself at Doug's side, hands raised like Yves' but balled into fists. Baz ran straight to Terry and helped him climb dazedly to his feet. Mark, too, stepped up into the ring but held back. He stood by the ropes, watching the other men.

"He's all right, Doug. Terry's all right, y'know. I mean, he's been knocked about a bit, but he's going to be all right," the man in the Johnny Deuce mask whispered out of the side of his mouth. "It's going to be okay!"

Doug didn't reply. He stood, breathing heavily, struggling to control himself. Finally, he spoke, but his words weren't for the man across the ring from them. They were for the assembled audience. "I know you," he said, and as he spoke he turned slowly so that all of the men gathered there could see and hear him. "Maybe not as individuals, although I'm betting some of you perverted fucks used to come and watch me when I...when I did this. But I know who you are. I know *what* you are. You're twisted bastards! Excuses for human beings, all of you. You make me sick!"

"*Non!*" Still hard, still proud, Yves Montaigne spat his defiance at Doug. "You make *me* sick! You hypocrite!" He spread his arms out wide to take in the ring and all of the shadowy area around it. "*This* is the real world. This is what life is really all about, *mon ami*. Fighting! Proving yourself as a man! Winning! Fuck or be fucked!"

"Kill or be killed?"

Yves smiled, a twist of his thin lips. "Not the childish pretence these fools hide behind." He gestured contemptuously at the other wrestlers in the ring with them. He shook his head as if pitying Doug, but his eyes were still cold. "You knew that once, but you ran away. You coward!"

Doug stared ashen-faced at his accuser. "No..." he began, but had to stop, his voice breaking. He glanced across at Terry, standing now, supported by Baz, and just for a moment Terry looked so like Geoff that Doug thought his heart would break. And next to him, Baz, supporting him, arm thrown round his shoulders protectively, the way Doug had longed to hold Geoff but had never been able to. Had Doug ever looked like Baz? Of course not! But had Doug never looked at Geoff the way Baz was looking at Terry right then? Doug shook his head. Baz was right. He really hadn't seen things that were right under his nose for a long time now. He turned back to Yves. When he burst into the room it was with only one desire burning in his heart: to kill Yves Montaigne. Now... "That's not what life is about," he said quietly, but with an intensity that carried his words out past the ring's ropes and into the darkness. "It's about...love."

Yves' laughter was a cracked thing. "What do you know of love, you stupid, lonely old man?"

When Doug replied, it wasn't Yves Montaigne he directed his answer at, but Terry. "This...madness cost me the life—" he swallowed, took a deep breath "—of the man I loved." Then he stood, oblivious of everything except Terry, his eyes fixed on Terry's, waiting nervously, fearfully, for the lad's reaction. When Terry nodded, just once, Doug looked down quickly so that his face was cast into deep shadow by the overhead lights, and no one could see his reaction.

"It cost me the life of my father. *You* took my father from me!" Yves' words were a howl of fury.

The reply, when it came, was firm and calm. "Then you're even," said the man in the Johnny Deuce mask. "In fact, more than even." He stepped closer to Montaigne, lowering his voice so that only the Frenchman and the other men in the ring could hear what he said. "I don't know just how far you were prepared to go tonight, Montaigne, but I'd say you've gone far enough. You've fucked with us all, one way or another, with your tricks and games. There's no need to go any further with this charade." He stepped back and looked across at Doug. "And believe me," he said, "I know a thing or two about charades...and the damage they can cause."

Yves' eyes narrowed. "Who are you?" he demanded.

Johnny Deuce sighed. "I'm sorry, Doug," he said as he reached up to undo the ties holding the mask to his face. "I should have done this long before now. Time to grow up and let go." And he let the mask fall to the canvas.

"Mark?" said Terry uncertainly. By his side, Baz rolled his eyes and sighed.

"No, I'm his twin, Martin," said the unmasked man, the mirror image of Mark. "Martin Mansfield."

Chapter Four

"Now will someone please tell me what the fuck has been going on?"

Crowded around the table, or sitting on the edge of the bunks in the tiny ferry cabin they had booked, the assembled men of the POWer posse grunted or nodded their agreement with Eric's exasperated demand. Events of the last twenty-four hours had left them exhausted but still determined to have answers.

Even after the assorted rescues and revelations in Yves' mat room, matters could have turned distinctly ugly. White with fury, Yves had reminded them they were still on his home ground and that his 'technicians' were paid very highly for far more than just their skills with audio-visual equipment. Indeed, three of them, sporting more muscle than was needed for carrying cameras, had even then begun advancing on the ring. It was the unmasked Martin Mansfield who stepped up to Yves again and quietly reminded him of three things.

Firstly, they were still surrounded by an audience, most of whom were unable to tear themselves away from the unscheduled spectacle in the ring. This audience's 'tastes' were only too obvious, but did Montaigne really think these suited men in the shadows would sit silently in front of an all-out gang fight, with the risk of being drawn in themselves, possibly even of spilling some of their own precious blood?

Secondly, there was the small matter of the web camera Yves had set up— linked to the laptop he had left for them. "By now," Martin explained, "it will be with our friends, Eric and Jonesy. My friend Baz here sent clear instructions on how to use the record function. Any attempt to prevent us leaving this place, and any *methods* used, would therefore be burned to disc and handed to the local police before the blood had dried." Only the men in the audience behind Baz could see the lad cross the fingers of one hand as he fervently hoped the technologically inept Eric and Jonesy had in fact been able to follow his instructions.

It was Martin's third point, however, delivered almost in a whisper to Yves, that, more than any other, secured the safe passage of the POWer posse from Montaigne's property. They were, Martin reminded Yves, surrounded by a number of very wealthy, very powerful men, men who prized their anonymity extremely highly. These men could not afford to be linked publically with anything as perverse and degraded as the 'entertainment' Yves provided for them. Currently, though doubtless alarmed by the evening's unexpected turn of events, they felt secure and safe from recognition and from the camera, in the comforting blanket of the darkness Yves had created.

But Martin had made a mental note of where the light switch was.

Seething, but outmanoeuvered, the still-naked and humiliated Montaigne was powerless to prevent the Brits leaving the ring and his mat room.

Outside, Baz let out a huge pent-up sigh of relief, but Martin's expression was still grim. "C'mon, we've got no time to waste."

Doug nodded, but Mark looked confused. "What do you mean? We're out, aren't we? No one's hurt. All's well."

"You are such an idiot sometimes, Mark," said the man with his face. "Montaigne couldn't do anything to us in there, but we're not safe here."

"What? Outside?" said Mark.

"In Switzerland," said Martin.

"In Europe," growled Doug, and he looked to Terry.

"Yeah, yeah, all right," Terry muttered. "Maybe you were right about that all along."

"And maybe you both just need to stop picking up the wrong guys when you're abroad. Now, move it! Mark and I will take our camper. Baz—" and Martin threw a set of keys to the lad "—you take Doug and Terry in the minibus. We pick up Eric and Jonesy and get the fuck out of here. Now, go!"

"I thought you were in charge," Terry grumbled groggily as Doug half-supported, half-carried him to the minibus.

"I thought you thought you were," said Doug.

Terry considered this as he was manhandled into his seat. "I don't know anything any more," he said ruefully.

There had followed the longest journey any of them had ever known. Eric and Jonesy were thoroughly bemused and at first downright rebellious at the thought of making such an unexpected dash for home. But a combination of clear, concise explanation from Martin plus no small amount of glowering and threatening from Doug had pulled them into line. They'd driven off at speed, refusing to turn back even when, after five minutes, Eric complained he'd left his favourite leotard behind in the rush.

Switzerland gave way to Germany, and Germany gave way to France in a succession of seemingly endless motorways and border posts, of snatched stops for changing drivers, for fuel and food, where none of them allowed themselves to be alone, and none dared meet the eyes of strangers for more than a few seconds. After thirty hours of exhausting travel, they were back at the ferry port. Then came the hardest part of all: four hours of enforced waiting to board the next available boat, sitting ducks as Jonesy gloomily kept reminding them.

"Don't be daft," Eric had scoffed. "We're practically home and dry. Nothing's going to happen to us here."

Baz, still the only one among them who knew all of Doug's story and how close he and Geoff had been to escaping Colline before tragedy had struck, glanced at Doug. But Doug's attention was fixed out of the minibus window as he endlessly scanned and rescanned the faces of passing men for signs of anything or anyone dangerous.

Baz turned to Terry who had been worryingly silent for almost the whole of the journey. "Terry?" His voice was low, trying not to draw the attention of the others, but Terry seemed not to hear him. Like Doug, his gaze was directed out of the window. Baz spoke again, louder. "Terry? Terry?"

Terry jumped and turned. His face was pale, drawn, and automatically Baz went to reach out for him, to hold and comfort him. But Terry flinched, and Baz let his arms drop. "Not yet," Terry murmured.

Baz nodded. "Okay," he said. "It's going to be okay."

Terry nodded, his lips thin, none of the usual devil-may-care about him that drove Baz mad, and that he loved so deeply. "It will be," he said, almost to himself, before turning back to the window and the passersby outside.

☆☆☆

Now, at long last, they were safe in their cabin and on their way home, and the time had come for all cards finally to be laid on the table.

"Okay, okay," Eric said, "I get the whole Yves Montaigne, twisted fuck out for revenge thing that was going on back there, I guess. But what did Johnny Deuce have to do with anything? It was you, wasn't it?" He pointed at Martin. "It was you all along."

"No, it was you, wasn't it?" Jonesy butted in, pointing at Mark.

Baz rolled his eyes. "For fuck's sake," he said, almost under his breath.

"It was both of us," Martin said, almost apologetically. "We were both Johnny Deuce."

Eric's jaw dropped. "Shut the fuck up!" At the sound of Baz's laughter, he turned to the boy. "Oh right, so I suppose you knew all along, did you?"

"Not all along, no," Baz retorted. "But by the time I'd realised that they wore masks almost always, even when they didn't need to, that they wrestled in completely different styles, wore a two of clubs on their boots which is a traditional symbol for disguise, and that one of them had slightly larger ears than the other, then yes, I did actually work out what was going on."

"Well, aren't you just Miss Marple!" Eric snapped.

"Not many people know about the two of clubs thing," Martin admitted.

"I didn't," Mark said sullenly.

"Okay, so I Googled that one," Baz confessed.

"No, but you are clever, mate," Jonesy said with grudging admiration.

"I know I am!" Baz exploded. "That's something else none of you worked out because you've all got your heads stuck so far up your own arses! I've just finished a degree in computer sciences, thank you very much, which I paid for by wrestling. But none of you knew that, did you? You know why? Because none of you ever bloody well asked!"

While Eric and Jonesy struggled to take in this latest in a string of surprising discoveries, Mark and Martin Mansfield, and Doug and Terry remained silent, the two pairs of men regarding each other warily, like tag teams weighing each other up before a bout. "So, said Terry slowly, looking at Martin, "you and I never...?"

Martin shook his head. "No. Sorry."

Doug glared at Mark. "And you and me...?"

"Not on your life!" Mark snorted.

"Thank God!"

"Amen!"

With Mark and Doug bristling at each other, Jonesy turned from the uncharacteristically heated Baz to Martin. "So," he asked, confusion evident through his lilting Welsh accent. "Why?"

Martin made a resigned face. "Dad," he said simply.

"Mansfield?" Terry frowned. "Mike Mansfield, I mean. I don't get it."

Martin gave a small laugh. "I don't suppose you do, given your family. But believe me, our family, our Dad, is very different. Dad's keen on wrestling if it brings in money. But it's just one string to his bow, just one part of the entertainment business he's building up, and there's just no way he'd have ever let his sons and heirs strip down to boots and trunks and jump into a ring in front of the public."

"He'd have ripped our balls off," Mark said glumly.

"He's had enough trouble accepting...other things about us, and the fact that the business he's spent his whole life building up isn't going to be left to any more Mansfields after Mark and me." Mark gave a snorted guffaw, and Martin shot him an irritated look. "He'll come round to that one. He's not quite the monster you think he is. But family is important to him, and to us—" and here he fixed Mark with a stern eye, and his brother shrugged a reluctant agreement "—and I for one didn't want to upset him any more."

"And I for another," said Mark, mimicking what the others were beginning to see as Martin's slightly more formal manner, "didn't want to have my balls ripped off."

"But wrestling was something we both really wanted to do, right from when we were kids visiting the halls with Dad," Martin continued, and as he spoke there was a genuine enthusiasm in his voice, a boyish eagerness that almost drew smiles from both Terry and Doug as it resonated with something deep in themselves. "We'd thought for ages about working our way into some of Dad's promotions somehow, so we'd already got our secret identity all worked out."

"Though I wanted to be called The Masked Mauler," Mark declared.

"Masked Moron, more like," Doug growled.

"But," Martin pressed on, with just the hint of a smile in Doug's direction, "we knew we'd never get away with it. Dad keeps too close an eye on his business. So, that's why we proposed the trip abroad, to 'broaden our business knowledge', but really it was so we could finally live out our childhood dream, for a while at least. And that's when we made contact with Montaigne."

Doug looked sharply at Martin. "He tried to recruit you? For his 'special' fights?"

Martin shook his head vehemently. "No. We weren't over in Europe long enough for that. I think his...recruiting methods take more time." He glanced at Terry, but Terry's eyes were turned downwards as if he were deep in thought. Martin went on, "And there's no saying if he would have tried anyway. I'm thinking you have to be pretty good to be picked by him for his 'private' matches."

"You're good," Doug said immediately. There was an audible gasp from Eric and Jonesy at such unheard of, unsolicited praise.

"Thanks!" said Mark with a huge grin.

"I wasn't talking to you, big ears," Doug said, his eyes fixed solely on Martin.

"Anyway," Martin continued, "our contacts with Montaigne were genuine business affairs. He seemed mildly interested in expanding his and our promotions in England and Europe. It must have been when he realised that gave him access to the Bacchus family as well that he got really enthusiastic. And that's when he started using us all."

"You used us, too." Everyone looked to Terry.

Mark stood up. "Now hang on a minute," he began, his voice rising.

Martin reached over and gently but firmly pulled him back down into his seat. "Yes," he said slowly. "We did. Montaigne would set up fights for us across Europe if we brought POWer along with us. Maybe we let ourselves be carried away by the chance to live out our childhood dreams, but we had no idea what he was really up to."

"And is that true for both of you?" Terry looked directly at Mark Mansfield as he asked the question, thinking of that night with Stefan, and that other night with Dieter and Kurt. Mark looked away and wouldn't meet his eyes.

"I'm truly sorry," said Martin. "Can you forgive us?"

"Yes," said Doug immediately, turning swiftly to glare at Eric and Jonesy so that, this time, their incredulous gasps died, strangled, in their throats.

"Thank you," said Martin simply. He turned to Terry. "Can you?"

There was a pause, a tension in the air that grew with each passing second. Terry rose from his chair. "I need to think," he said.

"Terry," Doug began, reaching out for the younger man.

Baz stood up, placing himself between them. "Just give him some time, Doug, yeah?" Doug hesitated, looked to Martin who gave a small nod of agreement, before very reluctantly letting his arm drop. "We'll be here when you get back, Terry, okay?" Baz said, adding very quietly so that only Terry could hear, "*I'll* be here."

Terry nodded and hurried from the room.

☆☆☆

By the time he was out of the door he was practically running. He had covered the length of two corridors before he finally came to a stop and leaned back against a bulkhead, his head spinning, panting as if he had run much further and much faster than he had. He stood there, eyes screwed shut tightly, waiting for his hearbeat to calm, for his breathing to slow. Waiting...waiting...

"I thought you were never coming out."

Terry kept his eyes shut. "I thought you might have knocked and come in."

"Under the circumstances that seemed...inadvisable. You knew I was here?"

251

"I saw you while we were waiting to board. And..."

"And?"

Terry opened his eyes and looked straight into the eyes of Yves Montaigne. "I knew you wouldn't let us go that easily. I knew you wouldn't let *me* go that easily."

"*Tu as raison, mon brave.* You are right. Shall we?" With the sweep of one hand Yves indicated the direction they should walk.

Chapter Five

"Money solves all problems," he said in response to Terry's expression of mild surprise when the cabin he brought them to turned out to be only one corridor away from the one the POWer posse had booked. When he'd last seen him, Yves had been incandescent with fury. Now once again he was the suave, sophisticated man Terry had first met in France all those weeks ago, and Terry found himself responding strongly to the man's powerful sexual charisma.

For a moment they stood regarding each other. Carefully, Yves reached out, keeping his hand low, his movements slow, as if Terry were some wild animal he was wary of scaring off. He reached behind the lad, resting his hand on the curve of his arse, lightly at first and then more firmly, more possessively. His face a mask, Terry did the same. The firmness of the man's buttock under his palm sent an aching pulse shooting right through his dick, which immediately stiffened and began to grow in his jeans. Another moment, and the two men were in each other's arms, kissing fiercely, deeply. Yves pressed in hard, pushing Terry up against the door, both hands on his arse as his crotch ground against Terry's, both cocks surging to full, hard erections. Terry pushed back and twisted so now it was Yves pinned against the door. Terry reached for the collar of Yves' shirt and the Frenchman smiled, letting his head fall back so that Terry could undo the buttons and expose his neck for kisses. Instead, Terry hooked his fingers into the shirt and pulled it apart with one clean jerk, silver buttons flying everywhere around the cabin. Yves went to protest but his complaints swiftly melted into guttural gasps of mingled pain and pleasure as Terry leaned into the exposed chest and began to fiercely suck and bite the hardening nipples brought to light. A yank of the shirt down over his shoulders and Yves' arms were pinned, leaving him unable to defend his perfectly sculpted and shaved pecs and abs, even had he wanted to, from Terry's hungry tongue and mouth.

"Doucement, mon brave! Plus douce, je t'en prie!" he begged, but Terry ignored his protests, sinking to his knees as he kissed, licked, and bit Yves' bucking body. Even as he worked the groaning Frenchman's navel with his tongue, Terry was reaching for his belt, tearing the trousers open and wrenching both them and the tight white cotton briefs beneath down to Yves' ankles. Montaigne's long, curved cock sprang free, hard and veined, and eager for action mere inches from Terry's face. Yves stood, eyes closed, breathing hard, waiting for the delicious closing of Terry's lips round his cockhead, their sliding down his long shaft, the exquisite pressure of Terry's tongue against his aching erection. "Please," he moaned softly. "Don't make me come in your mouth. There is so much...so much I want to do to your body before I come."

When he finally realised that Terry was not sucking him off—that, in fact, Terry was not even touching his cock at all, with tongue or finger, Yves opened his eyes and looked down at the blond head in front of him with a confused smile. The face that looked back up at him was blank.

"D'accord. Okay. We don't have to finish here," Yves said. "Come back with me."

Terry put his head to one side in an exaggerated pretence of thought. "So you can fuck me in your ring while guys watch? So that afterwards you can do...whatever it was you were going to do the last time?" He shook his head. "No, thanks."

Yves swallowed. The unsatisfied hard-on was a raging tease that made it hard to think. "Terry. I was...mad back then. I was *maddened.* By Doug. By what Doug had done to my father. I wouldn't do that again. Not to you."

"You want me to abandon my family? After everything they've done for me?"

Yves laughed. "You don't have a family. I don't have a family. We are made for each other, *mon brave,* in so many ways."

"I have a family," Terry said calmly.

Yves' eyes narrowed. "Who? Your 'uncle'? The man who wanted to fuck your father? The men in masks who lied to you? Or the others, who follow you around Europe because you are their meal ticket? That's not a family. That's a group of strangers using you for their own ends. You don't really know them at all."

Terry nodded slowly. "You're right," he said simply. "I don't really know them. I mean, one of them is actually two guys, one quite decent and one, quite probably, an utter shithead. I thought another one was a hard-hearted bastard put on this planet just to make my life difficult, and it turns out he loved my dad more than my mum did, which kind of makes him even more family than I'd thought he was before. And the guy I thought was just a pretty face, good for opening and closing shows, turns out to be a computer genius who...likes me." Terry paused, thinking about Baz, about what he had seen and learned about him during their trip, over the past two days in particular, thinking about that final comment as he had left the cabin. "And I think I like him, too," he said with surprised realisation. "So, no." He shook his head as if calling himself back to the matter at hand, and to the scimitar of a stiffy still mere inches from his face. "I guess I don't really know them. But—" and at this he reached up and gave the stiff dick a hard whack with his hand. It made a meaty slap against Yves' thigh, drawing a sharp gasp from the Frenchman. "—I do know you." Terry rose to his feet, firmly grasping Yves' cock at its root as he did so, so that both balls were in his hand. When he was standing fully upright again, he smiled into Yves' face, squeezed and twisted. Yves gasped, his eyes widened, and his mouth was a wide O of surprised pain.

"Now," Terry continued, "I'm going to keep this reasonably short, partly because I want to get back to my family—" and he gave a small squeeze of the balls in his hand, as if to underline the word "—and partly because, although this probably hurts like fuck, I think there is a part of you that quite likes that, and I don't what to do anything that makes you happy. Ever again."

"You'll regret this, *mon a...*"

Yves' words were cut off as Terry squeezed and twisted, pulling up for good measure, so Yves now had to stand on tiptoe in a largely vain attempt to lessen the pain. "No more French words. Please. I want to make sure we both completely understand each other. 'Cause, you see, I'm not very bright. I know that now. I mean, I *really* know that now.

And I thank you for that. Your little games made it really clear to me and to everyone else. But that's okay. It's good. We all have to learn sometime don't we? We all have to...grow up."

"Grow up?" Yves said through gritted teeth, unwilling to give the English lad any cause to make his situation even more uncomfortable, but unable to bite back the bile within. "That is just exactly what *they* do not want you to do. They will keep you as a child forever, doing what they want you to do, living the life of mediocrity and passivity and pretence they want you to live. With me you can be a *man!* Live like a man. Fight like a man. Fuck like a man!"

"No," said Terry, gently rolling Yves' cobs in his hands like stress balls, but not hurting him, yet. "You're the one who treated me like a kid, Yves. You're the one who led me by the nose, and the cock, through France, Germany, and Switzerland. Right up to the end, you had me dancing to your tune, fucking who you wanted, when you wanted, how you wanted, trying to turn me into a poor man's version of you. And then, in that ring, you just about beat the living shit out of me. And you know what? When Doug and the others got me away from that place, I didn't feel 'rescued'. I felt...cheated. Because I am the better wrestler." Yves sneered, the sound giving way to a sharp hiss as Terry twisted his sac sharply. "No, really, I am. I know that now. I'm the better wrestler, and I'm the better man. And yes, I know you beat the crap out of me that last time. But I know why now. It was because I didn't know just how stupid I was. I didn't know who I was. I didn't know what I had to fight for. That's when things go wrong, you see. For me. For Doug. Even for you. But I do know now. And I wanted you to know. That's why I didn't say anything back in the harbour when I saw you getting on the ferry."

Terry gave a short laugh. "So here we are. I've got your dick and balls in my hand. I could pull 'em off. I could turn you around and fuck you right here and now, up against the door. There's even a small bit of me that wouldn't say no to one last good fuck from you." For a good five seconds Terry stood as if weighing his options, even as he weighed the balls in the palm of his hand. "But," he said finally, "the answer is *none of the above*. And you know why? Because now, I finally know myself, and I finally know you. And you, *monsieur,* are a piece of shit."

Terry dropped Yves' balls as if letting go of something rotten, and watched as Yves gasped in relied, struggled out of the shirt that had held his arms pinned, staggered over to the cot in the cabin, and gingerly lowered himself onto it, nursing his abused jewels and glaring malevolently at Terry.

"You are a fool," Yves snarled. "What are you going to do back in England? Your petty 'company' is dying on its feet. Without my support, what future do you have?"

Terry stepped towards him, smiling in grim satisfaction at the way Yves flinched back away from him. "The future?" Terry considered. Was Yves right? The whole point of the trip had been to link up with foreign investors, and that had turned into a total crock of shit. On the other hand, the future owners of their main opposition back home had joined their team. From what Terry had seen, one of them looked set to actually join the family. Mike Mansfield might be a pain in the arse, but even he couldn't hold out against that sort of connection. Could he?

And, as he had made so very clear to Yves, Terry had indeed learned a great deal from his Grand Tour of Europe, a lot of it from Yves himself. The potential of online wrestling, for one thing. All Terry needed to help with that was someone with the relevant skills, a newly acquired degree in computer sciences, ideally, and preferably with a good knowledge of the wrestling business, too. *Now where oh where can I find someone like that?*

Whistling happily, Terry unlocked the cabin door and prepared to step out and return to his family and his future. He looked back just once at Yves, sitting, trousers and briefs still round his ankles, hand carefully massaging his mauled pride and joy.

"*Au revoir,*" Terry said, and he closed the door behind him.

About the Author

Jack Stevens read English at university, travelled the world, worked up trees, in factories and offices and now, when not writing or wrestling, tries to teach drama (which really helps with the wrestling). He would like to see more repeats of *World of Sport* wrestling bouts on television, please.

NineStar Press, LLC

www.ninestarpress.com